End of Pain

by

CA Humer

A Rob Adams Series

End of Pain

Cover Art by *Lisa Dawn MacDonald*

The Wild Rose Press, Inc.
PO Box 708
Adams Basin, NY 14410-0708
Visit us at www.thewildrosepress.com

Publishing History
First Edition, 2025
Trade Paperback ISBN 978-1-5092-6248-9
Digital ISBN 978-1-5092-6249-6

A Rob Adams Series
Published in the United States of America

Dedication

To all the heroes.

Acknowledgements

Alton is the imaginary site for this novel. The names and locations are a product of my imagination. Any resemblance to actual individuals or locations is coincidental.

No man is an island, and no author completes work without the help of friends, associates and professionals. I'd like to thank Officer Timothy Haywood, of the Arlington PD, the Arlington Citizens Police Academy, and all the officers that shared information about their work. The Academy program offers an introduction to each department and the individuals in charge. Every citizen would benefit from this opportunity to understand the workings of their local police department. It helped me paint an accurate picture of Rob's working environment.

Lastly, a book about crime and killing would never be possible without the input and feedback of professionals. Thanks go to Retired Grand Prairie Detective Alan Patton, and Dr. Tasha Zemrus with the Tarrant County Medical Examiner's Office, for their valuable insight into the crime scene process and terminology and the ME's involvement and responsibility.

Thank you for your purchase of *End of Pain*. I am truly appreciative of the support of The Wild Rose Press, my editor and guide, Lea Schizas, a wonderful writer in her own right, and my sweet and supportive husband, Don. Please look for my other books, including the Sam & Kate Slater series, *Art from Darkness, Artistic Deception* and *Dying for Art*, the next book in the series, coming soon.

Chapter 1

Rob groaned, pulling himself awake from too little sleep. Rolling over, he grabbed his cell phone to silence its obnoxious thrum. The vibrations caused it to dance across the nightstand, threatening to jump to its death. Rob swore under his breath, wishing it would. Having just dozed off after spending the night answering a call for a gang banger that looked like a pincushion, the last thing he needed was an unwelcome wake-up call.

Last night's case flashed through his mind. The victim's drinking buddy had stabbed him eleven times in a fit of jealousy over a nineteen-year-old stripper. Rob puffed his cheeks, expelling air through slack lips. What a man wouldn't do for a pair of double D's. Idiots! That's what they all were. Rob was just about over it. Nine years in crimes against persons and all he did was chase and catch worthless scum that killed each other in a variety of stupid, violent, yet highly effective ways. He wondered if the city should just cordon off the east end and let them all kill themselves. It would save taxpayer money and a lot of his precious time.

The cell display read Lieutenant Griffin, his boss. Swiping a hand through his hair, Rob answered.

"Adams," he growled into his phone. He rubbed his hand over his stubble, struggling to bring his mind into focus on such little sleep.

"Well, aren't we little Miss Sunshine this

morning?" Griffin's smoke-stained voice drawled. "It is morning and although I know you didn't get much sleep after the gang banger case, I have another one you need to pick up. Sweeney called in sick last night—flu or something. You're up on rotation and you're going to want this one, anyway. It looks like it's that missing coed. Unfortunately, she isn't missing any longer." Griffin coughed into the phone, causing Rob to pull it away from his ear, lip curling at the sound. Despite having quit smoking over 30 years ago, the lieutenant still hacked up phlegm. Although it could have been because of the allergies that plague everyone in the great state of Texas this time of year. Griffin cleared his throat and continued.

"She turned up at the waste water drying beds. You know? The ones on Greenway. Some birding enthusiast found her while he was out looking for a freakin' horned owl. Uniforms have secured the scene and cordoned off the area. The CSI team and Medical Examiner's investigator are on the way. Call Pete and get out there." Griffin hung up without saying goodbye.

"Yeah. Love you too, boss." Rob grimaced and rolled out of bed. After a quick shower, he grabbed last night's jeans off the chair where he'd tossed them just hours earlier, tugging them on. Pulling open his top drawer, he selected a clean black t-shirt from the pile of other clean black t-shirts. Splashing cold water on his face, Rob checked his reflection in the bathroom mirror. Dark circles and bags had collected under his eyes. Rubbing his hands over his tired face, he sighed and rolled his head on his neck, listening to the creaks and pops. He didn't bother to shave.

Picking up his Nikes, Rob walked barefoot into the

kitchen, where he stared dejectedly at the remains of yesterday's coffee in the pot. Normally, he set a timer, enjoying a fresh brew when he got up. Forgot to do it last night. He poured the left-over dregs into a to-go mug, and dialed his partner, Pete Bonnert. Rob didn't relish sharing this news. Even on the brief night of sleep, Rob knew his partner would be up cooking breakfast for his kids. Spending time with his kids was a priority for Pete, no matter what time they wrapped a case. Zapping the coffee in the microwave into something reasonably palatable, Rob asked Pete to meet him at the crime scene.

The morning had dawned hazy. Smoke from the wildfires in West Texas carried on the open-the-oven-door air, smudging the horizon. Rob figured it would blow off by nine and the temp would climb to an exceedingly hot August day. Every night, the local weatherman, a buddy from Rob's baseball days, counted off the number of triple-digit days and the records being set. Glancing at his watch, Rob noted the time at just after 8:15 a.m. On route, he called the uniform officer who had secured the crime scene to get a report. The cell rang twice before Rob heard Minton's youthful voice answer.

"Minton, it's Adams. I'm headed that way. I understand you were first on scene. Can you give me a rundown, please?" Rob listened, pulling down his visor against the morning sun.

"Yes, sir." Rob heard the rustle of a notepad being pulled from a pocket. "So, sir, the sun rose at 6:57 a.m. Mr. Gibbons, a birding enthusiast, discovered the body at approximately 7:15 a.m. I asked him to wait at my patrol car, expecting you will have questions. I've established the perimeter at twenty-five feet around the body. Crime Scene Investigators arrived five minutes ago."

"Thanks, Minton, Nice work. If I could only clone you." Rob hung up.

The Crime Scene Investigators would set up a grid search pattern to map the scene and search for evidence. After they transported the remains, they'd continue to look for additional evidence. Rob called Pete to get his estimated time of arrival and then turned onto the rough, broken asphalt drive that led back to the drying beds. Located just north of a prosperous neighborhood, most folks didn't even know the drying beds existed; unless the wind blew in the right direction. Rob could never figure out why someone would pay upwards of half a million dollars for a house, put in a stellar pool and outside entertainment area, then be stuck sitting inside half the months of the year because the outdoors smelled like a toilet. He figured they did it for the panache of living next door to one of the Texas baseball players, who favored the area. Rob guessed since they won the World Series, that probably added value.

The entrance to the Turner Creek Drying Beds wasn't marked or inviting to the casual passer-by. The area, a renowned birding spot, drew enthusiasts from around the country. Most regular folks drove by without a glance. He wondered how the killer selected this site. As he waited for Pete, Rob finished the last few swallows of his lukewarm day-old coffee. Pete drove up a few minutes later, pulling in next to Rob's smoke-gray 1977 Camaro. The two men nodded a greeting as they climbed out of their cars.

"Short night. Sorry to take you from your time with

the kids. Today is pancake day, isn't it?" Pete always made pancakes on Tuesdays. Eileen, his wife, worked the third shift at the ER and she arrived home in time to join them and send the kids off to school. Rob envied the ritual.

"Had time to slap a few flapjacks on each plate and kiss Eileen goodbye." Pete shrugged. "They get it."

The two men walked the rest of the way to the crime scene in silence. As the lead investigator, Rob knew the importance of recording his initial observations about the scene. Death investigators never got a second chance to process and view a crime scene as thoroughly as they wished. Knowing the crime scene speaks if one listens to what it tells you, Rob stopped to scan the area. He was a master at this. His quasi-OCD gave him a keen sense of observation. Pete stood back to let him establish the investigation's scope and identify potential sources of scene contamination. Rob noted the location of the evidentiary items. Items that might get lost, contaminated, or degraded. The victim lay face up at the edge of a containment pond; her naked body partially submerged in the muddied verge of the receding water. Countless hikers and birders had trampled the grass. His gaze moving over the scene, Rob saw too few small yellow tents placed at sites where evidence lay.

Rob watched as the crime scene techs performed their work with exceptional expertise and diligence. They photographed, took videos, and made detailed sketches with accurate measurements of the crime scene before moving or altering anything. They documented the location of anything collected on the site sketch, along with when they discovered it and the person who made the discovery. A CSI team could make or break the prosecution's case. Rob knew this team. He worked with them often. Their reputation for thorough and remarkable reports resulted in successfully closing cases.

Bud Gillette, the ME investigator, wiped the body temp laser on his shirtsleeve before returning it to his bag, then pulled off his gloves. Why he bothered to check body temp on a killing like this mystified Rob. The instruction manual said to do it, so he did. But body temp would be a moot point, considering the bag and tag, followed by storage in the meat locker at the medical examiner's office until they could work on it. Everyone knew that establishing time of death was a crap shoot at best. You asked when the victim was last seen alive and when they discovered the body. TOD was somewhere in-between those two events. In this case, so many other clues showed the time of death. Taking body temp just sometimes seemed like overkill, no pun intended. Of course, failing to do so could give the defense a significant advantage.

Rob stood at the perimeter, reading the frustration in Bud's expression, understanding all the hoops he had to jump through. He appreciated him for crossing every t and dotting all the i's as diligently as he did. Crime solving was a team effort and Rob respected Bud and the Fort Worth Medical Examiner's office for their work.

While the crime scene tech focused on getting every angle and close-up photo he needed, Rob and Pete looked at the body and the scene, taking in all the details. They patiently waited for Bud to finish up. He bagged the hands and feet, then laid the black plastic sheet next to the body so the CSI techs could roll it over to look at where the body had lain. Since this involved one tech having to step into the water, the two negotiated using rock-paper-scissors to determine which one would do it. Connors lost and good-naturedly flipped the bird to his partner for the honor.

This part of the operation was always dicey. Blood pools at the bottom of the body and fluid from rot and gases build up. Leaks form because of bloating from decomposition after 24 hours. It can get pretty gnarly. Rob and Pete stood back. Once rolled over, the technicians gingerly placed the remains in a body bag. The photographer took more photos of the ground. Rob and Pete watched them do their work as Bud walked over with a preliminary report. His black rubber boots, wet from the water, carried bits of leaf debris and algae. Rubbing the back of his neck, he frowned.

"She was a pretty girl, but you wouldn't know it to look at her now. My best guess is the victim's been in the water for at least a day. Luckily, the fish and turtles hadn't gotten too far with their grisly work, but the birds feasted on her when the water level dropped. Although gruesome, the damage done by the environment isn't too extensive." Bud slapped at an insect buzzing about his bald pate.

"Won't know for sure if it's the missing woman or not for a while yet. Elements and animals made a positive ID pretty difficult, but she was wearing a necklace with 'Kathy' on it. Hopefully, the ME will be able to lift prints. If not, we'll have to check the dental records. You took the missing person report, didn't you Pete? Sorry it turned out this way. The ME will confirm, but it looks like the cause of death is strangulation. There is some bruising on her face—looks like the killer beat her pretty badly. I hope we can get something from under her nails. There were defensive wounds on her hands. ME will do the post as soon as we get her to the morgue. Do you guys want to be there? If not, we'll get the report over to you ASAP." Bud looked over at the body bag being loaded into the transport van and shook his bald head. "This sucks. Sometimes, I really hate my job. Only good thing is that I don't have to do next of kin notifications. As soon as we know who we are looking at, we'll let you know. Take care, guys."

Bud waved and made his way to the ME's station wagon. His pear-shaped body, clad in wrinkled khakis and mustard yellow bowling shirt, showed a distinct disdain for fashion and matched the depressing, dirty white government issued vehicle he drove. It had a permanent slump to its chassis, similar to the slump Bud had to his shoulders. Dealing with dead bodies took its toll.

While the CSI team walked a strip pattern looking for additional evidence, Rob and Pete interviewed the man who'd discovered the body. Outside of an encyclopedic knowledge of birds, the man had little else to contribute. And, since the killer dumped the body along a popular trail and it lay submerged for at least a day, several people had hiked past the site without even knowing it. Footprints covered the area and were not likely to provide any leads. Rob suspected any evidence would be so contaminated by now, it would prove useless in a court of law. Outside of the body, finding any clues on site would be like finding a needle in a haystack. Whoever the killer was, that person knew where to dump a body and, so far, hadn't left behind any trace. Rob left Pete and the CSI team to finish up the grid and went to the morgue to check in with the ME. Maybe the body would yield something the crime scene hadn't.

Rob drove to the Tarrant County Medical Examiner's Office on Fulton. Alton and the surrounding cities used the county services near the Tarrant County Hospital. Snagging a parking spot a half block from the entrance on one of the side streets, he hoofed it to the single-story brown on brown brick building. Stepping through the glass doors, he greeted Tonya, the receptionist.

Tonya sighed, resting her chin in her hand.

At 6 foot 2 inches, 210 pounds, with broad shoulders and an athlete's physique, Rob caught the attention of most women without trying. His thick, dark brown hair, often in need of a cut, curled over his collar. Rob had one suit to his name, reserved for weddings and funerals. His uniform of choice was a pair of jeans, black running shoes and a black t-shirt. If a collared shirt was required, he chose a lightweight cotton, rolled at the sleeves. He wore a lightweight sports jacket to cover his shoulder holster. Not uniform dress code, but Rob's boss, Lt. Griffin, rarely said anything because Rob performed. Besides, the few times Rob walked into the precinct wearing a suit, every female officer on the force practically walked into walls or ran their patrol cars off the road, looking at him with lust in their eyes. Lt. Griffin didn't need the worker comp claims and Rob was a crime solving machine. The department called him 'the Mountie'. He always got his man.

Rob looked around at the new décor in the lobby. The county had finally gotten around to renovating the building where the labs and administrative offices were located, but had yet to make similar improvements to the holding and autopsy rooms. It needed live plants. Tonya gave him her usual hopeful smile.

"Hey, Tonya, did they start on Kathy Erickson yet?"

Rob was all business. Tonya, smile fading, gave him a head tilt, pointing him down the hall, and buzzed him in. When Rob darkened her door, it meant death and sadness for a family.

Walking down the impeccably clean, white vinyl floored hallway to the morgue, Rob acknowledged the orderly and signed in. He made his way down the ramp. The space smelled of disinfectant and death.

Noting Kathy wasn't in any of the four bays of what he called the autopsy corral, he walked to the auxiliary cutting room where Dr. Sumeesh, the Medical Examiner did his work. Grabbing a surgical mask off the counter, Rob walked into the room. Two dieners worked on Kathy's body, removing each organ and handing them to Dr. Sumeesh for weighing. Talking into the microphone on his headset, the ME recorded all the data as he placed the final internal organ on the scale and weighed it. Sumeesh, a small man with dark skin and thin hair, graying at the temples, inclined his head in greeting. His beat-up Reeboks and hospital scrubs belied his usual dapper appearance when he testified in court. He'd been in the position for eighteen years and rarely smiled. Maybe dealing with death daily stole the happiness. Seeing Rob, he paused the recording.

"Hi, Rob. I got to her first thing. I know how important this is to you. Don't envy you this one. Fingerprints weren't the best. Working on the assumption this is your missing person, I ran the dentals. According to the records, she'd just gotten her wisdom teeth out in June and they fixed a chip on her lower front tooth. It's Kathy Erickson alright. Twenty years old, social work major at the university. Reported missing on August 21st. Commuter student, she lived with her folks in Mansfield. But you know that after how much time you guys put in looking for her."

Anger flared in Rob's eyes along with a compassion that homicide cops hold on to even after years on the squad. But Rob's dedication burned hotter and brighter than most. Most of Rob's professional colleagues, including Dr. Sumeesh, wondered how he did it. The doctor himself readily admitted he found it difficult in his line of work, but then Rob was different. Rob viewed his work as a solemn, almost sacred duty. He approached each homicide prepared to use every tactic, tool, forensic technique, and procedure to find the killer. But for all that, Rob was a quiet guy. Likeable but hard; a loner. He did his job, often working sixteen to eighteen hours a day to solve a case, then went home while everyone else would head out for a mind-numbing drink or, if single, a quick roll in the hay with a willing partner. In this job, sex could be therapeutic.

Everyone liked and respected Rob, but he didn't have many close friends in the department. If a police department function required Rob's attendance, he showed up late, tracked down his partner, Pete, and then stood with his back to the wall. He always left as soon as he fulfilled the minimum social obligations. Several of the women on the force had tried their luck with Rob when he first started with the Alton PD, but outside of a few casual dates, nothing serious ever came about. Rob liked women, and they certainly liked him, but he kept his distance.

Rob's eyes scanned Kathy's body for a piece of the puzzle. Holding the mask over his mouth, he asked, "Find anything that will help us solve this case?" He wanted to know as much as the Medical Examiner could give him. Rob hated the look of the Y incision in Kathy Erickson's body, the emblem of the finality of death. It had been closed but not yet stitched. Sumeesh's assistant would handle that while he focused on the evidence available on the body.

Dr. Sumeesh lifted his compassionate and thoughtful gaze to Rob. Standing across the body from him, he walked Rob through what he'd found so far.

"Cause of death is manual strangulation. Notice the injuries here at the hyoid bone; the bruising? The killer used their hands. Which makes it personal. The killer wanted to see her face while they killed her. Whoever it is, dumped her body post-mortem, no water in the lungs. The contents of her stomach appear to be pepperoni pizza—store bought frozen—something generic and cheap. We're running the chemical analysis on the sauce and other ingredients to see if we can ID the brand. Based on her height, weight and estimated rate of digestion, I'd say she ate about five hours before she died.

"There is bruising on the face, and they fractured her cheekbone. Some of these injuries appear older. They had faded—others were more current. There is bruising on her wrists and ankles, consistent with being bound. She had fibers in her airway, which indicates that someone probably gagged her at least part of the time. I'm running an analysis to determine the type of material. I took scrapings from her fingernails. There are traces of blood and wood. I'm doing a type and DNA check, but I suspect it is hers. Based on the bruising on her palms, it looks like she might have been gripping something hard enough to tear her nails. She had splinters in her palms and fingertips.

"In addition to the contusions to her face, she has cuts on her breasts and inner thighs. The cuts are not deep enough to cause serious injury but designed to inflict pain. There was also what looks like a brand on her left breast. It didn't have time to heal, so it's difficult to make out. I'm running it through the system to see if I can find a match. There is vaginal bruising indicating violent and multiple penetrations. I'm running the rape test. It will probably be a miracle if we find semen. The killer hurt her. Whoever killed her hurt her bad. It's more than likely a male suspect based upon my observations. The perpetrator didn't leave a single hair follicle or flake of skin.

"I've got nothing, Rob. I'm sorry. The killer is smart. I don't think this came from a fit of anger or is a crime of passion. This is sick and methodical torture. It is pathological. The killer is a monster." Dr. Sumeesh's expression showed frustration, and if truth be told, fear. "I don't think this was his first and I bet it won't be the last. There will be another. I can feel it in my bones."

Rob had been staring at Kathy the whole time, taking in everything Dr. Sumeesh was explaining; absorbing it, internalizing it, chewing on what they knew, and thinking about what they didn't know. When homicide detectives worked on a case, they often referred to the person as the 'victim' or the 'body' or even the 'deceased'. Rob always referred to his cases by their name. Rob believed they deserved the respect and the humanity their name gave them. It also reminded him of the importance of his job.

Rob went over to the computer and scrolled through the pre-autopsy photos. He wanted to see what condition her body was in when they brought her in. The bloating made a hideous presentation, and the damage by the fish and fowl made his heart ache for the family. She had been a beautiful young woman. Now, she'd have a closed coffin.

Freezing the last photo on the screen, he studied it, rubbing his hand over his chin, pinching it in concentration. Thoughtfully, he raised his head and turned to Dr. Sumeesh, his normally brown eyes darkening with intensity. This wasn't happening on his watch. Kathy deserved better. "Thank you, Doctor. One more thing. Prior to your exam, did you or your staff wash and brush her hair?"

Dr. Sumeesh looked up, ready to defend his people. The question surprised him. He looked at the photo of Kathy Rob had frozen on the screen. He noticed that even though some leaf debris clung to her hair, it appeared clean and free of tangles. "No."

"Thanks, Doctor. Pete and I will let Kathy's family know. Send over the report as soon as you have it completed, please." Rob stepped out of the ME's workroom and called Pete. Next of kin notifications left a bitter taste in his mouth and a hole in his soul. He'd wait for Pete so they could deliver the news to Kathy's parents together. They agreed to meet at the station.

Rob returned to the station, arriving before Pete. He walked through the squad room, accepting commiserating looks and comments from the officers and detectives. No one enjoyed dealing with death, but when the killer cheated the young victim of a promising life, everyone felt it. He grabbed a cup of coffee and took a sip, grimacing at the bitter taste of the several hours old brew. Pulling up the standard form on his computer, he began the preliminary report on Kathy Erickson's murder. Rob stared at the screen, wondering once again why he did this job. He pooched his lips and snorted out a breath. He knew why. Justice and closure. Someone had to do the right thing, stand for the dead, giving them and the surviving family retribution.

Rob grew up in a home where his parents, both college graduates, instilled traditional values; loyalty, love, and moral obligation above all else. Before retiring, his mom taught first grade and his dad had been a firefighter, receiving several commendations for meritorious service, ending as a station chief. When Rob and his brother came along, his folks chose a more modest life-style, living on one income so his mom could stay home with them. They made the sacrifices necessary to give their boys a solid, stable home life and the opportunity to go to college.

Rob's dad always stressed the importance of service, honor and valor. 'If not me, then who?' he'd often say.

Rob's brother grew up to become an ER doctor and moved to Milwaukee. He had a beautiful wife and four kids. Rob's folks were crazy about their grandkids and, despite the cold, spent every Christmas with them. They hoped their younger son would follow his example. In their opinion, there could never be enough grandkids.

Rob slumped back in his chair and pinched the bridge of his nose, willing the impending headache to go away. He shut down the computer. Screw the report, he thought. He'd let Pete do it.

****

Pete sat behind the wheel of the department sedan. He took the surface streets to the Erickson's home, buying time. The clenching of his gut had him popping antacids like candy since leaving the station. Kathy's family had filed a missing person report on August 21st, seventeen hours after she'd left home and gone missing. Now the calendar showed August 29th and Kathy would come home, but not like anyone wanted her to. Rob read through the missing person report one more time while Pete drove along a route that had become all too familiar.

Rob remembered the details well enough he could have quoted them from memory. Kathy left for classes that morning, intending to stop at the library and pick up a couple of research books to help with the paper she was writing on the correlation between the single parent home and a child's mental health. Her parents had expected her no later than seven that evening. When she didn't come home, they texted, asking if everything was all right. Kathy, a dedicated student, often lost track of time when at the library. She was passionate about the topic she had chosen for her paper and planned to expand on it for her master's thesis. When they didn't hear from her by ten p.m., they began calling her friends. Maybe she had stopped by to visit.

No one had seen or heard from Kathy since their

last class finished at four. She hadn't mentioned she planned to go anywhere. While her father drove the route she usually took home from school, checking to see if her car might have broken down, Kathy's mom called the hospitals to see if they had admitted her following an accident. When both parents came up empty-handed, they called the police and filed the missing person report. Everyone thinks it works like on a television drama, but in reality, a waiting period is not required to file a missing person report.

Pete happened to be on duty that day and had seen the report when it came in. Although not officially his case, he took time to speak with the Ericksons. Processing the information, he passed it to the duty sergeant who made it part of the shift change briefings. When Kathy still had not returned home after 24 hours, Pete ratcheted up the urgency on searching for her and opened an active missing person investigation.

Rob and Pete spent several hours with the Ericksons gathering additional information and speaking with her friends and classmates. The police issued an All-Points Bulletin for her car. The APB turned it up at a small park next to a senior independent living community. University students often used the lot for free parking, so no one thought to say anything when it still sat there after two days. The lab did a thorough check, not finding anything to show someone had used her car for an abduction. If Kathy went somewhere with someone, she did it willingly; at least in the beginning.

When three days had passed and Kathy was still missing, Pete and Rob placed her on the FBI's National Crime Information Center list as an 'endangered adult'.

The computer network would provide information nationwide.

Keeping his finger where he left off, Rob blew out a frustrated breath. "Look, Pete, I know we combed through all her social network sites. Twitter, emails, and Facebook yielded little or nothing. Could we have missed something?"

"Anything's possible. We can revisit the homeless shelters and foster care agencies. Based on her social work major and research, someone might be angry or obsessed with her for shedding a light on mental health issues. With the transient nature of the homeless shelter, we might have missed someone during interviews. The envious classmate doesn't play and there is no evidence of her being romantically involved with someone who might wish her harm. The standard avenues of investigation lead nowhere."

As they drove to the Erickson's home, Rob closed his eyes, the pages of notes on the case floating within his thoughts. Going over everything now with fresh eyes, he saw one item that, in hindsight, troubled him. He returned to it several times, rolling it around in his brain. Kathy had posted a selfie on Facebook on the 8th of August, somewhere near the campus. 'I got away with a warning, but if all cops are that cute, slap on the cuffs and take me away, officer.' Kissy face emoji. Rob shifted his gaze to the passing landscape, seeing the message in his mind's eye.

"Pete, I keep going back to that stupid Facebook post. As crazy as it sounds, something tells me there is some connection. I'm thinking that's where we need to start." Pete glanced over at Rob, staring out the window, and calling forth whatever magic mojo he possessed for crime solving. He nodded in agreement as he hadn't any better ideas.

Parking in the driveway of the Erickson's beautifully landscaped brick home, the two men climbed out of the car and stood a moment, gathering their thoughts. The family lived in a gated community surrounding the country club golf course. Rob listened to the gurgling of a fountain splashing water soothingly. A floral wreath hung on the front door, its artificial flowers matching the scented ones in the pots flanking the entryway.

Pete rang the bell, listening as cheerful chimes echoed through the house. He and Rob waited for someone to answer, looking down at their shoes and wondering how to tell these loving parents that their little girl was dead.

Theresa Erickson answered the door.

No words were necessary. A mother could always tell just by looking at the forlorn expressions of the notification team. Mrs. Erickson cried out and collapsed to the marble floor of the foyer. Kyle Erickson was coming up behind her when her world turned black. He caught her, falling to his knees, holding her close. Looking into Rob's eyes, he knew the news they'd come to share. He buried his face in his wife's hair and they held each other, weeping.

Pete and Rob stood silently, waiting for the initial shock and grief to pass, knowing the parents would want as many details as they could handle.

Kyle Erickson recovered first. Suspecting that the eventual outcome would not be happy, he had been more prepared than his wife. He helped Theresa to her feet, and with his arm around her waist, led the way into the formal living room. The cream-colored plush sofas and French provincial tables with gold scroll made everything seem surreal—so clean, polished and perfect, waiting for the dark and devastating.

While Pete went for glasses of water, Rob settled the couple onto the sofa and explained what they had discovered. Pete returned with the water and a box of tissues he'd grabbed while walking past the powder room. This wasn't their first rodeo, and they had a system that worked. It didn't ease the pain and suffering for the family, but it made everything routine and helped Pete and Rob deal with the emotional aspects of the situation. No matter how often one did a notification, it never got easier. One just learned how to dull the knife so it didn't cut quite as deeply.

Chapter 2

Pete and Rob left the Erickson's with a sour taste in their mouth and the need for a cold beer. They had been partners for six of Rob's nine years in the department. The two men were tight—both on the job and off. Pete was a damn fine cop and a good match for Rob. He provided the soft side to Rob's titanium exterior. Married with twin boys and a daughter named Bella, daddy's little girl, Pete found time for life—his wife and family. He went to church on Sundays and grilled burgers for dinner. His wife Eileen was an ER nurse and their kids were their pride and joy. Pete coached his son's little league baseball team and attended every ballet recital.

Even though Rob spent most of his waking hours catching bad guys and solving crimes, he found time to serve as Pete's assistant coach and help train the little league pitchers. Rob played ball in high school and was on the farm league for the Texas Rangers before an overly ambitious and incompetent pitching coach caused Rob to blow out his elbow. Rob wouldn't let that happen to any of the kids he coached. But that was one of the few things Rob did that showed he was human.

Pete called Eileen and told her he'd be late. Both men headed for john Q's, a little tavern that offered a respectable selection of craft beers and sponsored the little league team Pete and Rob coached. The owner, John McKean, was a friend. When they walked in, McKean recognized the slump of their shoulders and automatically pulled two IPAs, placing them at the end of the bar where conversation, when needed, would be possible.

****

Pete stared into his pint and shook his head. "This one is bothering me big time, Rob. Every time I look at the photo of Kathy Erickson, all I can see is Bella in ten years. That same brightness and love of life. The job—it's eating me up. Eileen worries I might develop an ulcer. Thank God for family. As crazy as our life is, it keeps me sane." Pete raised his glass to his mouth, puffed his lips and blew out a sigh. He sucked down half his beer, lowered his glass and his head.

Rob couldn't say a thing to make it better. With secret envy, Rob soberly squeezed his partner's and best friend's shoulder, trying to offer whatever comfort that was worth.

By the time John came by to inquire about a second round, the images had faded and the hard edge dulled. Rob flexed his shoulders and released some of the tension he constantly carried in his shoulders. Pete flinched every time Rob's neck cracked, but never looked up from staring into his glass. John could tell this had been a bad one.

"News reported finding a body. From the looks of it, I'm guessing it was your case. I'm sorry for the family." John said as he thought, *and I'm sorry for you two that have to deal with the dark side of life like this.* He silently took his leave, wisely letting the two men debrief in their own way.

Crossing to the end of the bar, he smiled as he saw a professor from the university come in with her aunt and sister. The three women bellied up to the bar, greeting him with their bright, cheerful smiles. Although John immigrated to the United States from Scotland over thirty years earlier, he often let his brogue slip out, especially when it came to impressing the ladies.

"Well, a fine good evening to you. I'm always happy to have all three lovely Lawrence ladies join us. Tuesday girl's night out? What are you ladies drinking? The same?" he asked, readying a glass at the pull. Meg usually had a cider, Juju, an Ultra Light and Mary Margaret, M&M as they called her, always wanted a Shandy. She was a devoted Anglophile...

"How well you know us, John," M&M said, smiling in just the right way for John to know she was always happy to see him too. Meg looked from her aunt to John with raised eyebrows. M might be just shy of fifty, but she was still a stunning woman and a notorious flirt. Meg watched the sparks fly between M&M & John. It happened every time the ladies went to john Q's for their girl's night out. John didn't miss Meg's questioning gaze.

Leaning over, she whispered, "M, you're not setting a very good example. What would you think if Juju or I flirted with any eligible man that walked in the door?"

"Oh, Meg! If only you would!!!" Although M&M was teasing, John knew she wished Meg would flirt with a man, any man. A past relationship had left Meg broken hearted, but M&M confided in John that the time had come for her niece to move on, to stop building the walls around her heart. He smiled supportively as M brushed the concerned look from her eyes as she brushed back the hair from her face. Laughing, she blew kisses to John, which he deftly caught, then mimed putting in his breast pocket.

John always enjoyed the times Meg, Juju and Mary Margaret came in. Meg taught American History at the university. He enjoyed their many stimulating conversations about the revolutionary war. John considered himself an amateur genealogist and traced his lineage back to Thomas McKean, a signer of the Declaration of Independence. At least his research showed that. Meg knew her stuff, and they exchanged tidbits of information, much to their mutual delight.

While John readied their drinks, Meg touched his forearm to focus his attention. "John, I did some research into that coin you unearthed. It looks to be a British 1793 Conder Token. You know, of course, that Thomas Paine irritated the Brits with his 47-page pamphlet, *Common Sense*, probably the best-selling publication of the time. Many believe it to be what started the ball rolling to demand independence from Great Britain. Well, this coin references his support of France during the 1790s when he wrote a series of pamphlets, specifically *Rights of Man,* which in part defended the French Revolution. Britain worried that his writings would encourage a similar uprising in England. It led to the British holding a trial and conviction in absentia for the crime of seditious libel. The coin appears to reference Thomas Paine, who apparently angered the Brits with his talk of freedom. It represents the hope that they would hang him, thus ending Pain or, in this case, Paine with an 'e'. 'End of

Pain'—get it? They minted it in the 1790s. It is extremely rare and quite valuable. Where did you find it?"

"Well now, an old junker like me never tells, does he?" John said with a wink as he passed along their drinks. The three ladies took them to a table where they munched on pretzels, laughing as Juju regaled them with stories of her teaching observations class. John watched them with appreciation, polishing the bar top and whistling under his breath.

All the ladies made him smile. He thoroughly enjoyed their company. Juju was sweet as sunshine. A real musical talent. She was like a moonbeam; all silvery and delicate. A damn fine piano player, she'd occasionally sit at the old grand piano John had tucked in the corner, playing Billy Joel and Elton John tunes to the delight of the crowds. No impromptu concert was complete without a melancholy folk song or an etude by Chopin or Debussy that brought a hush to the room. The music always left the patrons feeling thoughtful and emotional. She rarely left a dry eye in the house, which encouraged them to buy another round. John appreciated the bump to his business.

Meg, the older sister, was smart as a whip. Her passion for history, especially the revolutionary war, matched his. M&M, or M as they often shortened it, was a stunning woman who caused his heart to skip a beat. Her insouciant smile came with a promising twinkle in her eye. It made one wonder what she was thinking. How she'd stayed single so long after her husband died was a mystery to John and one he often considered remedying.

They were a fun trio of ladies. The girls had lost

their folks when they were kids. M raised them and John contented himself the last year filling the role of affectionate uncle. He gazed over at the three women. Clearly, both Meg and Juju took after their aunt and got their looks from the Lawrence genes. The family had delicate features, thick hair, long limbs, good bones and brains. John smiled and sent a nod to Mary Margaret, who flirtatiously raised her eyebrows at the attention.

****

Pete sat, munching on pretzels and nursing his second beer. He stared at the football game on the TV over the bar, losing himself in the game. Rob looked at the screen occasionally, tracking none of the action. He kept being distracted by the nearby table of three women talking and laughing. Rob found himself drawn in by their obvious joy. Their smiles were bright and genuine and even though he couldn't hear what they were talking about, he found their laughter infectious and smiled along with them. Rob surmised the three women were related because of their striking resemblance. Maybe a mother and two daughters, he thought. The older one wore her hair in a French twist, accentuating her long neck and tall forehead. She was slender and toned for a woman who looked to be in her late forties. The one that was regaling the other two with her story had long blonde hair worn loose down her back. Her blue eyes sparkled with mischief as she threw her head back with a laugh, giving a fist pump of triumph and shouting out 'Yes!'.

But the third lady in the group drew Rob's eye most. She had her back turned partially away from him and he hadn't really seen her clearly until she got up to get a refill on their pretzels. He leaned back on his bar stool to enjoy the view. It appeared to take forever for her to unfold herself from her chair even though she couldn't have been more than 5 foot 5 inches tall. Every move flowed from one to the next. She was grace incarnate. Leaning over the table, pretzel bowl in hand, she made a final comment to her companions. Her hip jutted out just a little, showing off a nicely rounded bottom, snugly encased in stone-washed jeans. Long legs supported her slender frame. Allowing his gaze to trail down and then back up, Rob noted a trim waist and curves in all the right places. Her hair was a slightly darker shade of blonde than her sister, cut into a pixie style that curled around her ears. She wore a blue bandana headband to hold back her hair, bringing out the blue of her eyes. Her brows feathered up and away, drawing attention to her almond-shaped eyes. They didn't appear to miss a thing. She must have felt his eyes on her because she turned to gaze at him, an inquisitive tilt to her head and curve to her ruby lips. He revised his earlier impression of her eyes. They were deeper than just blue. More violet and they fascinated him. He was being drawn into their depths when Pete nudged him with his elbow.

"Hey, buddy. I need to get home. Eileen is keeping dinner warm. You want to join me for leftovers? The kids would love to see you. Bella is over the moon that you are coming to her dance recital. If I wasn't the love of her life, I might be jealous of her crush on you. You are her Prince Charming, you know."

Rob laughed and gave an 'aw shucks' expression. "No, thanks, Pete, although I hate to disappoint the kids. I'm good. Last night's takeout is waiting at home for me. Let's go." Rob caught John's eye and motioned for the check. He pulled out his wallet to pay while Pete went to the men's room. When Rob turned to leave, he collided with the third woman, who had caught his eye, knocking into her drink and splashing it all over his front. She bounced back and instantly looked up to apologize.

"Oh, geez, I am so sorry. How bad did I get you? Oh, oh. Hey, John, had a tsunami here. Call FEMA! Call the Red Cross! I need disaster relief, or at least a towel." She was blushing and laughing, and Rob couldn't help laughing with her. When John handed her the towel, she patted Rob's wet front, getting dangerously close to his crotch.

"I think I've got it, thanks," Rob said, quickly taking the towel out of her hand. Meg looked at him like she didn't get his meaning. Surely she wasn't that innocent, he thought. How could anyone that beautiful be innocent? But here she stood looking at him with those incredible blue eyes, smiling like nothing except happy filled her world.

Sobering a little, she put her hands up, palms out. "Well, I'm still sorry. Look, I'll pay for any dry cleaning."

"No harm, no foul. These are just work clothes. It'll wash out. I have to go. See you around." Rob walked toward the door and passed Pete, who was looking back and forth between his partner and the woman at the bar. Rob didn't miss the look in Pete's eyes.

"Hmm, now this is an interesting development," Pete said, and followed Rob out to their cars.

****

Meg returned to the table, still chuckling over the

28

cider spill and thinking about the map, just as John delivered a replacement cider. He hadn't missed a thing and neither, it seemed, had Mary Margaret. They exchanged looks, making tacit arrangements to talk about what had just happened and who that guy was. John could see Meg wasn't thinking of what had just transpired between her and Rob. From the instant she saw it, her focus had been on the map hanging on his wall.

Poking John in the chest with her index finger, she called him out on the incredible piece of history. "Okay, John. That is an amazing map. Where did you get it? We know Britain navigated the Mississippi up to the time they were required to cede the land to the newly victorious and independent America, but that map implies that the British may have expanded into Alabama before the Spanish or French opened it up. There have always been rumors that some enterprising loyalists fled the states and tried to build a new English Colony near present day Montgomery. No one ever found concrete evidence. Knowing you, that isn't the original. It's way too valuable to just hang on a tavern wall. Is it legit? Can you let me borrow it? I'd like to study it."

John looked at Meg's shrewd expression. He had an extensive collection of early American artifacts. When they'd first met, he'd invited her up to his apartment with hints of original signed silver works by Paul Revere. Initially, Meg thought he wanted to show her his 'etchings' but then he let her know he was more interested in Aunt Mary Margaret and just happy to know someone as passionate about history as himself.

John tweaked her nose and laughed. "You never

know, it might be a family heirloom. You know how much stuff I have squirreled away. Still haven't catalogued everything. My ancestor Thomas McKean lost everything he had after the revolutionary war, but the family had an attic stuffed to the gills and even more crap ended up being added over the years. They passed everything down to me. Might be he or some other distant relative met a traveler who gave him the map..." He turned angelic eyes heavenward and smiled like the little devil he was. Bringing his attention back to the map and then Meg, he showed his hands, palm up. "But honestly, I found it at a flea market. It looks authentic to the period, but I seriously doubt it. It would be at least two hundred and twenty-five years old. The colors would have faded by now. I just thought it made a pleasant addition to my décor here in the tavern."

John was right there. He'd transformed the small family restaurant into a museum of sorts, featuring replicas of revolutionary war items and framed documents. The furniture conjured up images of the taverns where the four founding fathers might have discussed writing the declaration of independence. The stone fireplace featured two Windsor chairs flanking a piecrust table; a favorite spot to sit on cold winter evenings.

John watched Meg's mouth curl into a sly smile. He kept his explanations for the origins of his collections plausible, but he knew she wondered how he came by so many. They couldn't all be family heirlooms. He was passionate enough about history that he could easily turn a blind eye to the source of his collection. That was one reason he and Meg got along so well. She had a similar passion and singlemindedness. When Meg found something or learned something, nothing would stop her digging into it. She had both the intelligence, training and dogged determination to find the answers. John had a great deal of respect and admiration for Meg. Not only was she a popular lecturer on Early American History, specializing in the Revolutionary War, she also co-chaired the history department at the university. A very impressive resume for one so young.

"I can see you won't be forthcoming with any info, but could I borrow the map? It might make an interesting example for my lecture on how NOT to get bamboozled by forgeries."

John laughed, picking up their empty glasses. He agreed to see what he could do and returned to the bar, thinking that would indeed be an interesting topic for a lecture. One that he'd be sure to attend since he'd be the source of many of the forgeries Meg would undoubtedly speak about.

The ladies ordered a pizza to share and switched to iced tea. They enjoyed dinner and continued the conversation, but Meg's eyes returned several times to the map on the wall. By 8:00 p.m., they were ready to call it a night and head out, Meg and Mary Margaret to the house and Juju back to campus. She had to pick up a music score from the library for an early morning class before heading home.

As the girls kissed and hugged goodnight in the parking lot, an officer in a blue and white squad car sat in the shadows of some cedar trees watching. He thought the long-haired blonde was cute and might have a broken taillight. Or at least she would, when he stopped her.

Meg and Mary Margaret pulled out first and turned toward home. Juju locked her car doors and checked her messages before putting her car in gear and pulling out going the opposite direction. She took Beardsly St. north and was turning on to Abram when she saw the flashing lights behind her. *Crap!* She thought. *Was I speeding? No way. Ewe, DUI? No, I only had one beer, and that was with food. What's with this guy?*

Juju looked for a safe place to pull over, then remembered the bulletin posted at the university commons. It warned of some wacko stalking female students. The university suggested everyone be careful. Well, Juju thought she would be safe rather than sorry. She pulled back into the lane and proceeded with her flashers on to the police station near campus, where she planned to pull over. Surely, he wouldn't fault her for being cautious. As she turned into the police station parking lot, the squad car tapped his horn, waved, and drove off. Apparently, whatever citation he'd intended to give her wasn't that important. She let out a sigh of relief.

Juju pulled out her phone and texted Meg. —Just escaped a brush with the law. LOL. Some cop wanted to pull me over. Remembering that wacko hanging around the campus, I drove to the PD station to pull over there, just to be safe. Once I turned in, he drove off. Thank goodness. I had that beer…I can just see the headlines—'New ISD music teacher arrested for drunk driving!' Eeek!!!—

Meg responded immediately. —Sounds like you dodged a bullet. Be safe and text me when you're headed home. I'll wait up.—

Juju smiled at her sister's worry, put her phone

away and headed to the library, watching her rearview mirror like a hawk.

****

No cop worth his spit would pass up the opportunity to rag on his partner when it came to women, and what Pete saw as an electric shock between Rob and the petite blonde turned out to be fertile ground. Walking out to their cars, he poked at his friend.

"Man, she really got you good, Rob. Is it cold and sticky? I bet it is, even though she made a valiant effort to dry you off. I could tell you hated every moment of that." He threw his head back, laughing.

"Ha, ha. Yeah, it's cold and sticky and I can't believe she called for FEMA and the Red Cross. The woman has a weird sense of humor." Rob wryly admitted. He thought about her laughing blue eyes and the soft feel of her breasts when she collided with him.

Pulling open his car door, Pete made the 'captain obvious' observation. "She's not too hard on the eyes either, is she, pal?" Then, taking on a more serious tone, "It's been a while since Carrie screwed you over. When are you going to get over it and move on with your life? I know you, Rob. I've watched you with my kids, how much Bella loves you. You're not the loner you pretend to be."

Rob's grip on the car door tightened when Pete mentioned Carrie and his jaw clenched, recalling the last time he'd seen her. She had left a major hole in his heart and it hadn't healed, even after all this time. Hell yes, he wanted someone special, the normal things in life; a mortgage, wife, kids. But he wasn't sure he was ready to risk another betrayal.

"Pete, yeah, don't think I didn't notice how cute she was, but the cider definitely put a damper on my interest. Look, man, when it's time I'll find the right woman and hopefully she'll be interested in me and, well, you know. I'll, oh hell, I'll move forward as you suggest."

Pete nodded at the sudden change in Rob's demeanor. He'd touched a nerve. Punching Rob in the shoulder in farewell, he climbed into his car, heading home to a loving family. Rob turned out of the parking lot toward an empty apartment.

Rob did his usual circuit of the parking lot at his apartment complex before pulling into his assigned space. He felt his pants sticking to the leather seat of his car and reminded himself to bring down a damp towel in the morning to clean it up. Climbing the stairs, he unlocked the door and stepped into a modestly furnished apartment. The complex, located close to Pete's place, only had 28 units. The owner liked the idea of an Alton police officer living there and discounted the rent. Most of the residents were older and long term, so his law enforcement services were rarely called for.

Grabbing a beer from the fridge, Rob walked out onto his balcony and looked up at the stars. A surprisingly cool night for the end of August, the fresh air helped clear his head. Picking at the label on his beer, Rob thought about Pete's comment. He was right. Rob was a loner and had been since Carrie screwed him over with his best buddy. He should have known she wouldn't be content with a minor league player after he saw how she reacted to his injury and assignment back to the minors. Picking up the pieces of his heart, Rob had refocused his future. He had always loved history and wanted to teach, but Rob was one hell of a ballplayer. He had put college and a teaching degree on the back burner when the Texas Rangers drafted him in his sophomore year. They sent him to the minor leagues to develop as a pitcher. Everything looked good for a career in the majors. He proposed to Carrie and things were going gangbusters. Carrie bragged to all her girlfriends that she was engaged to the next Sy Young winner.

Regrettably, the pitching coach that mentored Rob got overly ambitious. Called up half-way through the season, the coach let Rob throw eight of the nine innings in an insignificant game, screwing up his pitching arm. They sent him back down to the minors on the injured reserve list. He never fully recovered. Carrie realized her dreams of major league wifedom were going down the drain when the Rangers let him go. She hooked up with his best friend, a first baseman with more perceived promise. Rob walked away from professional baseball, hurt and disenchanted. He ended up finishing college with a double major in history and psychology.

During his time at school, Rob learned he had another calling and love. He read about Joe Brandt, a serial killer in Louisiana who had killed at least four women. The psychology of the case fascinated him, and he followed its progress. He discovered he saw things others missed. He had an uncanny ability to identify patterns and interpret information differently than others did. Rob possessed a talent for putting odd pieces together to paint pictures, tease out the answers. His research skills for finding killers and his desire to serve and protect made him a valuable asset to any police department. Joining the Alton PD as soon as he graduated, Rob rapidly moved up through the ranks to lead investigator. He was that good.

Standing and stretching his back, he walked back into the apartment and turned on the TV, channel-surfing for a game to distract the memories Pete's comments had awakened. He lay back on his recliner and found his mind drifting to the few details they had on Kathy Erickson's disappearance and now death. They didn't have much, and his mind kept returning to the selfie and Facebook post about being pulled over. Rob resolved to check all the traffic stops in a five-mile radius of campus on the mornings of 8/7 through 8/10 on the off chance something would make sense.

He dozed off dreaming of a blonde pixie dancing naked on his chest, laughing at him and pouring cider on his crotch. Startling himself awake, he realized his beer had dumped over dousing his pants and chair. *Just great. What a klutz and what the hell with the pixie?* Rob got up to get a towel and cleaned up his mess.

Stripping off his clothes, he stood in the shower, letting the hot water run over his head and down his neck, relaxing his tense muscles. He sighed, having one of his internal dialogues thinking about the pixie. A cider bath wasn't his idea of fun, but he sure enjoyed the feel of her breasts as they made soft cushiony contact with his chest. He smiled, recalling how she had laughed while using a towel to clean him up, getting perilously close to his tightening groin. Shit, who would have thought cider and an old bar towel could be so damn erotic? Rob shook his head and turned the water to cold. *No time for this nonsense. I've got a murder to*

solve and probably other lives to save from this sicko.
He stepped out of the shower and crawled under the
covers, hoping for at least four hours of uninterrupted
sleep.

****

It disappointed him that the little blonde outfoxed
him by driving to the police station rather than pulling
over. Not that he would have done anything tonight.
Sometimes he wanted to take them immediately, but
other times he only wanted to get a name and address
so he could plan the big event. That was often more
fun—planning, watching, and waiting for the ideal time
to strike. When he took the time to savor the moment,
he found the anticipation almost as arousing as the
actual taking. He'd get a boner tracking down his
victims on social media and sending them private
messages with flirty comments and compliments. He'd
type out, 'Your hair looked so beautiful today—like
silk. I'd like to bury my face in your long tresses.' He
sometimes read romances out loud to his guests. The
ones with the bosomy women and half naked guys on
the covers. He knew women loved it when you called
their hair 'tresses'. It came in handy for when he
approached them for the takedown. He considered it
priming the pump.

He'd post romantic comments and already have an
online relationship established, a familiarity. A mention
of one of the crazy compliments he sent and they
wouldn't see him as a threat but as the guy that they
knew from social media. They were all so gullible. Tell
them they were cute or hot and you were interested in
getting to know them better and they'd trip all over
themselves to get in your car to 'go for a coffee'. He'd

make light conversation as he headed toward the nearest java shop and then sheepishly ask if it would be alright if he stopped by his place to check on his new puppy first; telling them the little guy wasn't completely housebroken yet. Sometimes he'd pull out his cell phone and show them his screen saver of a cute furry little guy.

He didn't have any stupid dog. He hated dogs. The picture came from an animal adoption ad he'd found. "Ooh, he's so cute." Blah, blah, blah. He'd been running this con since Albuquerque. All it took was a picture of a cute puppy. They fell for it every time.

Chapter 3

Rob walked through the bullpen with a convenience store coffee early the next day. The overnight guys were rotating off, finishing reports after tossing a couple of road rage perps in the can. They'd have the next thirty-six hours to sleep off the drunk that caused their stupidity and meet with the court-appointed attorney in the morning to work out the fine and time. Pete came in around seven-thirty with a dozen sausage rolls and two large coffees, causing Rob's stomach to growl loudly. He wasted no time pouncing on Pete's thoughtful gift, mumbling his thanks around a mouthful.

"Yeah, I figured you didn't eat anything last night. Leftover takeout? Not your style, man. How many beers did you drink and how often did your mind stray to the cider queen?"

Rob rolled his eyes, and reached for a second sausage roll, avoiding the not subtle interrogation while Pete took a roll for himself and slurped coffee. He pulled Kathy Erickson's file and flicked to the initial missing person report.

The two spent the day setting up the case file, reviewing information. Besides the statements from Kathy's friends and classmates following her initial disappearance, Rob added the copy of the crime scene log and his initial report, including the interview with the bird enthusiast. The continuity form listing evidence collected on scene was slim. Kathy hadn't been killed there and there were too many contaminants to the scene. They'd have to wait on the autopsy results and ME's report.

Right now, Rob and Pete had a big goose egg. Nothing. Nada. No one saw her or communicated with her once she left class that last day. Her timeline just stopped. Rob knew they'd have to go back to square one. Any clues to her killer would be based on the ME's report and what happened before her disappearance.

When five o'clock rolled around, Pete pulled his jacket off the back of his chair. Shrugging it on, he closed his computer. Pete dedicated himself to the job, but that duty didn't consume him as it sometimes did Rob. It helped to have his priorities in the right order. God, Family, Country, Job. Placing a hand on Rob's shoulder, Pete urged his partner and friend to shut it down for the night.

"Rob, take a break. Until the ME turns over their full report, we are no closer to finding Kathy's killer than before. There isn't anything else to be accomplished working overtime. Come to the house. Eileen is making lasagna. There will be plenty and you need the down time."

Rob ran a hand over his face, stroking the stubble that emerged every evening at five o'clock, no matter how closely he shaved in the morning. He'd already put in eleven hours and felt the frustration of failing to find the one piece of the puzzle that would lead to solving the crime.

"Yeah, you're right. I'll just tidy up this last bit and

be out the door. Hey, I'll take a pass on the lasagna. I think I'll go burn some of this energy off at the gym, then get a good night's sleep." Rob stacked up the papers and inserted them into the file, waving Pete off. "Go, eat some lasagna for me."

"You know I will. See you in the morning." Pete flipped his keys in his hand and headed out the door, whistling "That's Amore".

Rob spent an extra hour at the precinct, going over everything he had on Kathy Erickson. Her social media had turned up some texts from some anonymous person. Looked like some guy had been coming on to her. Sounded like a damn swash-buckler. Rob rolled his eyes and shook his head, wondering what was with the 'kiss your dainty hand stuff'? Someone tried to delete others. The tech guys were trying to resurrect any others that might have gone missing from the ether net. Rob didn't know what that all entailed, but his guy was on it. Besides the hair being brushed, he had the brand. He kept this evidence hidden from the media. No sense letting the killer know everything the police knew.

Stretching his arms over his head, he rolled his shoulders and neck, listening to his vertebrae pop and crack from sitting so long. Rob needed caffeine. He walked over to the coffeemaker, only to find it empty, and the dregs from an earlier pot burned onto the bottom. Hell. He considered making a fresh pot, but passed.

A quick glance at his watch revealed the lateness of the hour, and the pangs of hunger stirred within him. Rob thought about the leftover takeout. Three-day-old Chinese sounded less than appetizing. He didn't keep a well-stocked refrigerator and didn't feel like fast food, opting to stop off at john Q's for a burger on the way home.

Choosing a table in the corner with a view of the TV, he slouched back, watching the soccer game while nursing a beer until his meal arrived. He noticed the three women from the other night walk in; observed how the room seemed to light up when they entered, greeting several patrons on the way to a table. He wondered how he never noticed them before. Cop eyes danced over the group. The family resemblance struck him again. The younger women were pretty, and he could tell they would mature into the classic beauty of the older woman. Rob watched as John gave personal attention to the three, focusing his charms on the older gal and sharing some serious conversation with the pixie. That was how he saw her now; a pixie or maybe a fairy who had danced through several of his dreams, teasing him. It made his shoulders tense up and he rolled them around, easing the ache. When John brought over his burger, he couldn't help himself.

"Looks like you enjoy the company of the three attractive ladies over there. I don't think I've seen them before. Friends of yours?" Rob nonchalantly inquired, gesturing with his chin. He sprinkled a generous amount of salt on his fries and poured out a big glop of ketchup on his plate.

When John raised his eyebrows in surprise, Rob tried to hide his motives. Typically he was a private guy and never showed interest in any of the women that frequented the tavern, even though several had asked John to introduce them. But now, he was interested. He wanted to know more about the pixie.

"That they are. Good friends, Rob. And, yes, I

enjoy their company very much and you might too. All three are intelligent and witty and bring brightness to the old place whenever they come in. I particularly enjoy talking with Meg, the gal with the short hair. She is a professor of American History at the University. That being one of my passions, Meg and I talk a lot about my family history and some items in my collection. She was making a beeline toward my new map when she ran into you the other night, spilling her cider all over your pants. I'm sure you remember."

Rob laughed and nodded. "It's hard to forget. That cider was cold and sticky by the time I got home. And Pete couldn't stop laughing at me. He thought I wore it well and enjoyed my obvious discomfort. So, what's her fascination with the map?"

"Oh, it implies that there might have been an English settlement in Alabama shortly after the War of Independence. She wants to study it. In fact, she is doing a lecture entitled 'Flea Market Find or Forgery'. She wants to use my map as an example. Would you like to meet them? Mary Margret, or M&M as she's nicknamed, is the older gal. M for short. Don't get any ideas, Rob. She's already spoken for. But her two nieces, Meg and Juju, are single if you're interested. Come over when you finish up and I'll introduce you." John offered and went back to the bar.

Rob savored his burger, splitting his time between watching the soccer match and the three women. He considered the names John had rattled off. M&M, Juju and Meg. Unusual. When halftime rolled round, Juju went to the piano and played. She kept it light. This didn't seem to be a novel experience for the crowd, who joined in singing to "Piano Man" and "Uptown

Girl". A couple of the patrons walked over to her to visit and make requests. Most knew the women by name. She ended her impromptu concert with "My Love is like a Red, Red Rose" and returned to their table. The social interaction he witnessed fascinated Rob. The ladies looked like a fun group and right now, he thought, he needed fun. By the time the second half of the match started, Rob finished his burger and walked up to the bar. He ordered another beer and a round for the ladies. He asked John to introduce him.

"I can still introduce you, but it's too late for the round, Rob. That fella over by the piano beat you to it, and now he's making his move. Come on, I've only seen that guy once before. I don't know him. I'd rather you make friends with them first." Rob could sense a bit of protectiveness in John's tone and understood it. The guy, good looking in a young Ryan Eggold sort of way, appeared very smooth. Rob ran his gaze over the man, taking in the details of his dress and mannerisms. He wore expensive clothes, an Invicta watch, and looked like he could handle himself if any trouble arose. Rob couldn't make out the conversation, but it looked like his interest lay with Juju, the long-haired blonde. John pulled a beer for Rob and led the way to the ladies' table.

John stood behind M&M with his hands on her shoulders, smiling broadly, saying in his musical Scottish brogue. "Juju, your piano playing and the beauty of you three ladies has earned you another admirer. May I introduce my friend John Robert Adams, little league baseball pitching coach extraordinaire and Dudley Do-right of Detectives. Rob, this is M&M, Juju, and Meg—the Lawrence ladies."

Rob shook his head and laughed at John, wondering if he could be any more embarrassed. But rising to the ridiculousness of the situation and John's ultra-formal introduction, bent the knee and bowed, flourishing his hand in a most courtly fashion.

Juju and M&M laughed and Meg's eyes sparkled. This was true 18th century gallantry, and she leaned forward, irresistibly drawn to him. Rob raised his head and looked into Meg's eyes. As they grew wide, her hand flew to her mouth, covering a gasp, recognizing this was the poor guy she dumped her cider on the other night. Rob's eyes twinkled with mirth as Meg blushed deep crimson. John continued his introductions, turning to the strange gentleman. "And you, sir, I don't think we've had the pleasure."

"We haven't. As I was just saying to the ladies, my name is Justin Whitman. Not a little league coach or a detective." Justin smirked tightly at Rob. He ignored the two men, drawn instead to Juju. He appeared inconvenienced by the interruption that John and the cop presented.

Meg stood to shake hands with Rob. "Hi, Rob. Please, join us and accept another apology for spilling my drink on you. Oh, Justin, why don't you join us too?" She scooted her chair back so the guys could pull a second table over. Rob felt Meg's gaze as he helped move another table and chairs to accommodate everyone.

Justin helped position the table and grabbed the seat next to Juju. Rob saw Meg stiffening when she noticed Justin putting himself between Juju and the others. The man skillfully cut her off from everyone but himself. Watching Meg's eyes narrow with suspicion,

45

Rob paused. He wondered what the deal was with the sisters or this guy. His detective instincts kicked in. Capable of multi-tasking, he observed Justin while getting to know Meg.

Rob settled himself between M&M and Meg and opened the conversation by asking what had piqued his curiosity since the introduction. "Okay, what's the story with your nicknames? I mean, it's candies, right?" All three ladies exchanged looks, smiled and nodded to Mary Margaret, who launched into the explanation.

"Well, Rob, I can see John's introduction of you is quite accurate. You are a first-rate detective. And, if you know the criminal mind as well as you know your candies, we'll all be safer and sleep better tonight." That got a laugh from the table. "So, first off, Juju's formal name is Julie. Her daddy started calling her Juju Beans when she was just a baby and it stuck. Fits her, don't you think?"

Rob and Justin turned appraising, and in Justin's case, adoring gazes toward Juju. She giggled and waved away her embarrassment, as she hid her smile at the special attention.

"As for me, well, Mary Margaret is quite a mouthful. My little sister, Meg and Juju's mom, could never say it when she was a toddler. Best anyone could understand was 'M-mumble-M'. Somehow it got shortened to M&M, which was also her favorite candy. That stuck too, see? Eventually that got shortened to just M—like in Bond, James Bond," M&M quoted in her best impersonation. Rob considered M quite a character. She knew when she had her audience enthralled. She smiled, waiting for the next question Rob was curious to ask.

"Okay, and what about Meg? There isn't any candy that fits with Meg."

Squeezing Meg's hand, M&M continued. "Ah, right you are. So, when my sister and her husband had Meg, they named her after me. We couldn't really call her M&M. After all, that is my name. Now, you may recall there are plain and peanut M&M's. I'm afraid we saddled Meg with Peanut, which did not suit her at all. But, and here is where it gets brilliant." M paused, waiting til she had everyone's rapt attention. "A peanut is a nut, so we called her Nutmeg. That got shortened to Meg. I think it fits her perfectly. I always put a little pinch of nutmeg in my Alfredo sauce. It adds just the right amount of nuttiness and that is what our Nutmeg does. So, there you have it." M&M dusted her palms together and raised them up, saying in her best French accent, "*Voila*."

Rob looked skeptically at all three women, wondering if they were yanking his chain, but for some odd reason, these three seemed incredibly genuine and the names did all make sense. He dusted his palms, raised them up, and attempting to mimic M&M's accent, said, "But of course!" laughing in agreement with her.

Business at the bar lightened, so John turned it over to his staff and came over to join the group, and each couple fell into their own private conversations. Rob turned his chair toward Meg, leaning in to be heard over the sudden cheers coming from the bar as the home team scored the winning goal. "John tells me you teach American History at the university. One of my favorite subjects; it was my major in college. How long have you been doing that?"

Rob discerned Meg's distraction when she turned just enough to speak with him while keeping an eye on Justin and Juju. "I joined the faculty four years ago, right out of grad school as an adjunct professor. I got my PHD, and they offered me full time. My dad taught secondary American History for years while he built an extensive collection of historical artifacts. He ended up writing books and touring the lecture circuit. I think I learned most of what I know from him through osmosis. He was the most amazing man."

Meg paused, her gaze thoughtful, eyes assessing. Tilting her head to the side, she smiled, as if recalling some past conversation. It made Rob question if he was being compared in some way to this paragon.

"I got my PhD and currently fill the position of Co-Chair of the history department. I write academic articles and do the lecture circuit just like my dad, although it is mostly for the university system to high schools here in the state. It helps with college recruitment more than anything." Meg relaxed a bit and took a sip of her cider. She leaned back in her chair, looking inquisitively at Rob.

"Rob, John introduced you as John Robert Adams. President Adams didn't actually have a middle name, but if he would have, Robert would have been very appropriate for the times. How did you come by your name?" She leaned forward, hands clasped on the table.

Meg adeptly tossed the conversation ball to Rob and now he had the chance to recount his family's history and the embarrassing tale that had once made him cringe.

"You are correct. My folks named me for President Adams but also for my father, who is John Robert

Adams II. I didn't aspire to be known as the III, so I opted to use Robert or Rob. I still have to sign all legal documents as John Robert III, though. My folks love history and as corny as it sounds, they fell in love when they were in the musical *1776*. Mom played Abigail to Dad's, John. It is pure coincidence that his last name actually is Adams. I grew up listening to the musical and my folks singing the love songs to each other. July fourth is crazy at their house, bigger than Christmas." Rob smiled and took a sip of beer, looking at Meg and warming to the subject. "John mentioned you are doing a lecture on 'Flea Market Find or Forgery'. That sounds interesting. Would you tell me about it? I'd like to attend."

"John was the inspiration. He has tons of recreations and several authentic pieces that he claims…" —Meg made air quotes— "he found in his attic or at garage sales. He is an astute collector, so I never fear someone will take advantage of him, but what about others? Hence a mini education on how to authenticate an item." Meg shared the outline of the lecture, holding some things back so she wouldn't spoil it if he came. She appeared to be enjoying his company and their conversation, but Rob saw she still kept her eye on the man with Juju. Rob had yet to see anything improper or threatening. Meg clearly had serious trust issues. He wondered if those issues extended to all men or just the ones that hit on her little sister.

****

To say it had bowled Justin over when Juju sat down at the piano was an understatement. Above and beyond her obvious beauty; her sunny disposition and innocence completely captivated him. Her long, slender fingers hypnotized him as they floated across the keyboard. He could read her emotions in every note and when she played her final piece; he could feel her touch, deep in his soul. Justin had closed his eyes and listened to the music ebb and flow over the crowd and into his heart. He wanted to meet her; to know her. As soon as she returned to her seat, he made his move. In tune with his surroundings, Justin found himself acutely aware of everything going on around him; every word, sound, and smell.

Approaching the table, he introduced himself and took Juju's hand. "You are a wonderful musician. May I buy you and your friends a drink in appreciation for the wonderful music you played this evening?" Justin waved a signal for another round at the bartender and turned back to Juju. "Listening to you play and seeing the smiles on so many faces gave me great pleasure. I am not usually so forward, but may I join you?" Juju drew Justin to her like a moth to the flame. He longed to find someone special. Yearned for happiness. Everything moved along according to plan. He envisioned spending quality time with Juju. Then the bartender and the cop interrupted.

Justin wanted to spend a little time getting to know this lovely lady and invite her for coffee. He didn't want to overplay his hand and scare her off. But here he sat talking with a remarkable young woman while sensing the scrutiny of an overly protective sister. And then the cop joined them. Justin speculated on the odds that this detective might be the one working on the recently committed murder. Justin felt the energy drain out of him with that thought. He had been alone for so long. To be sitting next to someone that might know all the nuances of the murder; someone who could solve the crime? Might help him put his demons to rest. He could finally close his eyes and not see everything he knew and feared. Justin felt haunted every time he saw a young woman with long, blonde hair. Would she be the next one? It had become a profile with which he was all too familiar. He longed for it to stop. How many more years could he go on?

Justin wondered how long it would be until he found the next victim. God! He was either extremely lucky or brilliant. They would write books about his ability to manipulate, deceive, and destroy. He was a master, and he was orchestrating the greatest sinister symphony ever composed. Somehow, Justin had to stop it.

He heard her voice and felt the lightest, feathery touch on his arm. Juju smiled at him with playful laughter in her eyes. "Justin, you know all about me, but what do you do?" Her fingertips ran up and down his arm, tickling the hairs like she tickled the ivories. He gritted his teeth. From the moment he saw her, he knew she was special. He felt himself getting lost in her. She was everything he wanted, but he wouldn't let his physical response overwhelm him. Juju wouldn't be a quick one and done. He knew the killer would want to enjoy the chase, the conquest, the destruction and end of pain. Justin turned his full attention to Juju.

"I own some used car lots. In my free time, I enjoy working on cars as a hobby. I've rebuilt several classics and drive them in parades. Maybe you'd like to ride in my GTO in the Fourth of July parade next year. I'm almost done refinishing it. I could match the paint to the color of your eyes. Of course, if I did that, maybe no one would notice the car because it would fade next to your beauty." Juju blushed, her innocence drawing him ever deeper under her spell. "I'd like to take you for a ride, Juju." She leaned forward with her chin cupped in her hand, looking dreamily into his eyes.

"May I take you to lunch on Friday?" Justin asked, hoping she'd say yes. He noticed the way Juju shot a quick glance at her sister as if to ask permission. He saw Meg giving her 'the look'. The one that seemed to say they needed to talk before she made any decisions or commitments.

"I'd like that, Justin, really, I would. I have to check my schedule. Can I let you know?"

Justin patted her hand and smiled, feeling disappointed. "Sure. You check. Hey, I need to go. I have a meeting in the morning. What's your number? I'll text you." Justin didn't have a meeting. He had someone to find. He stood and made his goodbyes to the group.

Justin stood, prompting Meg to glance at her watch. "Oh, look at the time. We should go too." Pushing back their chairs in synch, the three women rose like a murmuration of starlings following on the heels of Justin's exit. Moving as one, they said goodnight. Rob insisted he escort them to their car, unaware they were being watched.

****

The car sat under the same cedar trees, giving him an unobstructed view as everyone exited. Tonight, the ladies were in one car, so separating the long-haired blonde from the pack would not be possible. Slamming his fist against the steering wheel, he took a deep breath and drove to the shop to change into his uniform and seek a diversion.

He drove to the pizza joint on the north side of campus and waited patiently. He smiled, knowing that the next gift from the gods would exit shortly and she'd be his.

****

Debbie finished her mug of ice-cold brew and flashed a teasing smile at the guys. The tight jeans and her low-cut t-shirt didn't hide any of her better assets. Her blonde hair floated just past her shoulders. She wore it loose tonight. It had been fun flirting with the three frat boys who had been buying her beer all evening. Silly boys. They may buy her beer, but she wasn't easily bought. Blowing kisses at the hopeful fellows, she pulled her jacket on and walked out the door as steadily as the four beers she'd consumed allowed. Good thing she only lived a few blocks away. She didn't think she'd be able to drive. When Debbie reached the middle of the block, a blue and white pulled up next to her. A cutie in uniform rolled down his window.

"Good evening, ma'am. Nice night for a walk, but you shouldn't be out alone this late. It's not safe. How about I give you a lift home?" he asked in his most concerned officer of the law voice.

Debbie could hardly believe her luck. What a doll. He wore his wavy dark hair trimmed short around his face and ears, but left it a little long on top. He had a wonderful five o'clock shadow working and his dark eyes assessed her with an easy smile. Debbie sighed. After playing the tease with the three frat boys, she was horny as hell.

"That would be great, officer. Can I play with your

lights and siren?" she asked seductively as she sashayed up to his car.

"Honey, you can push my buttons and touch all my knobs. I'll even let you blow my whistle. Looks like I'll have to take you to the station and frisk you. Get in, ma'am," he said as he jumped out and opened the back door. Debbie giggled, pretending to be under arrest, playing along with the fantasy.

"Will you have to cuff me?" she asked, toying with her hair and pressing her breasts against him. She ran her hands down his chest and to his crotch.

"I'm sure I will, ma'am, I'm sure I will. I'll also have to hold on to your purse in case you are carrying any illegal contraband." He smiled from ear to ear. He couldn't believe his luck. Not only would she be fun, she'd be a willing participant—at first. He could do all the kinky things he liked to do. She was already doing the role playing he enjoyed so much. He was sure she'd be into some bondage based on the handcuff remark. She might even be willing to try a little S&M. Then, when she realized he didn't intend to let her go and his attentions grew more violent and cruel, she'd beg and plead. It would be even sweeter. God, how he loved it when they cried and begged for mercy.

Chapter 4

Juju set each plate down on the table a little harder than necessary, taking out her frustration. "I don't know why you insist on doing a background check on everyone that wants to date me. It's only lunch, for God's sake. I'm twenty-one, legal and I can make my own decisions, you know!" Juju followed the plates with a clattering of silverware, haphazardly placing them at each setting. "I bet you're not doing any background checks on your detective, and he is interested in you."

Meg sighed in exasperation. "Okay, first off, Mr. Adams is a friend of John's. Justin is a complete stranger to us all. Second, he is interested in history and we were discussing my upcoming lecture. We weren't flirting, and he wasn't coming on to me."

Juju barked out a laugh. "Not coming on to you? Come on, Meg!" M stepped into the middle of it and laid a hand over Juju's arm.

"She has you there, Meg. I watched his hand twitch as he fought to keep from touching yours. His gaze rarely wandered from your face, unless he observed the scene unfolding between Juju and her new young man. There were visible sparks. And do you know what? I am glad. It's about time you had a little romance in your life."

Juju raised her chin smugly, and crossed her arms

over her chest until Meg raised her finger to make her third and final point. "I shouldn't have to remind you about what happened to me. I know you don't have the details, but believe me, not everything is as it seems. Sometimes you have to dig a little deeper to see the true worth of an individual. All I'm doing is running a Spokeo on him and checking out his social media presence. It's not like I'm running him through the National Crime Information Center. Although if I ever want to, I bet Rob could run him through the NCIC." Meg was trying to make a joke, but Juju wasn't having it. She shook her head and rolled her eyes.

"Good Lord. It won't take long to get the info back and if he looks okay, we'll have him over for dinner and all get to know him better." Meg felt the intense stare M threw over her shoulder until she caved and added, "and yes, I'll run the same on Rob."

Meg returned M's look of silent scolding, watching as she stirred the marinara sauce, checked the pasta water. The atmosphere in the room heated. Meg hoped the water boiled before Juju's temper did. She saw M press her lips together, trying hard to suppress her laughter. She sighed inwardly. Meg had this conversation too many times with M. She knew her aunt didn't disagree with her caution, but appeared to applaud Juju for standing up to her big sister.

Yes, Juju was a legal adult. Regrettably, she was also more optimistic and innocent than Meg, at least now. Meg remembered the time when M had comforted her. She'd had stars in her eyes just like Juju, but the betrayal of one's affections changed things. Meg saw the world differently now. She had always been an old soul. As a student of history, Meg studied battles and witnessed deception, failure and destruction, even if only in the pages of a book. She had battle scars from a previous relationship. Her relationship experience made her more cautious. Trust didn't come easily anymore.

"Juju, please," Meg said, taking her hand. "I don't want to argue. I love you and care about you. You two have been texting all day. Why don't you invite him to dinner on Saturday night? We'll get to know him while we wait for the background info to come back."

"Ugh! You make me so crazy, Meg Lawrence, but it's a compromise I can live with." With a smile splashing across her lovely face, Juju jumped up and danced into the living room to text Justin.

Meg pensively straightened the silverware and tried not to cry. Even after six years, it still stung. He had been a professor at Oxford. She'd landed a scholarship to spend a year studying the British perspective of the American Revolution. Conrad was in his thirties, tall and devilishly handsome. His accent hadn't hurt either. They embarked on a torrid love affair almost immediately. He had been her first, and she fell head over heels in love with him. Meg became so caught up in Conrad she almost failed her courses that semester. She had been naïve and sure he loved her. She even contemplated moving to England and hoped to become his wife.

Then she met his actual wife at a student-faculty reception.

The woman cornered Meg on the way back from the loo. She was thin and stylish and everything an ambitious professor would want to advance his career. Meg remembered the wife had consumed a few too many drinks but was sober enough to give Meg a reality slap in the face. Her face flushed as she replayed the scorn in the wife's voice and her condescending sneer.

"Do you think he loves you? Did he tell you I'm a shrew, and he plans to divorce me as soon as he can? Do you think he is the love of your life? Your Mr. Darcey? Oh, my dear, you are one in a long line of naïve American students that Conrad has seduced. You'll go home, he'll come sniveling back to me, begging my forgiveness, and when a fresh batch of cute little American coeds comes over, repeat the process. You silly little fool." With that, the wife shoved past Meg and staggered to where Conrad stood, pontificating on the Magna Carta to a new batch of wide-eyed female students. She made a show of putting her arm around his waist and raised her martini glass to Meg in a triumphant toast.

Meg closed her eyes, humiliated by her ignorance, as the memories faded and Juju returned, looking disappointed. "Well, it turns out something came up. Justin can't make lunch Friday or dinner with us Saturday. He said he'll be unavailable for the next few days and will be in touch." M&M placed the platters on the table and poured wine. The women ate their dinner in silence, everyone wrapped in their own thoughts.

Chapter 5

Kyle Erickson had promised to let Rob know the date of Kathy's funeral. Sometimes the killer attended, looking to get another jolt of excitement, feeding on the family's grief. A text with arrangements tinged on Rob's phone two days after the ME released Kathy Erickson's body. Rob planned to attend out of respect and hoped to pick up additional clues.

They filled the Methodist Church parking lot to overflowing. Rob had pulled his one suit from the back of the closet and arrived at the ten a.m. service. The Ericksons were active members and the support of the paster and friends helped them get through this difficult time. Rob signed the guest book, scanning the pages for anything that seemed unusual. He then scanned the room, letting his gaze rest on the attendees. A simple walnut box containing Kathy's ashes sat on a pedestal surrounded by several floral arrangements.

Rob entered and sat in the back pew. He glanced around the sanctuary. Built in a horseshoe configuration, an altar rested below a frosted window in front of a simple wooden cross. Solemn organ music sounded softly. People visited, hugged, dabbed a few damp eyes. When the family took their seats, the pastor read the liturgy for burial. A family member read the lessons and psalms. A solo violin played a mournful adagio Rob didn't recognize. Then the congregation rose to sing a hymn before the pastor delivered his moving homily. He recalled confirming Kathy; spoke of her faith and devotion. Sharing touching stories of her love of children, her teaching at vacation Bible school, he drew tremulous smiles and nods. When he finished speaking, assuring them that Kathy rested in the Arms of the Lord, family and friends stood and spoke of Kathy's love of life, her joy and radiant smile. Her generous spirit and sense of humor. They loved Kathy and they would miss her. At the conclusion of the service, Kyle led a devastated Theresa out, followed by the rest of the family.

Rob waited until the crowd filed past before making his way toward the foyer. Several friends surrounded the Ericksons. When Kyle saw Rob, he gave his wife to her father's care and broke away.

"Thank you for coming, Detective Adams. I guess this is part of the job. Looking for the killer. If it will help, I'll make a copy of the guest book. Are you any closer to finding who did this?" Kyle asked.

Rob saw the raw emotion, the anger, banked by his deep sorrow, burning in Kyle Erickson's eyes, and wished he could give him something. Taking Kyle Erickson's hand, Rob placed his other on Kyle's shoulder. "I came because I care, Mr. Erickson. We'll find him, count on it. Kathy deserves and will get justice. And you are correct. Sometimes the killer attends the funerals of their victims, so we'd appreciate a copy of the guest book and if there is anyone you find suspicious, let us know."

Kyle's eyes shined with unshed tears. "Thank you. God, you have no idea how difficult this has been. She was our only child. Our baby." He teetered on the brink of breakdown. Rubbing a hand under his nose, he swallowed and regained control. "Oh, before I forget it. When the medical examiner returned Kathy's personal items, they included a necklace that didn't belong to her." Pulling a plastic bag from his pocket, Kyle held it out to Rob. "I guess because it said Kathy, they assumed it belonged to our Kathy. Can you return it?"

Rob's eyes widened as he looked down at the gold necklace in Kyle's hand. The one they'd found on her body. His gaze moved up to Kyle Erickson's eyes. He hid his shock. "I can see it would be an easy mistake to make. I'll be happy to return it for you." Kyle nodded his thanks and went back to his wife. Rob pulled his phone and punched in Pete's number.

Chapter 6

Rob's next few days and nights ran together. After confirming that the necklace was the one they'd found on the body of Kathy Erickson, he added this to the crime book as another piece of the puzzle. He and Pete mulled over how the necklace fit into Kathy's murder and began a search for custom jewelry sources until a drive-by shooting at a block party temporarily claimed their attention.

Canvasing the neighbors, hoping for witnesses willing to give up information on the shooters, proved to be a challenge. The gang dominating this part of the city generated a lot of fear in the residents. They had seen enough vandalism and senseless violence to guarantee their silence. Each door-to-door interview resulted in mumbled denials of having witnessed anything, followed by the door closing in Rob and Pete's faces. Pete noted the homes with ring doorbells. Seemed that no matter how poor a household, high-tech gadgetry flourished. Working with the DA's office, they wrangled three warrants for the footage, which took time and yielded nothing.

Running into one dead end after another, Rob and Pete dropped by a body shop that serviced a lot of the gang members. A brief conversation with the owner and the invitation to take their questioning downtown shook loose another thread to tug on. The possibility of a retaliatory strike loomed. The big break finally came after an elderly man who lived behind the party house walked into the station, asking for the lead detective on the shooting.

Rob escorted Mr. James Moss to a table in the breakroom. Rob watched the grizzled old man lower himself into the chair. Thin as a rail, a powerful gust of wind could have blown the old fellow away. He noted the faded anchor tattoo on the old fellow's forearm and made small talk, building rapport.

"Saw some time in the Navy, Mr. Moss?" he asked, beginning with conversation versus interrogation. Rob set Mr. Moss at ease while Pete grabbed coffee and a Danish, placing them in front of the old man, earning a gruff 'thank you'. "Where were you stationed?" he inquired, relaxing back in his chair, and drawing a mirrored pose from the potential witness.

Taking a bite of the Danish, the old man washed it down with half his coffee and muffled a belch with the back of his hand. "Did some time in Nam off China Beach. Mostly hauled out the dead and wounded. Saw too many shot up bodies. Stupid kids don't get it. Dead is dead."

Rob and Pete gave the old man time and respect, allowing him to come around to the meat of the matter in his own time. When Moss finished the Danish, he used his finger to gather up the remaining crumbs off the plate, then meticulously folded his napkin, making a coaster for his coffee cup.

"This isn't the first time they used that house for their parties. One time, they pissed on my wife's rose bushes. Ruth loved those flowers, and they nearly killed them. Then, another time, they climbed over the fence and stole my tomatoes. Hell, if they were hungry, that would be one thing, but the little shits threw them at each other. It was a damn game for them. No respect, no respect at all!"

Pete brought over the coffeepot and refilled the old man's cup. Moss nodded his thanks and continued. "That last night, the night of the shooting? I turned off my lights and sat on my back porch. I had my twelve-gauge filled with rock salt, ready to protect what's mine. Must a been around ten-thirty when the car drove by real slow like. They had their radio blaring out that rap shit music. Bass bouncing off the buildings. They shouted insults at the party house and threw some eggs. The ones inside came running out, cussing and waving their guns, holding them sideways. Wanna-be gangsters. Idiots. Can't even do that right."

Pete made notes while Rob dove in for details. "Your house is behind the party house, isn't it, Mr. Moss? How is it you could see the front yard and street?"

"Well, I'm not directly behind the house. I'm katty-corner and the lot directly behind me and next to that party house is vacant. Got a clear view. Saw everything." Mr. Moss pushed his lips out, pinching them between thick fingers. "That was the first pass. Some idiots ran to their cars, thinking they'd give chase, I guess. But the other car turned around when they got to the end of the street and came back. By this time, just about everyone was out front, yelling and acting the fool, waving bottles of beer or their guns around." Mr. Moss leaned forward now, intent on the telling. He rested his elbows on boney knees. "I may be old, but I still move pretty well. I figured out what might happen and ran to the corner of my lot to get a better look. Stood behind the pecan tree and watched it all unfold." Shaking his head wearily, Moss sighed and sat back. Another sip of coffee met lips, sneering in disgust.

"Two of them, leaning out the car windows, opened up with semi-automatics. The fools that had run to the street had nowhere to dive for cover. They opened up with their pistols but that ain't a fair fight, semis 'gainst hand guns. The others, the survivors, jumped behind cars."

"Mr. Moss, did you notice the make of the car?" Rob held his breath. "Anything to help us identify the shooters?"

"Well, it would have been a waste of time if all I saw was the shooting. You know all that." Moss turned hopeful eyes to Pete. "Got another Danish?" he asked, licking his lips. Pete jumped up to deliver. "You're looking for a light blue Mercury Milan. I'd know that car anywhere. My wife had one just like it. The right taillight is busted. Noticed that when the car was speeding away. You might also find a bullet hole or two in the trunk. One idiot ran into the street, shooting at them as they drove off."

Satisfied with his narrative, Mr. Moss sat back and finished the second Danish, then his coffee. "I guess you'll want to write this up for me to sign. Isn't that the way they do it on all the cop shows?"

Rob smiled and nodded. "Just like they do on *Chicago PD*, Mr. Moss. My partner, Pete, here is a wiz on the keyboard. Can you give us ten minutes?"

"Sure, son. Ain't got nothing to do anyway. Garden is done, and those punks pulled all my damn tomatoes off the bushes. By the way, read about that girl being killed. You working on that too?" Rob nodded, giving a little shrug. "What is the world coming to? Crime taking over everything. It's so a decent person can't live a peaceful life anymore. Nasty business, nasty. You all have your hands full. I'll keep my ears open. Let you know if I hear anything to help."

Rob smiled his appreciation, not expecting Mr. Moss to pick up any hot leads, but thankful for his support.

Knowing he and Pete had solid information to pursue the gang shooting, Rob focused on crime solving. It took the rest of his day and lead no where.

****

Rob pushed the damp sheets aside and sat on the edge of the bed, checking the clock. Four-thirty a.m. and muggy as hell. Standing, he stretched his long frame, arms overhead, then flexed shoulders and neck. He growled a groan. Between murdered co-eds, gang shootings, and a pixie that wouldn't leave him alone, he wasn't getting much sleep. Might as well make use of the time, head to the gym and get in a workout. Tossing his workout clothes into his duffle, he drove to the police training academy on Pioneer Parkway.

The dated, one-story building sat next to the old animal shelter. Rob recalled the barking of the caged dogs, the smell of the cremated remains. It sucked that people abandoned their pets. The city worked hard to find adoptive families for each animal, but some were unadoptable and had to be put down. Years before, when he was in the academy, he'd met a retired gentleman who donated his time to spend a last day of play and affection with the dogs slated for euthanizing.

Rob remembered feeling there was something incredibly noble in that act. Now it served as a maintenance building and parking lot for the private school down the street. Using his key card, Rob entered the training center, making his way down the hall to the locker room.

The place was quiet at five a.m. Rob's footsteps echoed off the concrete block walls. They remodeled the old building, adding classrooms and a shooting range. The department used the center to hold scenario and defensive tactics training. SWAT and the Canine Division used the building for a lot of their testing and training. The gym, with its wood floor, ropes hanging from the ceiling and wrestling pads hanging on the walls, reminded Rob of his elementary school. Selecting a locker, Rob stashed his gear and stepped into the weight room. He usually enjoyed the solitude. Weight lifting required concentration on the muscle group being worked to get the full benefit from the workout. Rob focused on his back and shoulders. Beginning with bench pressing 135 pounds and moving through three sets of repetitions, increasing the weight by twenty-five pounds per side after the first rep then forty-five for the final, Rob fought to stay in the moment but, his mind was all over the boards.

Rob racked the barbell and sat up on the bench, wiping the sweat from his face. Staring at his reflection in the mirror, he mentally kicked himself. What the hell did it matter if the weight he'd selected to bench press was more than the weight of the compact body of a pixie? How the hell did he know how much she weighed? Why the hell did he care? But, he knew how much, had looked at the sweet curves and felt the fullness of her breasts when they collided with his chest that first night. He cared enough to imagine lifting her. Lifting her in his arms. Feeling her weight. Carrying her to bed.

"Hey, Adams. No dead bodies to hang around with this early in the day?" Goldberg asked, startling Rob from his musings.

Rob rose and slapped the SWAT commander on the back. "Not since I left your girlfriend's place. She kept swooning something about la petite mort."

Goldberg considered Rob's smile, then pointedly lowered his gaze to Rob's workout shorts. "Yeah, Adams. With you, it would be petite!"

Rob guffawed. "Ha! Touche, Goldberg. Touche! Catch you later, man."

Chapter 7

Debbie missed another shift. Tom kept getting her voice mail when he called. "That's it. That woman is always late and now she's missed two shifts in a row. I've had it. She can whistle Dixie if I give her another chance." He huffed as he hung up on yet another unanswered call. Aggravated, he ran his finger down the employee phone list to see who he could call to come in and cover the shift when Barb walked up, setting down a trio of pitchers.

"Geez, Tom. You look like you're ready to stroke out. What's wrong?" Tom appreciated Barb's concern. Irresponsible employees frustrated him and he sometimes railed at them, but they knew his kind heart tempered his anger. He demanded a lot of his employees and then covered the cost of their college textbooks for a Christmas bonus.

"Oh, it's Debbie. She's not answering her phone and now we're going to be short a waitress again. What a flake."

Barb paused while putting ice in the water pitchers. She turned to her boss with a worried expression. "Tom, that's not like Debbie to miss an entire shift, let alone two. Sure, come in late. We all know that's her typical behavior, but she needs this job and the money too much to miss work. Have you called anyone else? Maybe her neighbor knows where Debbie is. If she doesn't, maybe we should call the police to do a welfare check. There is supposedly some wacko, stalking girls on campus."

Tom heard the worry in Barb's tone. As steamed as he felt about Debbie missing her shift, everything Barb said made sense. He took her concern seriously. Although Debbie was a flake and came in late more often than not, she rarely missed her entire shift. Now he worried, too. He called the police.

****

Officer Gillespie pulled the duty officer position for the shift and manned the desk when Tom Baker called in. A request for a welfare check on one of his employees seemed an unusual request, but something pinged as he took down the information. Logging in the call and recording the information, Gillespie walked over to Rob's desk. "This could be nothing, but I thought you might like to know about it, maybe check it out. This guy, Tom Baker, owns Lucky Lucy Burgers. Says one of his waitresses has missed two shifts in a row. He is concerned and called to ask for a welfare check. The girl's name is Debbie Crawford. She lives five blocks off campus." Gillespie had pulled her driver's license photo off the Department of Motor Vehicles. He put the report on Rob's desk along with the picture, tapping it with his forefinger. "She is young, has long blonde hair and fits the profile."

Leaning back in his chair, feet propped on his desk, Rob had been watching Pete's internal struggle over whether to eat a third blueberry donut when Gillespie showed him the photo. Dropping his feet to the floor, he sat straight up and grabbed the report. After a quick perusal, he jumped up and punched Pete in the shoulder. "Let's go, buddy. Donuts can wait—Debbie can't." Calling over his shoulder on the way out the door, he asked Gillespie to call the dean's office to get all the contact info for Debbie Crawford, class schedule, and any extracurricular activities. Anything and everything they could get on her.

Rob pulled up in front of a dated building holding two-over-two shoe box sized studio apartments on a postage sized lot with four street side parking slots. A ramshackle frame house about the size of a two-car garage sat at the back of the property. A sign by the torn screen door read 'manager'. Walking up to her apartment, Rob knocked on her door. No one answered, so he sent Pete to track down the manager for a key. Rob circled the building and checked her windows, looking for any sign of a break in. Nothing looked out of the ordinary. No forced entry, broken windows or footprints in the scant shrubbery surrounding the building.

Pete returned, dragging a frazzled landlord behind him. Rob explained the situation, citing the request for a welfare check. The landlord, whose face showed the broken vein ravages of alcoholism and breathed out the smell of rotten teeth, bowed his back.

"I have a responsibility to my tenants." The landlord crossed his arms over a bony chest covered by a holey t-shirt stained with arm-pit sweat and something else unidentifiable. A miasma of marijuana fumes drifted from the hovel the man called home. "You ain't got no warrant, you ain't getting in."

This pissed Rob off. He hated a-holes that pulled the civil rights card, especially when they couldn't spell civil rights. He made a judgement call. "I see. May I ask your name, sir? Because I can get a warrant to enter Ms. Crawford's apartment as well as yours for obstructing a police investigation and suspicion of being in possession of illegal substances." He politely informed the man, while opening the note app on his cell phone.

Rob's gaze never wavered from the landlord's dilated pupils. Two minutes later, the man's jittery hand reached into his pocket, producing a key ring. Rob nodded. "Thank you, sir. If you will kindly open the door and remain here, we'll complete our check and if all is all right, be out of your hair."

Rob and Pete stepped inside. The tiny studio apartment's décor was what one would expect. Hand me down couch and chair in the living room with a 42-inch flat screen on a TV stand made from boards and milk cartons. An unmade queen size bed sat tucked into a corner with clothes strewn across it and on the floor. The bathroom looked like a bomb had exploded, with makeup and hair products littering every surface, a robe hanging on a hook behind the door and dirty towels on the floor. The towels along with the shower and sink were bone dry. No one had used the bathroom for a few days.

The coffee maker in the tiny galley kitchen had about a half cup of coffee sitting in the pot with tiny spores of mold growing in it, showing it had been a few days since she'd brewed it. Nothing looked wrong to Rob, but nothing looked right, either. "Pete, let's seal it up and open a missing person report. I have a bad feeling about this."

****

Rob and Pete pulled into the parking lot of Lucky

Lucy Burgers. The small joint catered to the college crowd, offering burgers, dogs and grilled chicken sandwiches, all served with fries. A fire department occupancy sign stated a capacity of 40, but Tom squeezed in another four tables, bringing the total seating to 52. The place was jumping and Tom was humping to cover the shortage of wait staff.

Rob waited patiently at the door until Tom came up with two menus in hand. "Table for two, gentlemen?" he asked, surprised that two older guys would come in. Rob subtly turned his badge toward Tom, not wishing to call unnecessary attention to their presence.

"Detectives Adams and Bonnert. Are you Tom Baker?" he returned his wallet to his back pocket, taking in Tom's wide eyes.

"Ah, yeah. That's me. Are you here about Debbie? I just called for a welfare check. She missed a couple of shifts." Tom had backed up, blindly reaching behind him to put down the menus. His butt found a stool. He sank down, hand to his heart. "She's okay, isn't she?"

"We are looking into that. Do you have a few moments to speak with us?" Rob and Pete spent the better part of two hours talking to the owner and staff of Lucky Lucy Burgers. The place had regular customers and Tom cooperated fully, sharing the names and contact numbers he knew. The staff filled in several more blanks.

Rob and Pete were contacting all Debbie Crawford's class and workmates, friends, and family, getting nowhere fast. Plowing through her phone records and social media posts gave them nothing of note. They found one post from a guy saying how hot she looked when he'd seen her at Lucky Lucy. Rob figured the guy just wanted to get lucky himself. Rob was looking for a reference to a cop. It continued to be the one loose thread from Kathy Erickson's case that bothered him and would have been perfect had Debbie shared a similar experience. She wasn't pure as the driven snow, but, if the same creep that took Kathy had also nabbed her, she didn't deserve it.

They tracked her last known whereabouts to the beer joint on campus, where she'd teased three frat boys and enjoyed four beers on their dime. According to the bartender, the three guys had stayed after she left. Pete ran their backgrounds and found no major issues, outside of a few traffic violations and misdemeanors for drunk and disorderly conduct. No one else pinged their radar, and Rob was getting frustrated with the whole thing.

The one lead they had was an elderly lady that called in about flashing lights shining in her living room windows the night Debbie disappeared. Rob scheduled an interview for eleven a.m. He hoped she'd be credible and not some crazy old cat lady reporting aliens.

The small frame house sat on a corner a block from the campus pub where Debbie had last been seen. Rob pulled to the curb, shut down the engine and climbed out of the car. He stood, looking in the direction Debbie would have walked that night. Turning, his gaze moved over a vacant lot in desperate need of mowing. It held the remnants of steps and a cracked sidewalk leading nowhere. Across the street, an older commercial building held a dry cleaner and print shop. Katty corner to the house, a parking lot and garage catering to the maintenance of college vehicles, filled two lots. The street paralleled Abram and didn't carry a lot of traffic after dark. Rob's gaze landed on Loudale Evans' orange brick 1950's miniature ranch. Her home being one of the last residential properties on the street, flashing lights would have gotten her attention.

Pete led the way up the steps to the small covered stoop and rang the bell. Rob stood at the bottom of the steps. His gaze flicked to the front window when he saw the curtains twitch. Mrs. Evans didn't appear to be a fool who answered a door without checking.

A tall, rail-thin woman opened the door. She wore her silver hair short. It's waves creating a cap that hugged her skull. She'd pushed her reading glasses up on her head and held a book in her hand, a finger marking her place. Music drifted out from the back of the house. Classical and muted. A smile wreathed her face. Introducing themselves, Rob and Pete found themselves invited into a small living room.

"Come in, please. Have a seat. Can I get you some tea? Coffee?" Mrs. Evans set down her book and held her frail hands clasped to her breast.

Pete, being better at the small talk than Rob, declined the offer for them both. They glanced around the room and settled on the small sofa. Mrs. Evans returned to her rocker, feet planted together on the floor, looking expectantly at the two men. Rob exchanged a quick look with Pete, thinking, oh boy.

"Mrs. Evans, thank you for seeing us. You mentioned to our desk sergeant that you saw suspicious flashing lights on the night of September 22nd. Can you tell us what time that was?"

"Yes, I believe so. You know I am a participant in the university study on aging, so I hear a lot of the hubbub going on. I saw the posting about the wacko, the warning about being vigilant. When I saw those lights, well, I wondered if there might be a connection. So, let me see." She reached for a calendar on the small table next to her chair. Tapping her finger on the date in question, her brow furrowed in concentration. "Ah, yes. Tuesdays I watch my FBI shows. About half-way through *FBI Most Wanted*—that Dylon McDermott is a real looker." Smiling coquettishly, she dimpled at Rob. "You're not so bad yourself, detective." She winked broadly. Pete coughed to hide his chuckle.

Rob grimaced, rolling his eyes. "Uh, thank you. You were saying, Mrs. Evans?"

"Yes. So about half-way through the program, I see the flashing lights reflecting off my television screen. It was a good part too. They were chasing the bad guys. Lots of fast cars and shooting. That must have been about nine-forty."

Rob jotted down the information, hopeful. The old woman seemed to have all her faculties about her. If she saw something that would help find Debbie, they could close the case. He leaned forward, elbows resting on his knees. "So, you notice the lights reflecting on your television screen. Did you happen to look out the window?"

"Well, of course I did. A commercial came on, so I went to the window. Sometimes the tow truck brings in a vehicle at night, but this was a little further down the street. I couldn't see the vehicle, only the flashing lights bouncing off the windows of the dry cleaners and into my window. Besides, the tow trucks have yellow lights. These were blue and red. I'd swear on a stack of bibles."

Thirty minutes later, having reviewed and confirmed the information Mrs. Evans had to share, Rob and Pete climbed into their sedan and headed back to the precinct. The timeline for when Debbie left the campus pub lined up with the time Mrs. Evans noticed the flashing lights, and she was certain they were blue and red. They'd have to check to see which patrol was on that night and if they were in the area. But it formed another piece of the puzzle. A puzzle that was all one color right now, or maybe two.

Blue and Red.

Chapter 8

Debbie woke up. The hot cop turned out to be a real sicko. She hurt all over. He'd stripped her naked. Using a dog chain and handcuffs, he tethered her to the headboard. The cuffs cut into her wrists. She'd been given just enough slack to squat over the five-gallon bucket left for her to use as a toilet. The bucket smelled awful, precariously close to overflowing.

Five bottles of water sat on the nightstand, along with a bag of corn chips. She'd finished the pizza he'd brought her last night. It tasted like cardboard and hurt her teeth to chew it. Debbie wondered if the creep had knocked some loose when he hit her. She brought her hand up to her face and could feel the swelling around her eye and cheekbone. When they'd first arrived, they'd played bad cop and naughty coed; everything was fun until he got rough. When he hurt her and did things that were really perverted, Debbie protested. That was the first time he hit her. She'd shut up and let him do horrible things—touch her in gross ways and use sex tools on her. It made her sick and embarrassed. Then he made cuts on the inside of her thighs and on her breasts. He kept ranting about wanting to brand her like he had the others, but then got angry because he'd lost his stupid ring. He kept bragging about how the ring was a special gift from his dad and he wanted to share it with her. Debbie cried and begged him to stop, to let her go home. He just looked at her with his dead eyes and laughed. His arousal increased the more she cried, so she stopped. That made him more mad, so he hit her again. When he returned to the shabby little room where he held her captive, she pleaded again. "I won't tell anyone, I promise. I just want to go home."

He smoothed her hair back from her bruised face. "I know you won't tell anyone. You have been so much fun. Thank you, Debbie." Taking a brush from his pocket, he brushed her hair; long gentle strokes that calmed and soothed. He continued to brush her hair and Debbie closed her eyes, thinking he intended to let her go home.

Tears trickled down her cheeks. Licking her swollen and bruised lips, she rasped out, "Why are you doing this?"

"Oh, dear sweet Debbie." He put down the brush, sighing. "Because I can, that's why." He closed his hands around her neck and squeezed. Her eyes flew open with fear and realization.

"Because I can." Her legs kicked, her feet drumming, pushing against the foot of the bed as she fought for air. His body trembled with excitement. Smiling, he choked the life out of her pleading eyes. As her body convulsed for the last time, he came, spewing his seed into the condom he'd put on to contain his semen. There would be no traces of him on dear sweet Debbie. His last act was to bathe her, wash and brush her hair and prepare his composition of cruelty for the world to see. He clasped the necklace around her neck that read, 'Debbie'; his parting gift to her.

The call came in at 6:15 a.m. Patrol found the body of a young female near the 3100 block of Pleasant

Ridge Rd. Preliminary ID of the victim came back as Debbie Crawford. Rob rolled out of bed, showered and drove to the crime scene, repeating the same frustrating and unproductive steps he'd taken with Kathy Erickson. They'd found Debbie beaten, raped, strangled, and left naked; this time in a shallow ditch overgrown with shrubbery and hackberry trees. Once again, the scene offered few clues.

Chapter 9

M pulled into john Q's Food and Spirits a little after 1:15 in the afternoon. She'd called John and arranged to meet him for a late lunch. Whenever the girls were busy, she would stop by for a quick bite and chat. She liked John and knew the feeling was mutual.

They had a lot to unpack from Tuesday night and she looked forward to this lunch more than the others she usually enjoyed with John. Flipping down the visor, she checked her lipstick in the mirror, smiled at her reflection. The years had treated her kindly. After one last check of her hair, M walked into the tavern.

"Hello, gorgeous!" John greeted her with a kiss on the cheek. "When are we going to take this lunch date up to my apartment and have dessert?" John was an outrageous flirt, but M could give as good as she got.

"When you shave that wooly caterpillar you have growing under your nose and win the lottery, big boy!" she replied, turning her back so he could take her wrap.

"Baby, you'd love the feel of my caterpillar on certain parts of your anatomy if you'd let me show you, AND…when I'm with you, I feel like I've already won the lottery." John smoothly returned with a wicked gleam in his eyes.

"Oh, John. You're such a raconteur." M gave a throaty laugh, patted his cheek, and sat down, making herself comfortable. She fussed with the place setting to gather her thoughts and then got right down to business. One of the many traits John admired about her.

"John, we both know why I'm here," she stated.

John wiggled his eyebrows. "Is it sex?" When M gave him a disapproving scowl, he retreated. "Ah, hope springs eternal." Sighing, he nodded. "Yes, I know."

"So, who was the guy last week?" M watched as the waitress set down their waters and took their order. John wouldn't say anything until they were alone.

"Well, you can't blame a guy for dreaming my charm is what draws you to my fine establishment. But I take your meaning. To which guy are you referring?"

"Both, but for different reasons. Since you introduced Rob, I am sure you know him and he is an upstanding man. I like him and I thought he and Meg hit it off. They appeared to have mutual interests. I'd like to see her open up some. What can you tell me about him?"

"Fair question, M. I know how important Meg is to you. She is also important to me. I've grown to love her like a daughter, so I wouldn't introduce her to someone I didn't know and trust." With that said, John sat back and pressed his lips together, wondering how much of Rob's past to share. John drummed his fingers on the tabletop, thinking. "Rob is a very private man. He rarely lets someone in, especially of the female persuasion. A past love hurt him, M, betrayed him actually. I'm not sure he is ready to open his heart or even remembers how, but when he does, the depth of his love and commitment will be unshakable."

This was exactly what M wanted to hear. Meg always pretended to be strong but deep down she feared being made a fool like she had when she gave her heart and her innocence to Conrad. Her walls were tall and virtually impenetrable. M sensed a strength in Rob that might break through, should he be interested, and she hoped he would be. M wanted Meg to find a love with a man like that and hoped Meg would come to see beyond her own hurt.

"If you think Rob is okay, I'll support it. The other guy? That's a different story. I'm not sure. Too smooth, too…guarded, and not in a way that shows he had his heart broken in the past. We all know what that looks like. Meg is doing her usual research and if something isn't right, she'll discourage Juju. Unfortunately, Juju is smitten with the fellow and I'm afraid she won't listen. Had you ever seen him in here before that night?"

John sat back, waiting while the waitress set down their plates. He rested his elbow on the table and his chin in his hand, considering how to explain his thoughts. Using his fingers to smooth down his mustache, he blew out a sigh and gave M a serious look. "I've been in this business for a long time, M. I try to run a respectable, family friendly establishment. You know my crowd. We're not a pickup joint. I rarely get a lone gentleman coming in. I might have seen him once before, but Justin isn't a regular. Most of the guys that hang out here are part of a group. They come here to watch the game. Sometimes I get someone newly divorced and they don't cook. Those guys tend to sit at the bar, drowning their anger and sorrows. I get to know them and feel them out. A few single guys, like Rob, come in to eat a solitary meal, nurse one beer and leave. Heck, we're in a semi-residential area between a self-storage business and an auto repair shop. We cater to the neighborhood crowd. When he offered to buy drinks for you gals, I thought it was in appreciation for Juju's piano playing. It's not the first time someone has stood for a round for you, but they usually don't sit down and make a move on one of you either. Has he been pushing to see Juju again?"

M put down her knife and fork, pushing her plate away. She had lost her appetite. "No, and maybe I'm concerned for no reason. Apparently, he asked her to lunch on Friday and had to cancel. He also turned down a dinner invitation. He mentioned having other commitments. But he is still texting her like mad, and she is getting that giddy, school girl crush look in her eyes. If his schedule opens up and he asks her out, I'm afraid she'll accept and not tell us. If something goes south, we won't know and won't be able to protect her."

John shook his head and gave M a raised eyebrow, about to ask the big question that was bothering her. Before he could speak, M rushed on. "Yes, I know. She is an adult and capable of making her own decisions. Oh, John, I don't know. I heard about that young woman they found dead. Maybe I read too many murder mysteries. He just—I don't know—felt off. Kind of gave me the creeps; that's all." M brushed a hand over her hair, smoothing a stray lock back into place. Taking a sip of her wine, she blew out a frustrated breath.

John reached across the table and took her hand, giving it a little squeeze. "I can tell you're worried. Since you seem to approve of Rob and he is the Dudley Do-right of Detectives," John said, smiling to lighten the mood, "how about I ask him to see if he can pull some strings and do a more thorough background on

Whitman then Meg will get with Spokeo?"

M smiled and squeezed John's hand back. "Keep this up, John McKean, and we just might have dessert in your apartment sooner than you think."

Before M left following their lunch, John turned over the map Meg had spied hanging on his wall. She promised to pass it along. John knew the map wasn't legit and knew Meg would easily figure it out. Meg, damn good at her job, knew American revolutionary history like the back of her hand. Her dad had been a respected expert in the field and Meg followed suit. John wondered how she would react to the forgery.

****

Rob was in the middle of a coaching session with Ben and Alex when he got John's call. He called a timeout and turned the boys loose to practice fielding bunts. He listened to John recount his lunch conversation with M, asking him to look into Whitman. Rob wasn't surprised. That both John and M thought Justin was a little 'off' matched Rob's initial reaction. Something hadn't felt right from the moment he'd sat down. Rob wasn't picking up any direct threat or danger, but Justin's eyes were too wary. He scanned the room as if he was constantly on the lookout for some peril. It seemed like he was hiding something. His angling to separate Juju from the group, his evasive answers and glib replies to friendly conversation had made Meg uncomfortable and, for some odd reason, that made Rob uncomfortable. Maybe the Pixie persona he'd attached to her made her seem innocent and vulnerable. Rob felt the need to shelter and protect her and those she loved. Rob informed John he couldn't do anything legally, but he'd call in a favor or two and get some history on the guy if he could.

John's call had Rob thinking about Meg. He'd done a little background checking on her. A simple online search showed several articles she'd written about The Revolutionary War. Her CV was impressive. A doctorate at twenty-six and co-chair of the university history department seemed a little intimidating when he considered his lowly bachelor's degree. But for all that, Meg was humble and approachable. Her enthusiasm for her work didn't come off as stuffy, but as excited. She wanted to share that excitement with everyone. And she was damn cute. But Carrie had been cute, too. No, Carrie had been drop-dead gorgeous, and she'd screwed him over.

When his injury put him on the injured reserve list and they'd sent him back to the minors, he'd been crushed. Calling his dad to share the devastating news, he received words of encouragement. His dad talked him through the disappointment. Rob had been at an away game when it all came down. He flew home, expecting Carrie to be as supportive as his dad, only to walk in on her and his best friend naked, hitting a grand slam in his bed. On that day, he lost his pitching future, his fiancé and his best friend in one triple play.

So involved in his musings, Rob never saw the bunt coming until it hit him solidly in the solar plexus. Rob rubbed the sore spot. Good thing an eleven-year-old didn't hit with power. But, everything about Meg hit with power. Meg drew him in a way Carrie never had. Did Rob dare risk lobbing one over the plate? It could end up an in-field home run.

Chapter 10

The minute M delivered the map, Meg disappeared into her library, excitement vibrating off her. She pulled out her high-powered optical hand-held glass with a lamp magnifier to focus on the map and all its details. Several generations improved from the one her dad had used; the magnifier enhanced images far beyond what he'd enjoyed. Her dad's love of history had been what drew Meg to the subject. Meg loved her folks and missed them. While Aunt M had been a staunch and loving replacement, no one could take the place of one's mom and dad. She and Juju had lost their folks when they were so young. Juju hadn't been old enough to remember a lot about them, but Meg had been twelve and she remembered everything. She was at the age when moms knew nothing and dads were the knight in shining armor.

The day of the accident, she and her mom had quarreled over ear piercing. A stupid argument that Meg regretted to this day. She remembered storming up to her room, slamming the door. She hadn't bothered to say goodbye to her parents when they left for dinner with friends. Juju was with a neighbor and Meg should have felt proud that her folks thought her mature enough to spend the evening on her own. She spent the evening playing music and reading her book on Betsy Ross until she heard her aunt's voice calling for her.

When M opened her bedroom door, Meg's happy life changed forever.

Meg felt a surprising wetness on her cheek. She hadn't realized she'd been crying and used the back of her hand to wipe away the tears. It had been a long time since something had stirred those memories. Her emotions were too close to the surface, and she clamped down on them. *I must be tired from all the research.* She stepped away from the table, getting her emotions under control. Running her fingers idly over the spines of her father's books and humming softly under her breath, she remembered his words of encouragement. Meg pulled out his copy of the John Adams biography by Page Smith. The two volumes of small print and big words had taken her the entire summer of her freshman year in high school to read. She slogged through it, dictionary at her side, but she'd done it. That was when she knew she'd follow in her dad's footsteps, teaching history. Thinking of John Adams brought Rob Adams to mind.

Hugging the tome to her chest, she walked over to the French doors leading from her office to her private balcony. Rob was an enigma. Open and talkative when discussing history, he maintained his privacy about his personal life. He smiled and laughed, but his eyes remained somber. Meg thought him interesting, not to mention very attractive. She enjoyed seeing him and wouldn't mind getting to know him better. Shaking her head, she laughed at herself. Here she was cautioning Juju about getting romantically involved, and she was hoping for the same opportunity.

Gazing into the flower garden below, Meg thought about her first encounter with Rob. She hadn't seen him as he turned from the bar and after hitting what felt to her like a brick wall she bounced back. Meg had to tip her head back to see his face. She stared into the warmest brown eyes. Tall and rock solid, he looked startled. Of course, who wouldn't be? He'd reached out powerful hands to steady her, and she noticed the well-defined forearms leading to muscled biceps. She recalled the feel of a washboard abdomen and broad shoulders through the t-shirt he'd worn that night. And she remembered the sight of his long legs, trim hips and well-proportioned body as she attempted to wipe dry his clothes. When he'd taken the towel from her hands to wipe his own clothes, it drew her eye to his crotch and she remembered having somewhat scandalous thoughts. Mostly, though, she remembered his eyes. They were hooded and guarded. She didn't think he trusted easily, and that made her feel sad. In that split second when their eyes locked, Meg saw into a soul that she somehow felt had witnessed terrible things and yet held compassion. Somehow, she knew this man would fight for truth, justice, and the American way. No, wait, that was a comic book superhero. Putting the book back on the shelf, Meg set aside such silly thoughts and sat down, once again, prepared to read a map allegedly from the late 18th century.

John had entrusted her with the original document, knowing she would safe-guard it. He'd placed it between two acid free cardboard panels and covered it with more acid free tissue to protect it during transport to her home office. If this was a fake, he'd gone overboard with the packaging. Mumbling to herself as she was wont to do when researching, she set out her legal pad and pen. Carefully unwrapping the precious package, she shut out the worldly distractions and began her inspection with the obvious.

"All right, John, let's see what we've got here. The fibers in the paper appear to be macerated cotton. Consistent with the time. I don't see any chain lines, but if they printed it after 1775, it might not have them. The discoloration looks authentic. Of course, an accomplished forger can do that with coffee grounds. Hmmm, the wear along the creases looks genuine, and the small holes and finger smudges at the edges are consistent with what one would expect. Of course, that doesn't guarantee authenticity. Overall, everything on the surface, without the benefit of carbon dating or extensive testing, appears to be original. If so, this is an incredible discovery. But what are the odds it would still exist in this condition after all this time?" Meg knew better than to bet on those odds and so did John, although he hadn't said so.

"Umm-hmm." Meg made little ticking sounds with her tongue, thinking out loud. "Let's see what else we have here. It looks like an early lithograph to which an artist added color after the initial printing, but. Hmm…that's unusual, and I don't see any show-through. It lacks the dimensional feel an engraved map would have, placing its making after 1800."

Meg jotted down all her observations and sat tapping her index finger to her lips, thinking. Based on just the physical characteristics she observed, she estimated the age of the map to be around 1800, but that isn't everything one needs to consider. Meg knew forgers could be very creative. Next, Meg looked at the style of the cartography—was it consistent with other maps of that era? Even though mapmakers had their own distinct style, most maps used similar patterns when notating rivers or mountains. Some symbols used were questionable, but still not outright proof of forgery. Once Meg had given the materials and style a solid going over, she moved on to other basics to prove its legitimacy. The names of landmarks or any settlements—were they correct and did they exist during the time the map was suggesting? Smirking to herself, Meg sat back with a laugh. She didn't think so. Someone had inserted a small town by the name of Alexander City, along with a symbol for railroad tracks. Ha!

True, this area, and potentially this town, might have been an English trading post in the late seventeenth century. But, incorporated as Youngsville in 1872, it didn't get its current name, Alexander City, until The Savannah and Memphis Railway came to Youngsville. Whoever created this map didn't do their research. Youngsville changed its name to Alexander City, named for the president of the S&M Railway, Edward P. Alexander in 1873, approximately 73 years after the purported creation of the map. Certainly, the English had a presence in the area and laid claims to the area north of the Gulf of Mexico. However, so did the French. The English were more successful in developing alliances with the native tribes, one based on trading with the Indians. The French ceded the area to Great Britain in 1763 after their defeat in The Seven Years' War. Then, during the Revolutionary War, Britain ceded the region to the Spanish. It's possible some English established a settlement hoping to rekindle the conflict with the American Colonies, but they surely would not have used a map with a town named Alexander City.

Blowing out a sigh, Meg settled back in her chair and ran a hand through her hair, her only thought being *Oh, John, what am I supposed to think?* Meg would bet her bottom dollar this was a forgery. A damn fine one. Now all she had to do was get a straight answer out of John about how he came to possess it. Picking up her phone, she sent him a quick text asking if she could come by to discuss her findings. His immediate reply was a thumbs-up emoji.

Meg took her purse and drove to Q's. Traffic got jammed because of construction on Ashton Lane when someone attempted a left turn on Duluth Dr. The thoughtless driver blocked traffic for anyone wanting to continue straight. The A/C in her car coughed and spit, adding to her frustration. When she pulled into the parking lot, the clock showed 4:45. Thankfully, the lunch crowd had left and the evening rush wouldn't start until 5:30. Plenty of time to nail John down on the provenance of the map, real or otherwise.

"John, I've looked at the map. I think it's safe to say you and I both know the map is a forgery. The sixty-four thousand dollar question would be, did you know it before or after you acquired it? Or, maybe I should ask, did you really find it at the flea market?"

John busied himself cleaning glasses and wiping down the bar, avoiding for the moment responding to her question. He shrugged his shoulders.

"Maybe a wee bit of scotch and a sit down with no interruptions is in order here, Meg," he said, pouring two fingers into a glass. He turned the bar over to his staff and motioned Meg to a table in the corner. Once settled, John took a sip and looked at Meg. "I have an impressive collection, Meg, you know that. Most of it is authentic. But several pieces I create as part of the décor for this place. People notice. I've become somewhat of a celebrity in the area and so when I go to all the historical society functions folks naturally come up to me looking for particular pieces. They seem to believe I can conjure up what they're looking for. You know me well enough to know that I always explain the importance of provenance. I make no guarantee that what they are holding in their hands is real, stressing again that provenance is required for all historical documents. But, if you could see the looks on their faces when they hold a document in their hands that supports what their great Aunt Edna has been saying for years…Well, they won't be selling their collections to anyone and most of them are just so damn proud to have a document to confirm their antecedents. It doesn't seem such a bad thing to be doing. I don't do it to make a profit, just to make folks happy. I know it's silly, but it makes people proud to be American and God knows we need that right now." He looked at Meg, looking only a little guilty.

Meg studied his face. She knew that, in reality, he wasn't bamboozling anyone. He set his prices based on the potential genuineness of the piece. Every time he sold an item, he provided a disclaimer, stating that without provenance, he could not verify its authenticity. He had plausible deniability. "John. your recreations are incredibly realistic. I just hope you are careful not to give anyone the wrong impression. I'm sure your clients are happy knowing these items are faithful recreations of documents, possibly from the period. And I know you tell them that if the item was real, this is what it would look like."

John smiled, knowing her love of history and soft heart wouldn't allow her to dash the hopes and dreams of his buying public as long as he didn't cheat them. "Okay, you have figured out my secret, although I would bet you've known for quite some time. I don't always sell fakes. Many of my finds are real and I come by them honestly. It's not my fault folks don't know what they have, and it comes up in estate sales at a fraction of the actual value. I do the legwork and my buyers reap the benefits of my efforts. When I don't have exactly what the buyer is looking for, I offer to recreate it for them. Most are happy to just have something to set on the bookshelf or frame and hang on their wall. Folks yearn to be connected to history and the founding of this country. Who am I to deny them the pleasure?" He nodded, and they struck a reasonable bargain about his sales pitch and the use of several of his pieces in her upcoming Flea Market Find or Forgery Lecture.

"*C'est la guerre.*" John tipped his glass to Meg in approbation. "Sometimes things happened because of incompetence or circumstances beyond one's control. I'm not worried my clientele will lose faith in my work. After all, most of my simple recreations are more affordable and sell in greater number than the authentic ones. And, when luck is with me and I find that authentic piece, it only adds extra luster to my recreations. That End of Pain coin, for instance? I found that in a most unlikely place and you authenticated it. I'll keep the original and use it to recreate more pieces for the customers that do reenactments or period documentaries. Thomas Paine is a popular rebel figure.

I've gotten quite a few hits on my website from interested parties for that one."

"John, don't you feel just a little concerned you might be taking advantage of people? What if they try to pass their recreations off as authentic? We both know you could enable something that isn't ethical. With your permission, I'd like to use several of your pieces as examples in my lecture; both the authentic and the recreations, but I don't want to negatively impact your business. Will that be a problem for you?"

John was perfectly okay with that. Raising his glass, he sipped, considering. "Meg, your calling attention to the quality of my recreations will only enhance them. It's not like I'm breaking the law. It's just 'art' and I'm a damn talented artist. You know, people believe what they want to believe." They clinked their glasses in agreement and talked about her upcoming lecture and which pieces she wanted to borrow.

With their heads burrowed in conversation, neither Meg nor John noticed Pete and Rob entering with a pack of hungry, rowdy ball players jostling each other, looking forward to their game of victory pizza and soda. Pete's twins saw John and ran over to say hi and tell him the big news.

"Mr. McKean, we won, we won. If we keep this up, the next stop will be the city-wide playoffs. We're going to add another trophy to your shelf over there!" They were jumping up and down, high-fiving each other when they noticed Meg. "Oh hi. Sorry to butt in. We're Alex and Ben." They stuck out their hands in greeting.

"Hello, Alex and Ben. My name is Meg." She

shook each hand offered, and smiled at their excitement. "So, you won your game and you're pretty confident you're headed to the play-offs. That's impressive. What positions do you play?"

"Alex is the pitcher and I play first base. Mr. Rob says our height is an advantage for both positions. Sometimes we switch positions and I get to pitch, but Alex is better than me. We're the best damn, I mean darn, twosome there is. We can read each other's minds and…"

Rob walked up behind them to corral their enthusiasm. "Yo, boys, inside voice, okay? Hello, John. Hi, Meg. Didn't expect to see you here. It's a pleasant surprise." Rob shook hands and sent the boys over to the table with the rest of the team. "John, the kids were amazing this afternoon. I wish you could have been there, although if you can spare a few minutes to visit with them, I'm sure you'll get a play-by-play. We're here for our victory pizza."

Meg felt a moment of indecision from Rob. She hoped he was trying to think of a way to invite her to join them when Ben ran up and grabbed his hand.

"Mr. Rob, Alex wants to order pineapple on his pizza. Is that even allowed? Sounds like something a girl would like—gross!"

Rob ruffled Ben's hair, forming a shocked 'O' with his mouth. Narrowing his eyes, Rob looked over at Meg, seeming to consider the providence of Ben's interruption. "I couldn't say, Ben, but if pineapple sounds like girl pizza, perhaps Ms. Meg would like to join us. She could give us her authentic opinion on the matter. How about it, Meg? Would you like to join a rowdy bunch of smelly boys?"

Meg looked at Ben and the lively bunch of boys sitting across the room. The boys were laughing and jostling each other as they blew the wrappers off their straws, attempting to sink them in an upended ball cap propped at the end of the table. Meg smiled. She couldn't think of anything she'd rather do at the moment.

"That sounds like fun and I could get a play-by-play of the big game." Ben grabbed her hand and practically dragged her to the table, shouting out that he was bringing a girl to help Alex with his pizza. Rob followed.

Pete's face split into a wide grin when Rob introduced Meg to him and the team.

"Oh, yeah. You're the cider lady. I enjoyed ragging on Rob that night. He kept muttering something about his bath and that damn pixie. That has to be you. Nice to meet you," Pete said with a lazy smile and sparkling eyes. "I see my Ben has taken a liking to you, too."

Meg smiled and gave a puzzled look to Pete. Rob scowled at his partner, who only smirked in return.

"Sit here, Ms. Meg, next to Alex and me! You can have my share of pineapple," Ben generously offered, pulling Meg away from Pete and over to the chosen chair. Clearly, he was ready to monopolize her attention.

Sending a quick text to M and Juju about her unexpected dinner date, Meg settled in for fine dining with Ben, Alex, and the rest of the team. They enthusiastically recounted every inning, amazing play and hit of the winning game. The boys celebrated each other's accomplishments and were refreshingly supportive of the few plays that hadn't gone as well as hoped. Rob added a few comments when asked, but mostly sat back and proudly watched the sportsman-like behavior of his charges.

Overwhelmed by the boisterous and energetic boys bouncing up and down, Meg watched with admiration as the two men interacted with their team. Pete used a gentle hand to remind each one to wait his turn to share their perspective. Rob engaged each young man with respect and used certain parts of the play-by-play as an opportunity to teach. He took the sting out of the failures and pumped up the players with positive observations, building their confidence.

Pete leaned over to share the coach's perspective with Meg, drawing her into the team dynamics. "The team has a batting practice scheduled on Saturday. Rob and I will work on ways to improve each player's individual performance. The boys are like sponges when it comes to Rob's teaching. His time with the Texas Rangers gives him an unmistakable aura of mystery and expertise, and the boys love him. I am so blessed to have Rob as a co-coach, partner and friend. I want only the best for him."

Meg heard the sincerity in Pete's comments, saw the affection on his face as his gaze settled on Rob. He appeared to see something in Rob's expression that caused Meg's gaze to shift. She noticed the softening around Rob's eyes and a contented curve to his mouth.

Meg's mouth curved in a similar fashion as, even when talking with the boys, Rob seemed aware of her, but in a relaxed and pleasant sort of way. In that moment, something crumbled just a little within her.

Pete leaned over to Meg, determined to nudge along the attraction clearly obvious between the two.

"Is all this baseball talk overwhelming?" he inquired. "The boys are always pumped after a victory, which is why we take them out for pizza. Gives them time to decompress and Rob has a genuine talent for using the time to help them grow as players." Gesturing with his glass of tea, Pete confided, "He's a good guy with a hard job."

"It looks like you've stolen Ben's heart. He would enjoy nothing better than if you'd join us tomorrow afternoon. My Bella has a dance recital and the more people I can sucker into coming to it, the happier she'll be. Seems odd to invite someone I just met, but would you like to come?"

Meg turned to Pete and smiled, imagining the warmth and love he'd invited her to share. "Thank you, Pete. It sounds like fun, but I wouldn't want to intrude on a family afternoon."

"No intrusion at all. Rob will be there. He dotes on my Bella almost as much as I do. I'll ask him to pick you up at one-thirty, okay?" Without waiting, Pete turned to the table and called out, "Hey, Ben, I got you a date for Bella's recital tomorrow with Ms. Meg. Rob will bring her." Rob turned a surprised look at Meg, who simply shrugged.

Pete chuckled, having out-foxed both Meg and Rob. Little did he realize, he possessed skills equal to M's for matchmaking. But Meg wasn't completely unhappy about it and missed the knowing glance Rob sent his partner.

The early evening wound down and everyone made their farewells to John and headed home. John called M and made a full report on what had happened, both deciding they needed to coordinate their efforts with

Pete as he seemed to have an inside track on 'nudging'.

Meg took her time driving home. She needed time to think. The evening with the boys had been sweet and fun. She thought Ben was absolutely adorable. It was obvious he had developed a big crush on her, but it was Pete's comment about 'liking too' that had Meg's heart doing flip-flops. From the first time she had made contact with Rob's hard chest, Meg had experienced a tremendous attraction. And then she'd looked into his eyes! Immediately, she'd felt the circular swirl of a whirlpool pulling her in. What if opening herself to that attraction made her drown? Did she want that? Would it be safer to step back rather than put herself out there to be hurt again? Meg arrived home and walked in to see M enjoying a cup of tea and a favorite book in the library. She looked up with a hopeful expression which Meg tried to ignore and M would have none of.

"Hi, Meg. Nice evening? I was thinking of getting another cup of tea. Would you like to join me?" M put her book down and rose to head to the kitchen. Meg dutifully followed, knowing full well there would be a third-degree interrogation. "Your text mentioned baseball. Not your usual choice for entertainment. What was that all about? I tried to text you back, but I guess you didn't get my message. I finally texted John, and he said you were sitting with Rob and his partner Pete and their little league team. Said you were charming the pants off a young man named Ben. Want to tell me about him?"

Meg smiled. John loved to tease and would choose to share just enough information with M to make her curious. "Why, yes. I have a new boyfriend. His name is Ben, and he is quite the charmer, although he thinks pineapple on pizza is 'girlie'." At M's raised eyebrows, Meg laughed and continued. "He is a first baseman and took great pains to explain the importance of that position. Ben is very handsome, makes me laugh and is quite tall–for an eleven-year-old. He is Pete's son. We have another date for Sunday afternoon. But I don't think we'll be eloping any time soon so you can stop your worrying." Meg took the cup of tea M offered and hugged her.

M looked abashed and smirked. "I'll get John for that one and you too, for playing along. You are both little stinkers!"

Chapter 11

Rob followed Ashton toward the lake. He sometimes ran along this route and admired the stately older homes with their lush landscaping. Peeking between them to the water, he spied a small sailboat cutting across the water, heard lawn service equipment buzzing and avoided the Amazon delivery truck double parked on the side of the road. When he reached Meg's street, he turned onto a lane that left city streets behind. The lack of curbs lent a rural feel to the neighborhood. Tall oaks shaded the street. Mothers pushed strollers and called out greetings to their neighbors. He smelled wood smoke from grills and heard music and laughter from celebrations around backyard pools.

Pulling up in front of the address, Rob saw Meg step out her front door. Stopping short, he put the car in park and stared. She was stunning. Rob knew Pete had played matchmaker when he told him Meg would attend the recital and he should pick her up. His first instinct had been to feign illness and back out, but he knew it would crush Bella if he didn't come. He finally reminded himself to breathe, thinking maybe this wouldn't be so bad after all. They had a lot in common and she wasn't hard on the eyes.

Rob climbed out of the car. Coming together on the walkway, they shared an uncomfortable moment where neither knew if they should shake hands or buss cheeks.

Rob cleared his throat. Feeling a little awkward, he reminded himself he wasn't Ben and not eleven years old. Rob held the car door for Meg and once she settled in, walked around the back of the car, sucking in calming breaths and giving himself a pep talk. Heading to the performance, they made small talk, then lapsed into companionable silence, arriving at 1:50 and tracking down the Bonnert family.

Rob scanned the entrance to the auditorium where he soon found Ben dancing from foot to foot, awaiting their arrival. Knowing his partner like he did, Rob knew Ben's assignment would be to show them to their seats. The crowd surged past Ben, who craned his neck to see around all the bodies. Rob held the door as Meg stepped through and watched an eager and terribly shy Ben run up, grinning toothily. He grabbed her hand, pulling her along, leaving Rob to trail behind. "Hi, Ms. Meg. Come on, we're sitting down front, over here."

Rob watched Meg swallow a smile when Ben seated her next to him and left Rob to fend for himself. Ben's crush must be very serious indeed, he thought. He caught Meg glancing over at him at the far end of the row. Pete jabbed Rob in the ribs, laughing at some private joke. After introducing Meg to Pete's wife, Eileen, the lights dimmed, and the recital began. The show opened with the younger students and was blessedly short. One can only consider the confused looks and absolute stage fright of the performers cute for the first couple of dances. When the time came for Bella to perform, she was the star of her class.

Rob noticed Pete and Eileen clasp hands and lean heads together as they watched their little Bella skillfully execute each step. He saw Meg's gaze softened, and a wistful smile touched her lips. Everyone seemed surprised at how poised and focused a child of only eight years old could be. At the conclusion of the dance, Bella flashed a dazzling smile and curtsied. Both Ben and Alex watched their little sister take her bows, jumping up to give a standing ovation, complete with whistles, fist pumps and hoots of appreciation. After the final curtain, Bella came running out, all smiles and excitement. She leapt into Pete's arms, who swung her around, kissing her on both the cheeks. She was every bit of Daddy's girl. The family surrounded her with hugs and compliments. Bella turned a bright face to Rob, who dropped to his knee and pulled a bouquet from behind his back. Rob worked the moment, knowing that it would have bowled most adult women over. At eight, flowers clinched the deal.

"Oh, Uncle Rob. You are my favorite Prince Charming. I'm going to marry you when I grow up." She threw her arms around his neck, hugging him for all she was worth.

Rob pulled back and looked at her with consternation. "Wait a minute! Did you say 'my favorite' Prince Charming? Is there more than one 'Prince Charming'? There isn't anyone else moving in on my gal, is there?"

Framing his face with her hands on his cheeks, Bella nodded, her expression serious. "Only my daddy and I can't marry him–he's married to Mommy." Then she hugged Rob again.

Rob couldn't hide the rise of color in his face. Thankfully, Pete jumped in and saved the day. "Come on, everyone! The smell of all that buttered popcorn has my stomach growling. On to Casa Bonnert for burgers and dogs." He took Eileen's hand, Bella took Rob's, and the boys flanked Meg as they made their way to the parking lot.

Pete led the caravan of two cars to a modest home in an older neighborhood with large yards and lots of trees. Meg felt like family, entering the house through the garage. The children ran up to their rooms to change out of their dress clothes. Meg stood in the kitchen, gazing out the windows at a wide grassy lawn with a pitcher's mound and a swing set. A tree house in the large oak in the back corner of the lot overlooked a green belt leading down to a small creek. It seemed a perfect place for adventurous boys to play. In no time, the kids tumbled down the stairs and out the door, looking for a cold drink and the opportunity to throw the ball.

Eileen called to their retreating backs as the storm door slammed shut behind them. "You guys hung your clothes up, right?" She sighed when no one replied. "Kids. Every day is a new day and a new challenge. You'll see when you have your own." Meg unconsciously turned a questioning glance toward Rob, sweet yearning evident in her gaze.

While Eileen handed out assignments, Pete started the grill. Rob iced down drinks, and Bella set the table. Ben and Alex did Rock, Paper, Scissors to see who'd get to light the citronella candles. Meg felt at odds until Eileen handed her the hand mixer to whip cream for the strawberry shortcake. Soon, everyone was productively engaged in preparing the meal. In no time, Pete was calling for burgers and dogs.

"Fire is ready. Where's the meat, wench?" Eileen rolled her eyes as she handed Meg a glass of white wine and carried the tray out to the grill.

Eileen supervised to make sure Pete didn't burn anything either down or on the grill. Bella used the monkey bars to practice her ballet moves, and Meg watched Rob play catch with the boys, giving a mini pitching lesson with each throw. The laser focused attention each boy gave Rob as he showed the proper grip for a knuckleball and reviewed the steps elevated Meg's attraction to the man.

"Now remember, you need to push the ball toward home plate. Don't rotate it. Don't worry about speed right now. Ready to try it?"

Alex was up first. He placed his fingers in the grip Rob had shown him. Rob nodded and walked to home plate. Squatting down, he smacked his glove, waiting for the windup and the pitch. Alex took his stance, wound up, and let the ball fly. Rob snatched the pitch out of the air.

"Awesome, Alex. That was right in there. You have a great start on it. It's not an easy one to learn because you don't do the rotation. It goes against your natural instincts and you can't forget the follow through. Ben, you try it now." The boys took turns until they had each thrown five pitches, then Rob pulled them back. "Okay, let's not overdo it. Show me your splits."

The mechanics of the pitching and Rob's handle on training fascinated Meg. The boys were like sponges. Rob must have felt Meg's eyes on him. He glanced over. With a laugh, he tossed her a glove. "Hey, guys, how about we see how Ms. Meg does?" Meg looked at the worn leather glove and picked up the metaphorical gauntlet. The four played catch until Eileen rang the dinner bell.

"You don't throw like a girl, Ms. Meg," Ben said around a mouthful of cheeseburger. "Did you play when you were a kid?"

"Well, that's high praise indeed, Ben. Thank you. I used to play catch with my dad. We'd toss the ball around and go to the games when he wasn't traveling. I like baseball. My dad taught me to score the games." Meg smiled nostalgically, and Pete took advantage of another opportunity to nudge. He gave Rob a jab with his elbow.

"Rob, we need someone to score our games." Scooting closer to Meg, he continued. "Rob usually does it, but it's tough to do that and focus on the pitching. Meg, what do you do on Wednesday nights and Saturday mornings? Want to sign on to the team? I'll even throw in a team jersey."

Ben jumped in eagerly. "That would be so cool, Ms. Meg. You could come to all our games and our pizza parties. Could ya do it? Huh? Could ya?" Ben's eyes gleamed with puppy love.

Meg's eyes grew bright with interest. "That is a sweet offer and, Ben, you make it difficult to decline. Let me check my schedule before I commit. I wouldn't want to agree and then have to let you down. And, I'm a little rusty. I'll need some help to get up to speed."

"Aw, Mr. Rob can teach you. He can teach anyone anything, can't you, Mr. Rob?" Ben asked hopefully. Meg could sense her approval rating in Ben's eyes had gone up about fifty points. That was all it took. Meg was now the scorekeeper for the john Q Patriots.

While she and Eileen cleaned up the dishes, the men enjoyed another beer and talked about baseball.

The boys were half listening, wrestling with the dog. Bella crawled into Rob's lap and fell asleep. He tucked her head under his chin and stroked her hair. It had been an exciting day and Bella was down for the count. Eileen called to the boys, telling them to say goodnight and head for bed. Rob offered to carry Bella to her room and he and Eileen left, leaving Pete alone with Meg. They enjoyed a comfortable silence until Pete let go a sigh.

"He's a good man, Meg," Pete quietly observed. "A good man."

Chapter 12

Tuesday found Rob and Pete working on the murders of Kathy and Debbie, as well as two others. Luckily, the other murders were easier to solve. One was a drive by shooting that killed a 17-year-old playing basketball in his driveway. The kid had been cutting his marijuana with oregano and one of his buyers wasn't happy. It helped that the neighbor had a ring door bell and the license plate was easy to read. They walked up to the front door with a uniform and Mama gave her son up, only to call a bail bondsman and put her house up for collateral. The son skipped town, and because of that, she'd soon receive a foreclosure notice, unless she could come up with the scratch.

The second was a husband who'd beat his wife when she neglected to pick up a six-pack of beer while grocery shopping. This was a two-inch putt. The husband went to his favorite bar and bragged about how he'd taken enough bitchin' from his wife. It only took the idiot four beers until he felt macho enough to brag about cracking her head open with his pipe wrench, showing her who was the boss. The bartender called it in. Uniforms went by the house and found the woman lying in a pool of blood. They picked him up and slapped him in a cell, booking him for the murder. He squealed like a pig and cried to his kids. This wasn't the first time the old man had whaled on his wife. They refused to put up bail. He'd be stuck in jail until his trial and likely plea it down to second degree manslaughter. Not the justice Rob wanted, and it rankled him some that with the legal system and the courts backed up like they were, the A-hole could get away with that. Rob rubbed at his 2-day stubble. He'd had a long, sleepless night.

All killers are idiots except the one they hadn't caught. Kathy and Debbie continued to haunt his dreams. There had to be some link with the necklace and the hair. But what the hell was it? And what was with the brand? The ME hadn't had any luck identifying it. He could make out a couple of letters, E & P. Maybe someone's initials? And why did only Kathy have the brand? Hell, who knew? All the questions were giving him a headache. He grabbed his jacket and kicked the waste can on his way out the door.

Rob arrived at john Q's a little after seven and smiled when he saw the Lawrence ladies at their favorite table waiting on their drinks. Justin had joined them a few times, but not tonight. He traveled a lot for business. Rob still hadn't had time to call in any favors to have a background search done on the guy, so whenever Justin was there, he listened and observed, looking for anything that might be helpful. So far, it had been squat.

Lately, Rob made it a point to join the girls on their night out. It turned out to be the one bright spot in his week and he needed some of that brightness. Just being in proximity to the three Lawrence ladies felt like being surrounded by light and laughter. As he approached their table, Meg saw him and her eyes lit up. She waved him over, inviting him to join them.

"Ladies, nice to see you again." He bent to give each lady a peck on the cheek in greeting. He didn't know why. It just seemed the natural thing to do. Meg beamed; her blue eyes radiant. When the waitress came with the drinks, Rob told her to put the round on his tab and ordered an IPA. When the beer arrived, he downed half before he turned to the gals, saying, "So, what's new? Tell me funny stories and make me laugh. After the day I've had, I could use it."

M, as usual, took the lead, launching into her latest observation on climate change, world politics and movie star scandal. Her dry wit and caustic sense of humor offered endless entertainment. Nothing and no one were sacred. When John swung by the table, she fired one across his bow and they traded barbed compliments, tit for tat.

Rob watched Meg, delighting in her laughter and sparkling eyes. He smiled into his beer and relaxed into the sheer normalcy of the evening. "And, Meg, how is the preparation for your 'Flea Market Find' going? I'm looking forward to hearing your thoughts on the subject."

Meg shared her progress with the lecture, sighting the map on John's wall as a prime example of a forgery and teasing him mercilessly. John looked sheepish but not repentant. "It's just historical art," he insisted.

Juju took the last turn to report the latest happenings in her life. The contract with the ISD had been signed, sealed, and delivered. They assigned her to split her time between Little and Dodd Elementary Schools. She would be responsible for first through sixth grade music and start in January. "Oh, and I found a stray kitten at a friend's apartment complex. We've been feeding it. He is solid black, so we named him Pitch Black, Pitch for short. I hope we can trap and adopt him if he isn't too wild." She sat with her hands clutched at her chin, an eager smile on her face.

Then she went on and on about Justin, bubbling over with excitement about his business trips and how much he told her he missed her. Rob had spent a few evenings with him. Without the background info M asked for, he tried to keep an open mind. Juju kept coming back around to how romantic he was. It sounded odd. All fluff, no substance, as far as Rob could tell, but it had been a long time since he'd felt romantic. Glancing over at Meg, he thought that might be changing.

M remarked about Juju's being Cinderella, and not all romantic men were prince charming. It brought a blush to Juju's face and a firm denial.

"M, you just don't know him yet. It's like a fairy tale. He is handsome and successful and he thinks I'm beautiful." She crossed her hands over her heart and pouted prettily.

Being gallant, John spoke up. "It's a three-way tie between you ladies for beautiful, as far as I'm concerned." That earned him a playful slap on the shoulder from M and laughs all around, before John turned away to work the room, greeting other customers.

Rob raised his glass to salute John in agreement and noticed how Meg pressed her lips together, clasping her hands in her lap. She was holding back her comments with difficulty.

"Rob has asked me to score the john Q Patriots games," Meg said, changing the subject. "You remember when Dad taught me to do it? Well, I made the mistake of mentioning it and now, well, I'm trapped."

John returned, catching the end of Meg's announcement. "The Patriots are getting a mighty fine addition to the team, Meg. And the team photo will look a lot better with you in it."

"Well, we'll have to see how well I do. If Rob can't bring me up to speed, they may regret the invite."

The happiness in Meg's eyes didn't go unnoticed by M. She sent a wink to John. "Oh, Meg, that sounds like so much fun. Perhaps we can join you at the games."

"That would be great," Rob chimed in. "The Patriots are enjoying a winning season. You just might see a future Hall of Famer in the group, and the boys would appreciate the support. How about you, Juju? Any interest in baseball? Maybe Justin would like to come, too." Rob attempted to maneuver the conversation around so he could probe for more info on Justin. He was curious about Juju's infatuation. "Speaking of Justin, where is he this week? We haven't seen him around lately. You said he has some car lots. Do you know which ones? From what I can tell, that's a lucrative business to be in."

Juju lit up with the opportunity to talk more about Justin. "Oh, yes. There are four. The biggest one is JW Motors on Davidson. He tells me they handle high-end vehicles there. Traveling is a big part of Justin's work. He attends car shows and salvage auctions to buy cars for the lots he owns. He knows so much about cars.

Makes, models, motor size, tires, ground effects. When he talks about them, I get so confused."

"I see. He must know a lot about mechanics and such." Rob tucked away this bit of information. It gave him another avenue to explore for background. "Does Justin enjoy sports? Little league might bore him, but Pete and I come up here to catch the occasional game. Maybe he'd like to join us. He appears to be important to you and it would give us an opportunity to get to know him better."

Juju shrugged. "We don't talk about sports, so I don't know, but I'll ask him if he'd like to come."

Rob felt Meg nudge his foot under the table, but he took a sip of beer and plowed on. "That could be fun. A real guy's night out. Does he like music? I mean, he obviously enjoyed your playing that first night when he bought you a round of drinks. That's such a big part of your life. It's always nice to have someone special to share something that is your passion. That's one thing I enjoy about spending time with Meg." He put his arm across the back of Meg's chair, giving her a quick squeeze. "Meg and I both like history. Although she knows a lot more about it than I do. I also enjoy spending time with you two as well." Rob inclined his head to Juju and M. "Where else can I enjoy the killer sense of humor M has or your love and knowledge of music? I really look forward to seeing you three every week." Rob raised his glass to the ladies, looking expectantly at Juju. He hoped she would have more to share about Justin.

"Oh," Juju stammered. "I know Justin enjoys being with us, too. Outside of the times we have all been together here, we mostly text. I don't know if he likes sports or what kind of music he likes. He told me on the night we met he enjoys working on cars, so that is one of his hobbies. That other stuff never came up. I mean, he asks me about what I am doing and what I like, but he hasn't shared his likes and dislikes of stuff with me. But he was very complimentary when I played Billy Joel the night we met. I'm sure he likes the old classics."

Rob nodded supportively and took another sip of his beer. "That's a good guess. I bet he likes Billy Joel. I don't see you as interested in working on cars, though. But it sounds like you are both looking forward to seeing each other more. Has he mentioned what he'd like to do when he gets back into town from this business trip? I know this little Italian restaurant. They have a piano player. I think you'd enjoy it. It would be a nice date night. Perhaps the six of us can go out for dinner, give John an opportunity to eat some decent food for a change."

John gasped as he brought over another bowl of pretzels for their table. "I heard that disparaging remark 'Boyo' but then it might be nice to be waited on by someone else."

Juju shook her head, a bit flustered. "That sounds like fun, Rob. I'll have to ask. You know, listening to you talk, I guess I don't know Justin as well as I thought. I mean, he knows a lot about cars and he says sweet things. We really haven't talked that much about ourselves. I mean, I talk about me, but he doesn't share much. He says I'm what is important. I guess that says something, doesn't it?"

Meg had been watching Rob attempt his not-so-subtle interrogation. Rob knew he was treading on thin ice, risking Meg thinking once a cop, always a cop. He hoped she appreciated his effort, but then she placed a hand on Juju's and dashed that dream.

"I, for one, think knowing about you *is* important; just like you want to know about him. M and I look forward to having him over for dinner to get to know him too. Has he said when he'll be returning?" Juju shook her head.

Rob laughed. "Oh well, no group date then. That's a shame. I was looking forward to their manicotti."

John returned to their table. Things had slowed enough that he could sit down to enjoy some time with Rob and his favorite ladies. "Rob, the boys are homing in on that championship. Young Alex has already instructed me to clear a space for the new trophy. You've done a heck of a job with them. I thought I'd organize the regulars to form a cheering section to root them on to victory. "

"Funny, we were just talking about that. That would be wonderful, John. I'm sure the kids would appreciate it." Rob placed his arms on the back of Meg and Juju's chairs, leaning back expansively. "We've got four more games in the regular season and then play-offs start. The championship game will be on October tenth. Young Ben initially thought that since Meg went to see Bella dance, it was only fair she come to watch them play ball. Of course, when Meg talked about knowing how to score, Ben jumped on it. It was very entertaining to watch him charm her into scoring for the team. Our next game is this Saturday. If you all are available, why don't you come?" Still questioning his feelings for her and hers for him, Rob was happy to have the safety in numbers that, including M and Juju, provided. "I know the boys would love to have everyone there."

Having extended the invitation, Rob watched Meg's face brightened. "It will be a fun and interesting way to spend a Saturday morning. Is it all right if I come a little early so you can go over the scoring with me? It's been a while since I've done it. M, Juju? What do you say? Can the boys count on the Lawrence ladies?"

Both M and Juju agreed, and John even promised to find time in his schedule to join them. Rob smiled, looking forward to spending time with Meg. He wanted to share more with her, but talking about his work felt inappropriate. He wanted to let her see a different side of him than the badge. Rob remembered how she watched him at the pizza party, his approach to mentoring the boys. He'd felt her observing him when he held the mini-pitching clinic with the twins following Bella's recital. Rob wanted Meg to see him doing something that brought joy rather than darkness.

"Good. Having Meg scoring will give me time to support Pete and the boys. John, can you manage the stats book until Meg is comfortable handling both? That way I'll be able to focus entirely on the pitching."

John had been whispering in M's ear, startled by Rob's interruption. "Oh, well, yes. It would be my pleasure and I'm sure M will help me with it. Then, when the team wins, we can come back here to enjoy our victory celebration pizza party."

"Sounds like it's a date, at least for John and M and Meg and Ben. Juju, you and I must be odd men out. Would you be my date?" Rob teased.

"I wouldn't dream of missing it." Juju agreed. "If

Justin is back and free, maybe he can come too."
Meg's eyes darkened with concern.

Chapter 13

Saturday morning saw temperatures starting in the low-eighties and climbing to the mid-nineties. Everyone joked about the cool front moving in. The Lawrence ladies dressed for the weather. M donned dark blue capris and a white camp shirt, while Meg wore denim shorts and her Patriots jersey. Juju brought the color, wearing pink shorts, a mint green and pink stripped t-shirt, and pink sneakers. A pink baseball cap topped off her ensemble. They swung by and picked up John, planning their arrival thirty minutes before game time. John would help M and Juju claim their spot on the bleachers while Meg went to review the scoring procedures with Rob. He had the team doing their stretches and warming up. Meg, walking toward the dugout, watched as Ben jumped up from his quad stretch and ran over to say hi.

"You're here. That's so cool." Ben blushed. She noticed the indecision in his eyes, struggling with wanting to take her hand but not sure if it would look sissy.

"Good morning to you too, Ben." Meg flicked the bill of his cap good naturedly and gave him a side hug that maintained his manly mien.

Continuing toward the dugout, Ben danced around, talking ninety-to-nothing. "Having you score is so exciting! Hey, Mr. Rob said you teach history. It's my favorite subject. Alex likes math. Go figure. I'm building a model of the USS Columbus. Most people don't know about the continental navy. I bet you know all kinds of stuff about it."

"I can tell you're excited. I'm excited too, and no, I'm not that familiar with the USS Columbus or the continental navy. Perhaps you'll share what you know with me." Ben turned his cow eyes to Meg, the pink of his blush reaching the tips of his ears. Thankfully, Rob walked over to meet them and rescued the shy adolescent.

"Hey, Ben, time to warm up your pitching arm. You and Alex throw a few while I talk with Ms. Meg." Rob and Meg watched Ben trot off and followed more sedately. "He has it bad for you. Pretty stiff competition from the looks of it." Rob gave Meg an easy smile. She felt a flutter in her heart. "Come on, let's go over those forms. I'll be nearby to answer questions until you get the hang of it. By the way, I like the jersey. Fits you."

Embarrassed by his observation and comment, Meg pretended to brush it aside. It had been a long time since a gentleman had given her a compliment about her appearance. Even though she wore simple shorts and a baseball jersey, she enjoyed hearing it. With their heads bent together, Rob explained the scoring forms. The proximity flustered her. Meg hadn't felt like this in quite a while. When his hand brushed her arm, she felt an electric zing. Pulling her attention back to Rob's instructions, Meg was relieved to learn the scoring all came back to her, like riding a bike. When the ump flipped the coin to determine who would bat first, Alex, as captain, took the field. Pete and Rob nodded their agreement.

Meg found herself too busy at first to pay much attention to anything but her score card. When things settled down, she took time to study Rob. He had on athletic shorts and a team jersey. Admiring his muscular legs and arms, a warm flutter of desire unfurled in her belly. When he turned his gaze to her and flashed a dimpled smile, the heat moved lower. Meg found him sexy and sensitive. Her attraction to him bumped up to a ten on the Richter scale.

Six innings go pretty fast and by 11:30, the Patriots exuberantly threw their hats into the air and cheered. All the players ran out onto the field for a group hug, jumping around in a circle. Final score, eight to three. Alex had struck out six batters. The fielders caught the two flies hit to center field and in the final inning; the boys executed a double play that had the fans on their feet. Pete and Rob grinned from ear to ear, proud of their boys.

****

He sat alone at the far end of the bleachers, a ball cap pulled low on his forehead, shielding his face. His lip curled when the victory dance carried onto the field. Stupid kids. Stupid cops. He knew he was better than them. He had his quarry in sight. They had no clue.

Once he'd learned her name, it was easy-peasy to track her on social media. Heck, how many college girls named Juju were there? And she hadn't set up any security. Most of her posts were public. Hacking into her profile had been ridiculously simple. He chuckled and silently scolded her for her carelessness. A couple of clicks and he discovered her home address and school schedule, two things that would help in his planning.

Dark sunglasses hid his calculating eyes as he studied her and the others. He seamlessly blended in with the crowd. No one noticed the single guy in a ball cap. He applauded when those sitting around him did, but did not cheer too loudly or call attention to himself. During the brief hour the kids played, he watched, gathering tidbits he could use when he tagged her on social media. When the last out was called, he walked over to the trees near the Lawrence car. He watched from his sheltered position as his precious Juju carried a small cooler and talked animatedly with an older woman. She looked adorable in her little shorts and tank top. God, he loved the color pink. The sneakers were so damn cute. He took a swig of coke, wiping his mouth with the back of his hand. Yeah, he'd have to post to her Facebook page about how adorable she looked. He'd plant the seeds, so when he made his move, she'd fall for it. Smiling, he imagined having her in his little room all to himself.

Chapter 14

Juju strolled through the mall, a happy bounce in her step. She admired her manicure. The soft shade of pink she'd selected gave her hands a healthy appearance and called attention to the delicate length of her fingers. Playing the piano required she keep her nails short, but that didn't mean they couldn't be lovely or that she couldn't pamper herself. Now if she could only find the right dress. Window shopping, she sighed over yet another dress she couldn't afford. Turning, she swung her hair over her shoulder and saw Justin across the way.

Leaning against the wall, with his arms crossed over his chest, Justin watched her, desire in his gaze. When their eyes met, he brightened with delight. His face wreathed with a smile. Watching her float across to him, he marveled at her innocent beauty. Justin stood mesmerized. His eyes proclaimed his affection, his joy that this delicate woman could be his. He held out his hands in greeting.

"Hello, Juju. What a pleasant surprise running into you like this. You look amazing. I've missed you so much." Justin leaned in to give her a kiss, pressing his cheek to hers, drinking in the scent of vanilla on her skin. "You smell good enough to eat." He breathed in next to her ear before releasing her.

Juju looked down, appearing shy at this special

attention. Justin knew women found him attractive and romantic. But with Juju's innocence, he didn't want to overwhelm her with his devotion and compliments. He watched her recover her equilibrium, slapping at him teasingly.

"Oh, Justin. You probably say that to all the girls. What are you doing here?"

"I was stopping in to see about some custom work I'm having done by a jeweler here. It's not ready yet." Taking her hand in his, Justin started walking them toward the mall exit. "Are you on your way home?" he asked.

"In a little while. I had some time and thought I'd window shop a little. My student recital is coming up and I want to get a new dress. Dillard's is having a sale. I'd invite you to join me, but it would probably bore you to tears."

Justin stopped and turned to Juju, tucking her hair behind her ear. "No time spent with you could ever be boring. I enjoy just watching you smile. I live for your laughter. Juju, you do not know how much joy you give me. Why don't we grab a coffee or something and visit a little before you have to head home? Surely dress shopping can wait for another day." He gave her a sweet smile before tucking her hand in the crook of his arm, and turning her toward a small bistro. Justin found them a little table in the corner where they sat with their coffee and a piece of cheesecake to share. He gazed at her adoringly, holding her hand in his, playing with the simple gold chain she wore on her wrist.

"Justin, the other night when we were at john Q's, everyone talked about their hobbies and interests. They asked me about you; what you do for fun. I didn't know what to say. We talk a lot and text, but it's always about me and what I'm doing. I want to know about you. Do you have family, Justin?"

Justin took his hand back and sipped his coffee. "My mother is the only family I still have. She's been living in LA since my dad died. I don't get out to see her very often. I've been busy for the last ten years." He huffed a frustrated breath. "Taking care of business."

Justin found it difficult to hide the sadness in his eyes. He read Juju's concern and saw the flicker of realization in her eyes she had touched on a sensitive topic. "Do you have a favorite type of music? And tell me more about your cars. You said you were rebuilding a GTR, right?"

Justin laughed. "Juju, you are the cutest thing. I love all music when you are playing it, but if I had to pick a favorite, I'd say I enjoy the classics: Beethoven and Brahms. My contemporary tastes lean toward Alicia Keyes or Adele. The Beatles and the Eagles are also on my list of favorites. I'm afraid you'll think me weird but when I turn on the radio, it's usually talk radio. I'm a bit of a news junkie. And as for my GTR– it's actually a GTO." He tweaked her nose and leaned in, taking both her hands in his, a flame of passion building in his eyes. "Juju, you wouldn't believe what it looked like when I first saw it in this guy's barn. It was probably more rust than metal and dirty as sin. The leather upholstery rotted and ripped; it looked like rodents had been making a nest in the stuffing. But the chassis was straight, and the structure still solid. I bought it right then and have been restoring it for the last nine months. The engine seized, so I had to rebuild the entire thing. I have been buying original parts and working to be as faithful as possible to the original 1969 model. I wasn't joking when I said I'd like to paint it the color of your eyes. Why don't we go to my workshop and I can show it to you?"

His excitement pulled Juju in. He was clearly as passionate about his car as she was about her music, but she heard Meg's voice in her head cautioning her that things are not always as they appear. "I'd like that, Justin. Oh, by the way. The little league baseball team Rob coaches may make the play-offs. We went to watch their game on Saturday. It would have been fun if you'd been able to come. Do you like baseball?"

"I do like baseball and I know you were there. I saw your post on Facebook. The selfie you took of yourself and your aunt M was adorable. You look so cute in pink." Changing to a more serious tone, Justin pointed out all her Facebook posts were public. "You should change it so you are only visible to your friends. There are too many wackos out there and one of them might pick up on your posts. You are too pretty not to get noticed."

Juju giggled and tilted her head flirtatiously. "If they weren't public, you wouldn't have found me and sent me a friend request. I'll change it to friends only now. Hey, we're going to go to another ball game next Saturday. It would be fun if you'd join us. There's a victory pizza party following at john Q's. Are you available?"

"I don't know. I've been out of town for a few days and have some work to catch up on. Plus, I'd rather do something else, just the two of us."

"I'd love to, Justin, but you know how protective Meg is. She wants to get to know you better. If you can't make the game on Saturday, she and Rob asked if we could all go out for dinner one night. Of course, if it's better for your schedule, maybe we can make it lunch instead and include a stop to see the car. I bet Rob would be interested in seeing it. He drives an old car. And Meg and I can pretend to be impressed, even though we won't understand a thing you're talking about."

"If it means I can spend time with you, I'd double date with Atilla the Hun. Let me check my schedule and we'll set a time." Juju's phone beeped, and she looked down at the text from Meg. Justin's face fell in disappointment. "Sounds like you need to head home."

She nodded, and the two walked hand in hand out to Juju's car. Justin took Juju's face between his hands, gazing into her trusting eyes. He gave her a gentle kiss on the lips, wanting to do so much more. He moved his mouth to her temple, once again breathing in her scent. Opening her car door, he made sure she'd buckled in, then closed the door and watched her drive off.

Chapter 15

Rob paced outside Meg's office, waiting for her to return after her last class. He had been talking with the campus police department about safety and security for the female students. Rob agreed that the chief, an experienced officer of the law, had implemented all the precautions they could under the circumstances. Policing a 420-acre campus with over 42,000 students is a significant challenge for a department, despite having 44 sworn officers and 47 public safety officers. As a professor, Meg insisted she wasn't in any danger, but Rob knew better. He hoped to convince her to be more careful. The more time he spent with her, the fonder he grew. He might as well act on his feelings and ask her out to dinner.

Rob stopped his pacing and stared hard at the door to Meg's office, like he could conjure her presence with a magic spell. With everything going on, he felt harried and overworked. The abduction and murder of young women might be concentrated on students, but Meg was also young and could easily pass for a student. Running his hand repeatedly through his hair, it became tousled and wild. His five o'clock shadow darkened his cheeks. He kicked at the baseboard in frustration. Where the hell was she?

As he turned, his gaze landed on Meg at the top of the stairs. Carrying an armload of books, she smiled, her eyes alight with joy.

"Hello Rob. What a pleasant surprise. What are you doing here?" She juggled the stack of books, trying to get her keys out. Rob took the books from her, freeing her to dig through her satchel, find them, and open the office door. The scent of cardamon and nutmeg floated through the air, igniting his senses. He followed her into a cramped 10x12 space that barely had room for a desk, chair, and side chair for guests. A quick survey showed every wall held a floor to ceiling bookcase filled to overflowing with more books and papers. "Oh, here, let me take those." She grabbed the stack and plunked it down unceremoniously on top of a three-legged stool in the corner. Removing her coat, she hung it on an antique rack tucked behind the door. Patting her hair and brushing at her skirt self-consciously, she turned and moved several other books from the side chair. Stacking those on the floor by her desk chair, she motioned for Rob to sit.

The old courtroom chair showed wear from years of sweaty student palms gripping the arms and bottoms sliding on and off. The patina revealed the age of the piece. It looked like the set dressing out of a Perry Mason episode. The look fit the Hodge-Podge eclectic style of her office, as did the abundance of books and research materials cluttering every surface. Rob took in the sturdy, reliable style of the office. It presented a direct contrast to the beauty of the woman who worked there. Meg's delicate frame juxtaposed the heavy weight of the furniture. Her sunny disposition contrasted with the dark wood and banker's lamp on the desk, shedding a circle of light on her work surface. The windows faced south. He imagined the sun would cast a mellow light over the books during the day. Dusk brought creeping shadows that softened the room.

Leaning forward, Rob prepared to explain his visit when Meg continued.

"What are you doing here? Thinking of auditing some history classes?" Meg teased. Rob liked it when she joked. It made her eyes sparkle and her nose scrunch up in the most adorable way. Giving himself a mental forehead slap, thinking *'Geez, I've got it bad'*, he told Meg about his appointment with the campus police.

"Meg, the campus police have a good handle on security here but, I'm still concerned. Just because you're a faculty member doesn't mean the killer won't target you. I'm worried about your safety, Juju's too. In fact, look at tonight. You have class till five p.m. You work in your office till six and then walk at dusk to your car, which is four blocks away in the unsecured faculty parking lot. It's really not safe and you do this four out of five days a week. You have a shorter day on Wednesday, but hold office hours in case your students need anything."

Rob had spent too many years reading a crime scene and interrogating witnesses. He saw Meg processing the information. Apparently, knowing the details of her schedule disconcerted her. Rob watched her stubborn independence kick in and her back bow. He perceived Meg thought he was overreacting, his concern silly.

"Thank you, Rob. I appreciate you watching over me." Rob looked at her, wondering if she was being sarcastic, but saw only sincerity in her gaze. "What would you suggest Juju and I do to stay safe?"

Choosing to believe he'd just imagined her tone, he leaned forward in his chair. "First off, promise me you and Juju won't walk anywhere on campus alone. The police chief is organizing groups of volunteer student escorts. They will work in groups of two and three, making sure no female student is ever alone and vulnerable. Juju can get an escort to your office and the two of you can walk to your car together. You carpool often. If there is ever a time when you don't, then both of you should take advantage of the escort volunteers."

Rob's sincerity and thoughtfulness touched her. "Thank you, Rob. You are sweet to have thought everything out. I promise both Juju and I will heed your advice."

"Good. I already spoke with Juju. She's on board starting tomorrow."

"Tomorrow? What about tonight?" Meg asked, confusion marking her expression.

"I asked Pete to drive Juju home. You and I are going to get that manicotti I talked about the other night." Rob stood up and held out Meg's coat. He wouldn't take no for an answer. Watching the gears turn in her head, he breathed a sigh of relief, when smiling, Meg turned and tucked her arms into the waiting coat.

He never believed he could have another chance at happiness. If you'd asked him ten years ago if he'd allow someone in his life again, he'd have told you to 'F' off. He had been angry and hurt when he'd learned his fiancé was screwing his best friend. Rob turned his back on any emotional entanglements from that time forward. But Meg was different. She had a hold of something deep inside that Carrie had never touched, and he hadn't let himself feel in years. His thoughts regarding Meg confused him. They ran the gamut from protective to playful to pure lust. God, she was so incredibly desirable; intelligent, beautiful, innocent, sexy. This was a woman that could fill his heart and life. Maybe this time would be a real chance at love, instead of the fantasy chance he'd had with Carrie, a woman with the emotional depth of a mud puddle. Taking a deep breath, he almost felt himself smile.

****

Meg didn't want to say no–to dinner or whatever else Rob might come up with. Rob Adams had something that attracted Meg. M would say she was smitten with him. From the moment she'd collided with his washboard abs and looked into his brown eyes, she'd found him intriguing and attractive. He possessed a quiet strength, a depth of character he rarely let others see. She saw it when he coached the boys. His eyes rarely missed a thing. He praised performance and softened criticism with humor and affection.

The two walked to Rob's car, conversing about history; a topic Meg always used as a protective buffer when she felt unsure of herself. It had been years since Conrad. The entire affair hurt and embarrassed her. The only saving grace was that it had all happened in England, so her colleagues here knew nothing about it. M was the only one that knew all the dirty details. She had been there to hold Meg when she cried and grieved for what she was sure was true love lost. The sordid affair had left her disenchanted with love overall. So, Meg built strong defensive walls around her emotions. Sometimes it frightened her that Rob could effortlessly chip away at the stone fortifications she'd erected around her heart. But then she looked into his eyes and felt a kindred spirit. Rob was real, and she saw something in him that made her know he was a deeply loving man. She wanted to feel that love from him and reciprocate.

Rob opened the car door, and Meg settled into her seat. He pulled the seat belt out, handing her the buckle. She considered this simple gesture. No one had ever done that for her before. He made his way around to the driver's side. Engaging the engine, Rob pulled away from the curb. She felt him cast a glance at her out of the corner of his eye and wondered what he was thinking.

Rob turned out of the faculty parking lot onto University Boulevard, then hung a left onto Canton Street, heading north toward Lamont Blvd. They crossed over Abram Street, then Davidson, passing the main police station where Rob worked. She reminded herself to ask more about his work. Meg was keenly aware of everything, the way Rob's hair curled over his collar, the shadow of his beard, the scent of his cologne. She watched Rob's powerful hand grip the five-speed floor shifter, two square-tipped fingers curling around the knob, almost caressing its smooth ball. His hand flattened, as if palming the handle, then flexed around the knob as he changed gears. She felt the smooth clutch work as he moved through the gears from first to second to third. Everything about how he handled even simple things spoke of his awareness, care, and control. Meg began to believe that he would handle her heart as expertly. She felt a few bricks in her walls loosen.

****

Antonio's felt like home and was one of Rob's

favorite restaurants for 'fancy food'. Family owned, it had an intimate lounge with an eight-seat bar and seating area barely able to hold the baby grand piano he'd squeezed in. The small dining room held a scant two dozen tables that Antonio typically turned two to three times a night. Reservations were always recommended. His folks introduced him and his brother to the restaurant when they were old enough to sit at the table without spilling their milk. Rob only took important people to Antonio's, since the likelihood of his folks learning about it scaled high on the gossip meter. The owner loved Rob like a second son and made sure he and Meg received the best of service. The food tasted amazing and Rob proved to be an engaging dinner companion. They shared little secrets about their past. History wasn't the only thing they had in common. Neither had ever married. They were both dedicated to their careers but wanted children. They shared life priorities of valor, honor, family, and country.

Meg chuckled and raised her glass in salute. "Rob, there is more to you than you let on. John's description of Dudley Do-Right may not be so far off the mark."

Meg's fingers circled the rim of her wineglass, a soft smile lifting the corners of her mouth. "Rob, Ben never fails to mention you played professional ball for a while. He worships you. All the boys do. I understand it was an injury that side-lined you. Do you miss it?"

Rob put down his fork and wiped his mouth. Leaning back in his chair, he twirled the stem of his wineglass and took a moment to frame his answer. Wanting Meg to know everything, the entire truth still felt a little too raw for him to share. "There is a special sort of camaraderie I enjoyed when I played pro ball. Unfortunately, it lost its luster. I had a buddy, a best friend actually, that, well, he didn't feel the same sort of friendship and his actions soured me on the team aspect of the game." Rob drew in a deep, thoughtful breath. "When they cut me, I no longer cared to be involved in anything team related. I took a step back, closed myself off. It took a while, but now I enjoy that camaraderie with the boys and encourage them to share it with each other. There is nothing like being part of something special. I see a similar relationship between you Lawrence ladies." Rob reached out for Meg's hand.

Meg trembled with his touch, causing his blood to heat. His throat worked to swallow the dryness in his mouth. His hand engulfed hers. The roughness of the calluses on his palms and fingertips brushed against her soft skin. Even though the touch was brief, an electric energy rushed through his veins. He squeezed her hand, fighting to control the urge to sweep everything off the table and take her. Breathing deliberately through his nose, he surrendered his hold, returning to his manicotti.

Meg took another sip of wine. Rob wondered if she was equally undone by the brief contact, skin to skin, soul to soul. She responded with a slight catch in her voice. "Umm, so, you double majored in history and psychology? How did you transition to police work?"

Rob smiled, back in control. "Yeah, seems a little odd, doesn't it? I always loved history, as I've mentioned, so I went back to school, thinking I'd get my teaching certificate. Research became my drug of choice. I spent hours in the library reading and found an article about a serial killer in Louisiana. The psychology of the case and others I uncovered after that intrigued me. There is something fascinating about watching and understanding the workings of the inner mind. I profiled everyone in my class on the first day to see how close I came to being correct about them at the end of the semester. I learned I have a knack for pegging people." Rob shrugged, embarrassed by the telling.

"Have you profiled me yet?" Meg asked, a hint of nervous laughter threading through her voice. She clasped her hands in her lap. Rob's gaze locked with hers. Was she afraid of the answer?

He held out his hand palm up, inviting Meg to place hers in it. She did so, tentatively. He rubbed his thumb over her knuckles. "I reserve in-depth profiling for my criminal cases, but I have thought a lot about you, Meg. From the first time I saw you at the table with M and Juju, I saw joy and love. I saw laughter and wit when you hit me with the cider. When you shared your passion for history, I saw keen observation and intelligence. When you spoke about your accomplishments, I heard modesty." *And when you look at me, it feels like my heart stops beating. I stand at the precipice of a great chasm; afraid I'll fall into its deep blue depths.* Rob brought his hand to her wrist and felt the rapid beat of her pulse.

Meg swallowed and hitched in a breath. "Oh, my," she whispered.

Rob could and would have said more, but Antonio chose that moment to take away their empty plates.

"So, my young friends, you must enjoy some tiramisu and coffee, yes?" Antonio smiled broadly.

The evening ended too soon, but Rob didn't let

Meg get away without making another date.

When he drove her back to her car, they sat in his front seat, holding hands. His thumb made lazy circles on her palm and he could hear her breaths become shallower. He felt the racing of her pulse. It matched his own. He wished he had the courage to take her home with him to show her how she drove him crazy. But he wasn't ready, and he wasn't sure she was. Rob knew that the odds of a long-term relationship for him had been slim to none in the past. Heck, even if he could get past his mistrust of a woman's fidelity, cops weren't known for long, stress-free marriages. The divorce rate was ridiculous. Pete's marriage to Eileen was an anomaly. Rob wasn't sure he had what it took and didn't know if he dared risk it.

Rob helped Meg out of his car and escorted her to her own. Holding the door open, but before she could get in, he turned her to face him, cupping her cheeks with his strong, warm hands. He stroked her lips with his thumb, feeling frissons of heat flickering through his body. Looking into her eyes, he felt he looked into her soul. Lowering his face to hers, he kissed her tenderly. Her lips parted for him. As their tongues touched and danced, he savored the light taste of garlic, the tang of the wine they'd enjoyed with dinner, and the heat of passion that was building between them. Rob pulled back to gauge her reaction. Meg had her eyes closed, her lips parted, inviting more. He kissed her again, this time with greater passion and possessiveness. They were both panting when they broke apart. Meg smiled up at him. He read the trust in her expression.

With a small laugh, she placed her hand on his

chest. "I think you should go before one of the escort teams sees us and thinks you're accosting me."

Pulling her closer, Rob held her a moment longer, then whispered in her ear, "Goodnight, Meg."

That night, as Rob lay in bed, he couldn't get her out of his head. She was his last and only thought as he fell into a sleep filled with erotic dreams. He woke with the sheets tangled around his sweating body. He had imagined the feel of her soft skin under his hands; felt her pulse race when his lips brushed her hairline and he whispered into her ear all the things he wanted to do to her. He thought once again about his long-term relationships and cop divorce rates. Realizing he was a betting man, and he liked to fight against the odds, he sighed in contentment and fell back asleep with a smile on his face.

****

Meg rose early. Pulling on her robe, she wandered down the stairs. While waiting for the coffeepot to finish brewing, she watered the little pots of herbs on the kitchen windowsill, thinking of the promises in the goodnight kiss she had shared with Rob. She dreamed of him, of his thumb tracing little circles on her palm and rubbing against her bottom lip. She sighed, imagining it tracing little circles and rubbing other parts of her body.

Meg sat still as a statue; her hand poised on the cream pitcher while her coffee grew cool. With her eyes closed, she revisited the evening. It had been more than she could have imagined. Occupying a dream world, Meg was oblivious as M walked into the kitchen and set a box of donuts on the counter.

M's hesitation to interrupt the moment ended when

Juju came bouncing into the kitchen, jolting Meg from her reveries. She grabbed a Boston crème out of the box and a cup of coffee on her way to the table. Juju was smiling from ear to ear. Meg couldn't help but notice. Laughing, she asked, "Okay, what did tall, dark and handsome text now?"

"Oh, Meg. Justin is so sweet. He has been busy buying cars from some auto auction so they can put them on the lots. He also says he is finding parts to restore his GTR. No wait. GTO. I always get them mixed up." Juju waved her hand in the air, laughing away her confusion. "He talks about how every night he sits in his hotel room, eating fast food or Chinese takeout and thinks about me. I asked him about his family. It's so sad. His dad and sister passed away and his mother lives in California. With his work, he hasn't see her in a long time." JuJu added milk and two sugars to her coffee and continued telling all the things she'd learned when she and Justin met at the mall.

"And, Meg. Justin said he misses my music and wants to buy a piano when he comes back into town. Then I can play for him when I visit him."

Meg sent an alarmed look to M. Things were moving more quickly than anyone realized. "That's very nice. Did he mention our invitation to dinner?"

JuJu, oblivious to the tense tone in Meg's voice, plowed on. "I asked about that and Rob's suggestion we triple date to that Italian place. He'd love to, but Justin might not want to share me with anyone. Isn't that precious?" Juju danced in a circle and gave Meg a hug.

Meg turned away to hide the worry in her eyes. Juju acted over the top about this guy and none of them knew anything about him but the 'sweet' things he kept texting to her and now a tidbit of info on his family. "So, when *will* he be available? Did he say? M and I would like to have him for dinner so we can get to know him as well as you seem to have."

"By the end of the week or even sooner, he thinks. Oops, gotta go. I have prep to do for student teaching. It isn't all notes and rhythms, you know. See you tonight." Juju grabbed her jacket and headed out the door.

Chapter 16

One of his favorite things was to walk around an auto auction, looking at the cars up for bid. This was how he made his living, and few were better at it than he was. He recalled the times his dad took him along to the auctions when he was a kid. Auto auctions comprised a variety of cars. Some were the trade-in cast-offs from larger dealerships, the ones that didn't make the grade. They would usually sell these to smaller dealers who'd put them on their tote-the-note lots. Included in the lots were cars the insurance company had totaled. The repair costs didn't equal the blue book value, so they dumped them with a salvage title. Some were just old and others were parts only material.

He and his dad would scope out the different cars determining which would sell to which buyers, either small dealerships, restoration businesses, or those picked up by salvage yards for parts, crossing them off their list. Then they considered the ones destined for the crusher. These were the ones his dad preferred and often bought. Very few bidders had an interest in these cars and they'd go for pennies on the dollar. His dad had vision, and he passed that vision on to his son, along with his savvy mechanical and body working skills. His dad knew his stuff and could usually tell what the sale price would be. That was a key component to buying any vehicle off an auction; seeing the value before buying and the potential for upsell after a little work. They'd pick up the ones bound for the crusher and salvage parts, some for resale and others for collision repair work done in their backyard and garage. Sometimes they'd pick out a couple of cars, take them home and refurbish them. They'd stick with a particular model, using pieces and parts from several vehicles to rebuild a 'new' used vehicle they'd sell. They had a fun time and turned a tidy profit, selling them to private buyers. His dad knew the business, applying for a re-built title, so everything was legitimate for the buyer. Sometimes, though, if the new owner wanted, they could wash the title and have a basically untraceable car. In most of those cases, the new owner didn't care if the car was legal or not. The buyer made the money right and his dad never asked questions. Time working together on cars was the best. All the guys in shop class envied his skills and his dad was damn proud of him.

When he was fifteen, his dad gave him five thousand bucks and told him to pick out the cars to buy at the next auction. He found a couple of Honda Accords. One with a bent axle and the other with a smashed side panel and trunk. Knowing their existing stock of parts at the garage, he bought both for $4,875. They hauled them home, and he got to build his first resale vehicle. Between the two totaled Accords, he salvaged enough parts to patch together one solid car. The engines had some miles on them, but Accords with as much as 70,000 miles on the odometer were selling like hotcakes. When he turned it back to 56,000, the value skyrocketed. His initial investment netted him

$11,000 when he sold it to a nursing home aid from Nigeria. His dad was so proud of him. To celebrate, his dad gave him his first beer. They toasted his success, and his dad talked about his legacy; how he was destined for greatness. The old man showed him the ring and said he'd get that when he became a man. It looked so cool. A genuine antique, his dad told him. What he especially liked was the hanging guy engraved on the face.

He and his dad continued to work together, share their beer and eventually his dad's collection of porn. Working together on cars felt great. It turned out to be one of the few things he did right. His dad didn't hit him when they worked on cars, even if he had been drinking. He and the old man would put away a couple of six-packs pounding out dents or fine tuning an engine. About halfway through the day, they'd take a break for lunch. His dad's latest girlfriend would put together sandwiches and chips. Sometimes she'd be wearing little shorts and a t-shirt. Other times, she'd wear a pink lace halter that left little to the imagination. She'd smile at his dad and run the tip of her tongue along her lips. Walking up to her, his dad would grab her breasts and give a little squeeze, pinching the nipples. She'd melt into his arms with a giggle. Then his dad would laugh low in his throat and work the belt of his pants loose. The two would head up to the bedroom, leaving him to his bologna sandwich and corn chips. Oh, he could imagine his dad stroking her long blonde hair and running his hands down her shoulders, across her breasts. He'd get a boner thinking of them touching. He'd imagine her mouth on his dad's body and then he'd imagine it on his. God, he wanted to have a girl like that. Wanted to squeeze and pinch and suck at her breasts. He wanted a girl with a pink pouty mouth.

One Saturday, he sat eating a bowl of sugary cereal when his dad came down the stairs, buttoning his shirt. Vickie, the latest blonde to take up residence, followed behind him wearing one of his dad's t-shirts and little else. Some old lady was selling a classic El Camino dirt cheap and his dad was heading out to pick it up. He downed his coffee, slapped his girlfriend on the ass and gave her a kiss with lots of tongue and a squeeze of her size C knockers. His dad told him to hold down the fort and headed out the door. He heard the engine turn over, and his dad drive away. Shrugging his shoulders, he turned his attention back to his cereal and the centerfold he was studying. He heard the soft whisper in his ear.

"You can look at the real thing if you'd like." She'd taken off the t-shirt and snuck up behind him, running her fingers over his neck and up into his hair. He turned in surprise only to find himself face to face with those size C's. She took his hands and placed them on her breasts, showing him how to cup them and tease each nipple. Then she placed her hand behind his head and guided his mouth to her nipple. "Suck on it, honey, suck it." She cooed. "Oh, baby, that feels so good. Suck harder. Oh, yeah, baby."

He thought he'd come right there. He pushed up with untamed urgency and pushed Vickie against the wall, fumbling with the zipper on his jeans. Laughing, she put her hands against his chest, pushing him back. "Hold on, honey. There's plenty of time and you are a big, healthy boy. You'll have multiple opportunities to play today. Let's go upstairs." She took his hand and brought his middle finger to her mouth. She circled it with her tongue, running the tip up and down his digit. When she sucked it, he almost exploded. Then she led him up the stairs to the bedroom and heaven, as far as he was concerned.

Vickie let him touch, squeezing and pinching like he'd seen his dad do, but she kept pushing him back when he wanted to move in for more. He watched her as she pleasured herself. She smiled at that and continued to run her hands over her breasts and touch herself. He felt he'd cream his pants when she reached out her arms in invitation. He tried to be cool, but when he came, prematurely spurting his seed across her naked belly, she'd only pushed him away, laughing at him.

"God, you are so pathetic. Look at your wee Willie Winkie. You couldn't satisfy a woman with that excuse for a cock. You're such a loser!" Turning away, Vickie reached down and finished the job herself, watching smugly as he practically wet himself again as she brought herself off.

His dad returned later that evening hauling the El Camino on a trailer, none the wiser.

That night, lying in bed, he could hear his dad and Vickie doing it in the next room. His dad liked it rough, and he liked to talk dirty while having sex. "That's right, baby. Roll over! You want it, don't you?" He heard the sharp slap as his dad's palm smacked against Vickie's bottom. He heard her moan in ecstasy. "Tell me you want me to do you. Tell me, baby, tell me!" he heard him say.

He buried his face in his pillow, thinking how soft and lovely she was and how she'd laughed at him. She called it his wee Willie Winkie. He felt a burning hatred building deep inside. She would regret what she said. No woman would ever do that to him again.

Chapter 17

Rob finally got back the information on Justin Whitman from his department contact and called John. They met at the tavern after Rob's shift ended. The two men settled into a booth at the back of the restaurant. Rob pulled the report out of the manila folder and summarized the information for John. "This is what my buddy could pull. It's only preliminary and very basic. Justin Whitman, thirty years old, DOB January 14, 1991. Lives at the Jefferson Apartments on Center St. Expensive digs. Born in Cleveland, Ohio, to Walter and Susan Whitman. One younger sibling, a sister. Mother is the only one still living. He moved around a lot as a kid. Family finally settled in Los Angeles where Justin was a better-than-average student. He got an associate degree in business from a Los Angeles County junior college but didn't pursue a bachelor's degree, although he had the grades to do it. Where he really excelled was as a shade tree mechanic. He bought old junk cars and fixed them up with his dad in the garage and then sold them for a nice profit."

"His sister disappeared and not long after that, his dad died, suspected suicide. Whitman took his meager inheritance and moved to Lake Havasu City, Arizona. He bought a 'tote-the-note' car lot that he built into a fairly successful business. He's moved several times in the last ten years, never staying in one place longer than two years. After Lake Havasu, he sold his car lot, moved to Phoenix, where he bought two. He sold those and moved to Albuquerque, same deal. Next stop is San Antonio and now Alton. He moved here in May of this year. He currently owns four lots. Doesn't do a lot of hands-on work or management. He hires most of that out. An accountant handles the financials for him. He travels around to various auto auctions to purchase his own stock. The lots contribute a significant amount of profit to Whitman's bank account every month. Can't tell you how he spends his free time. No hobbies or friends. No social media presence we can find." Rob sat back. He knew what he thought. He waited for John to react.

John took a sip of his club soda and stared at his glass, swirling the ice around. He pressed his lips together in concentration, clenching his jaw. The entire situation frustrated him. "It's not much to go on and won't convince Juju not to go out with him, especially as hard as he is pursuing her. M says he had some commitments and hasn't been physically present as much, but he is texting her like crazy and he even sent her flowers. M says Meg is running a Spokeo and financial background check on him. Don't know how much she'll get without a social security number. She insisted Juju invite him over for a family dinner so they can all get to know him better. You're the detective. What do you make of it?"

"I can't say with this amount of information. So, he moved around a lot. There just isn't enough to go on. Nothing on the surface looks suspicious. Look, the family is tight. They seem to have a handle on it. I don't want to butt in where I'm not wanted. If Meg is taking that close a look at him, they can decide."

"But I think you'd like to…butt in, I mean. Don't tell me you're not interested in Meg or getting to know her better. I might be old, but I'm not stupid and I'm certainly not blind. I also know that you are a still–well, you know. Look, Rob, Meg would be good for you. Give it a chance," John quietly suggested.

Rob shrugged. "They have it handled, John. I'm here for them if they need me. You are right. I am very interested in Meg Lawrence. It would be easy to get lost in her, but I also have a killer to catch. I have plenty of other issues to focus on."

John knew about Rob's past–the stupid social climbing broad that threw him over for his best friend because Rob wasn't going to be a big-time baseball pitcher. When Rob's best friend didn't make the big leagues, she dumped him too. Last they'd heard, she was whoring herself out with some professional football player. Rob needed to move on. John didn't realize that Rob was.

"Well, I'll see you tomorrow for Lawrence ladies' night out, I imagine," John called out as Rob exited the door.

Chapter 18

Justin thoroughly enjoyed the evening he'd first met Juju and the other Lawrence ladies at john Q's. He was getting to know Juju better and hoped Meg felt less suspicious and protective. He wanted to spend time alone with Juju. Checking in at the car lot, he made sure the delivery of the new inventory made it. The car carrier was off-loading when he arrived. He'd scored big time with the two Mercedes and Audi he'd picked up. Having paid top dollar for them, the profit margin would be slim, but the turnover would be fast. They'd draw in potential buyers to the lot, creating an opportunity to sell other cars in his stock. He considered it a lost leader purchase; something he had success with in the past.

The special shipment of custom auto parts he acquired were shipped to his private workshop. Justin locked up and crossed the parking lot to john Q's. The ladies had arrived. He smiled in anticipation of seeing Juju again. He longed to hold her hand and listen to her melodic voice as she shared her adventures with her young students. Justin's mouth twisted in disgust when he saw Rob already there. The cop stood when Justin approached the table.

"Hello, Justin. Juju was just telling us you'd be back any day now, but we didn't expect to see you tonight. Hey, I've got the first round. What are you

150

having?"

Justin shook hands and greeted each lady finishing with Juju, brushing her cheek with his warm lips. She shivered and turned shining eyes on him in worship. He noticed Meg tense up.

Waving to the waitress, Rob ordered, then inquired, "Was your business trip successful?"

"More than I'd hoped for. I picked up a new toy along with some spotless used cars for the lots. I also completed the negotiations with the Vandenburg car dealership. They've contracted with us to do their collision repair work. I'll refurbish the used cars they take in trade and have the first dibs on the ones they don't want to keep. I bought the auto repair shop next door, so John and I are now neighbors. After so much moving around, I hope to settle down and make Alton my permanent home." His eyes locked with Juju's as he spoke permanent home. "I'll take everyone for the nickel tour when it's ready to open."

Justin noticed Meg's surprised expression. She obviously hadn't expected this. It made him feel defensive. Was she judging him? Mocking him? He worked hard to build a successful business, one grounded and respectable. Justin sat back in his chair, hoping this evening would give everyone the opportunity to get to know him better. He felt Rob's scrutiny and knew the man constantly watched for anything suspicious. Casually mentioning the Vandenburg contract had Rob's brows furrowing. Yes. He'd prove he had it all together to both Rob and Meg. Justin watched the emotions flash across Meg's face; puzzled, envious, sad, hopeful. Tamping down his building anger, he hoped Meg would come to realize he was all right and Juju had found someone that worshiped the ground she walked on. Someone who would make her happy. Seeing Meg glance at Rob, he wondered if she felt a little envious of her little sister. Did she hope to be as lucky? Justin was successful, handsome, and what women in the past had always found attractive, but things had changed since meeting JuJu. Everything he held dear in the world was under siege. He only hoped he could destroy the demon he'd been chasing for so many years.

When the evening wound down, the ladies rose as one to leave. Juju looked over at Meg and then asked if Justin would take her home instead of riding with her sister and aunt. Meg hesitated. Justin's delayed decision appeared to please Meg.

"I would love nothing better, but I'm driving an old work vehicle tonight, and it's loaded with greasy auto parts. I wouldn't want you to get your clothes dirty. We'll do this another time when I have my regular car, okay?" Juju pouted, but Justin just put his arm around her and walked her out to the ladies' car, whispering in her ear and making Juju giggle with delight. Meg and Rob followed while M stayed behind, saying goodnight to John.

Meg stopped several feet from the car, letting Juju and Justin have a few moments alone together. The evening was cool and a light breeze lifted her shawl away. Tucking it more securely around her shoulders, she turned to Rob and asked the $64,000 question.

"What do you think? Every time I talk with him, he seems more responsible and grounded. He clearly thinks the world of Juju. I think he might be more protective of her than I am, and that's hard to do. M said you did a background on him. I know you had to call in some favors to do that and I thank you. What did you find?"

Rob shook his head and shrugged. "Nothing of note. He is building a business and appears to be doing a damn fine job of it. He's smart, well-off, and attractive. Most women would fall all over themselves to date him and he wants Juju. She apparently also wants him. Look at the two." Meg and Rob watched as Justin played with Juju's hair and stroked her cheek with the back of his hand while they stood close, talking to each other, saying goodnight.

Meg gazed at the two young people. "They look like they are falling in love, don't they? How can that happen so fast? They barely know each other."

Rob heard the sorrowful tone coloring her comment and wondered what thoughts ran through her mind. Did Meg have feelings for him? Because Rob believed he might have feelings for her. Feelings he never expected to have again.

Not so unexpectedly, Meg was thinking the same thing.

Chapter 19

Justin woke early on Wednesday morning. He had a back-load of work to do, papers to sign, properties to visit and people to see. He called Juju and asked if she could break away later in the day, maybe grab a coffee.

"I'd love to, Justin. Java Coffee is right by the Methodist church on Canton Street. Do you know the one? I could meet you there after my last class–about three o'clock. I can't wait to see you!"

Justin used his most persuasive tone. "Aw, Juju, I was thinking of some place more private where we can be alone together. I have something special for you." He heard Juju draw in her breath in excitement. "How about I pick you up at Java Coffee?"

"Okay, that sounds wonderful. I can't wait. I'll watch for you at three." Juju giggled, bouncing up and down on her toes with excitement.

"I can't wait either, baby. See you then." Justin hung up and smiled to himself. During his time away, he'd thought a lot about Juju. As crazy as it sounded, he thought he might be falling in love with her. Interesting, a man with his background falling in love.

****

Meg grabbed her sweater and headed over to Java Coffee. The student helping her with her graphics for the Flea Market Find or Forgery lecture had just handed her the flash drive. He'd mentioned some questionable

154

images and wanted Meg to review and approve it all prior to completing the PowerPoint and handouts. Contrary to her usually rigid schedule, Meg chucked office hours this one time. She wasn't in the mood to deal with whiney students. All Meg could think of was a double expresso. Pulling into the parking lot, it surprised her to see Juju standing outside the coffee house like she was waiting for a ride.

"Hey, Juju." Meg walked up and gave her a hug. "What are you doing here? I thought you were heading home to help M with dinner. Didn't you guys say you were going to try that chicken with tarragon cream sauce recipe you found?"

Juju looked around and then back at Meg. "Oh, Meg, I didn't expect to see you here. What a coincidence. Justin called. Now that he's back in town, he suggested we grab a coffee. He's meeting me here any minute. We'll have coffee and I'll get home in plenty of time to prepare the meal with M."

Meg scowled at her. She knew Juju too well. Juju was acting like Meg had caught her hand in the cookie jar. "Well, that's great news," Meg said, a little perturbed. "We can invite him to come home with us for dinner. What I planned to work on can wait." Meg put on her best cheerful expression. They waited for Justin together.

****

Justin smiled, thinking about Juju as he drove to Java Coffee. It felt so odd. This was the first time he'd met someone that made him this happy. He couldn't explain why. Pulling into a spot well away from the other cars, he parked, then took a moment to survey the lot. He noticed the two women standing together at the entrance to the coffee shop and reined in his disappointment. As he walked toward them, he hid the frown and split second of frustration. He knew Juju's family doubted his sincerity. Now that he was back in town, Justin hoped for the opportunity to change their minds. With his original plans to have Juju to himself thwarted, he figured now would be as good a time as any to do just that. Leaning in, he brushed a kiss on Juju's cheek and turned his warm smile to Meg.

"Meg, what a pleasant surprise. I thought I'd be having coffee with only one beautiful woman and now I see it will be double the pleasure. Juju, you didn't mention Meg would join us." His tone was light and friendly as he smiled and took each lady by the arm, leading them in the door.

"Hello, Justin. It's good to see you too. Actually, I was coming over for a coffee myself. It surprised me to see Juju here. We were just talking about how nice it is to have you back in town. You know, we Lawrence ladies love to entertain. We were thinking about having a small dinner party and hoped you might join us. We could invite John and Rob. That way, you won't feel outnumbered. It could be a couples evening. Are you available Friday?"

"Oh, Justin, I hope you can come. I want everyone to get to you know, like I do." Juju held Justin's hand and was running her slender fingers up and down his forearm as if she were playing an arpeggio. He felt the hypnotic effects of her touch rippling over his skin. His response was strong and undeniable.

"How can I say no to such a sweet invitation?" Justin replied before turning to the barista. "Now, what can I get you ladies?"

Meg smiled and seemed to relax a little. Justin thanked the gods. If he earned their approval, Meg and M would stop worrying about Juju going off half-cocked, head over heels with a what they defined as a complete stranger. Ordering their beverages, the three enjoyed a brief visit. Their conversation revolved around the recent murder and the university's plan of using escort teams.

Justin showed concern for Juju's safety. "I agree with the plan. Juju, you must be vigilant and never walk on campus alone." His hand patted Juju's delicate one. "I would be happy to be your personal escort when I am available."

Meg didn't miss the heat suffusing Juju's fair face. "I'd fear nothing if you were always with me, Justin."

Meg shook her head and finished the last of her latte. Standing, she smiled a thank you to Justin. "Well, I think we should go if we're going to be home on time. Justin, we look forward to having you for dinner. I'll let Juju text you the details." Tugging her love-struck sister to her feet, Meg shuttled Juju out the door and home.

****

He sat alone in a non-descript, typical college student compact car. Tracking Juju had been child's play. He drew in a satisfied breath, seeing her standing outside the coffee shop. All his instincts told him now was time to make a move. Following her from class had been easy. He had been watching her since last week, but still hadn't been able to get her alone. Those stupid volunteer escort groups were keeping the ladies safe after dark. During the day, he tracked her on campus, dressing scruffy, baseball cap pulled low over his face, and carrying a backpack to blend in with the other students. One time he walked so close to her he could almost reach out to touch her hair. He thought she had caught him when she turned, but with a quick tug on his hat and averting his face, she looked past him, smiling at someone walking the other way. He was just any other guy; not *the* guy.

On the weeks he didn't go in to john Q's during the girls' night out, he sat in his blue and white car across from the parking lot. He obsessed over the women. His nightly dreams, filled with the fantasy of taking both sisters, intruded into his days. He envisioned himself doing one while the other watched, or maybe he'd do both simultaneously. The fact that the older sister had a cop sniffing around her only added to his fixation. Knowing that he was operating right under the nose of the police added an element of risk that he found intoxicating.

Everything had gotten so boring of late. Usually after the first murder, the papers were printing so many interesting and lurid things about him. They'd give him a cool moniker. His favorite had been 'the hairdresser'. Nothing had made the headlines. What was wrong with these guys? He ground his teeth. There hadn't been a lot of media coverage, and that irked him. He liked the way the community reacted to the news, how the women huddled together; whispering the myths and legends that jazzed him. He mocked them when they abruptly became uber cautious and thought they were being safe only to fall victim to his scams.

A long-term relationship hadn't been on his radar before. Getting to know the families of his other girlfriends never occurred to him. But he wanted to get to know Juju and her family. Everything had grown so expected and mundane. Maybe the allure of playing to a larger audience enthralled him. He found most women bored him after four days. The lucky ones got to enjoy his company for a week, but all that crying and pleading, blah, blah, blah. His lip curled in disgust at that thought. He felt Juju would be different. She'd be entertaining in more ways than one. He'd heard her play the piano. Maybe he could have her play for him when he did her sister or when they weren't having their special fun together. He bought a piano with that in mind. Polished it up and placed candles on top of it. It would be romantic when she played for him. He liked it when she played the piano.

He hummed "Uptown Girl" as he pulled into the coffee shop parking lot, only to have the song die in his throat when he saw the sister standing with Juju. Instincts or not, he'd have to delay his fun. Their time would come.

He drank his coffee, listening as the women chatted about this and that, lectures and dinner invites. He chuckled to himself when they talked about the escort teams. How ridiculous to think something that simple could protect them. He was so much more clever than that. When the ladies left, he headed out. Cruising around campus, he selected a parking space near Iron's Hall. Shutting off the engine, he gazed out the windshield, zeroing in on all the opportunities walking by. He'd take a stroll to see what fun he could find.

Her pink sweater caught his eye. He watched her wave goodbye to her girlfriends and cross the park, taking a shortcut to the lot on the far side. A light drizzle started falling, and she quickened her pace. He ran up with an umbrella.

"Hey, here, let's share."

She paused, initially alarmed, but he gave her his boyish grin. "Oh, yeah, I know. Not to worry. Hey, I'm one of the escort guys. Just finished my turn and I'm headed home. I'll make sure you make it to your car safely."

The girl in pink smiled, scooting under the shelter of the umbrella.

By the time they'd walked across the park, he learned her name was Mia and convinced her to go for coffee. Bringing the new puppy into the conversation served as icing on the cake. She was his for the taking and he wanted to take. It had been too long since his last fun.

Chapter 20

Rob got the call at 9:35 a.m. Sargent Williams, with the campus police, received a panicked call from one Brenda Darling. Her roommate, Mia Hansen, hadn't come home last night and wasn't answering her cell phone. He asked if Rob would talk with Brenda.

"On my way," Rob quickly responded. Pulling Pete away from his current search for like cases, Rob threw him his jacket and shrugged into his own. "Pete, potential at the university. Let's go."

Brenda sat in Sargent Williams' cluttered office. Rob watched her eyes roam the room, landing last on the desk, set in front of a pair of windows. There, neat stacks of files occupied the out-box, while loose papers overflowed the in-box. The visitor chairs in front of the desk were hard, unrelieved wood. Despite the homeliness of a finger-painting proclaiming 'best dad ever' hanging on the bulletin board, the office would intimidate the inexperienced.

Rob accepted Mia Hansen's student registration and ID from Sgt. Williams. He looked at the face in the photo, feeling his stomach clench. Setting the information face down on the desk, he turned his gaze to the young woman, nervously picking at her cuticles. Brenda, a chubby brunette with an acute case of acne, wore thick glasses and fidgeted, clearly uncomfortable under the scrutiny of law enforcement. Being in the office of the campus police was a novel experience for this shy, bookish co-ed. Looking from Rob to Pete, she brought her fingers to her mouth and nibbled the nails. Rob gave her a calming and encouraging nod.

"Hi, Brenda. My name is Detective Adams. This is my partner, Detective Bonnert. Thank you for coming in. You told Sargent Williams your roommate, Mia Hansen, didn't come home last night. Can you tell us about that and your concerns?"

Dropping her hands into her lap, she twisted her fingers, pressing her lips together. She gave a tiny cough to screw up her courage.

"Mia has a late class on Tuesdays. Sometimes she goes out for a burger with her friends. And she's got lots of friends. Lots of boys talk to her and ask her out. I went to bed about nine-thirty. I have this stupid head cold and took some medicine to help me sleep. A bomb could have gone off, and I'd have slept through it. When I got up this morning, I made coffee and called to Mia when it was ready. When she didn't come out, I looked in her room. She hadn't slept in her bed. I mean, it was perfectly made, like always, even her stuffed tiger. I didn't know what to think and, well, that weird guy is out there, you know?"

Rob patted her nervous hands and smiled at her. The air of the campus station smelled like citrus, probably the cleaning solution they used to mop the floors. Sargent Williams passed two soft drinks to Rob and Pete, juggling a third for Brenda. Popping the tab on a can of cola, he set it by Brenda's chair. Brenda's hand shook as she brought the can to her lips, taking a tentative sip, then took a larger swallow. It seemed to help calm her nerves.

"You made the right call on this, Brenda. You say her bed was perfectly made. Is it possible she just got up earlier than usual? Went out before you were up?"

"No, sir. Mia isn't really a morning person, if you know what I mean. That's why I always make the coffee." Brenda sipped more of her soft drink, her eyes tracking back and forth, searching for more information to share. Rob saw this as a good thing and prompted her to continue.

"You mentioned Mia was popular. Do you know if she is seeing anyone special? Someone she might have spent the night with?" Rob wasn't discounting the possibility that Mia had spent the night with her boyfriend, even though his gut told him differently.

"Oh, no, detective. Mia is a nice girl. She wouldn't do that, even with Todd. That's the guy she's mainly dating. He's majoring in economics." Brenda's eyes grew wide as her brain registered the implication of Todd being a killer. Setting down her drink, she vehemently shook her head. "No, no, detective. Todd is really nice. He goes to church and everything."

Rob exchanged looks with Pete. If this was the work of their killer, it would be the third one in less than two months.

"Do you think Mia is all right?" Brenda's voice quivered and her chin wobbled.

"I don't know, Brenda. But reporting this as quickly as you did will help us a lot. We'll look into it. You keep yourself safe and let us do our work, okay?" Rob stood and watched Sargent Williams escort a tearful Brenda to the door of the police station. When he returned to his desk, he handed Rob the file he'd put together on Mia, tucking the registration and ID photo in with her class schedule, home address, and parents' contact info. Rob and Pete had another missing person report to file and parents to speak to. Mia's photo showed a pretty girl with a radiant smile and long blonde hair. Sometimes he hated his job.

Chapter 21

Meg and M focused on dinner preparation as Juju sat at the kitchen island snapping green beans. Besotted, completely besotted. She kept going on and on about Justin this and Justin that. The two older women looked at each other and rolled their eyes. They wondered how she knew all this about him. For goodness' sake, despite a couple of evenings at john Q's, they hardly knew each other, only speaking briefly on the phone and texting. None of that stopped Juju from gushing in anticipation.

"I think I'll wear the blue sweater tonight. Soft and feminine, but still casual. I don't want to be overdressed. This is so exciting. Finally, you'll get to know Justin like I do and you'll stop your worrying and I can actually go out on a date with him—ALONE—no chaperones. I mean, geez, I'll never get married if all the men interested in me have to pass your inspection. Did you get the Spokeo report back? I bet he is solid, isn't he? Good financials? I mean, you heard him the other night and the huge deal with that car dealership, for goodness' sake. That must be a big business opportunity, don't you think?" Juju put the bowl of prepped beans to the side.

"Yes, Juju. His financials look good. He is fairly new to the area, though. He moved here just last spring. There isn't a lot of information available. The only thing we can actually verify is that he has four used car lots. It all looks good on the surface, but remember, not everyone is as they appear to be. I'm sure he is wonderful and everything is all right. M and I just want to get to know him better. He will date someone very precious to us." Meg smiled and pressed her cheek against the top of Juju's head in affection.

M laughed and stated the obvious. "You know, while we are getting to know Justin better, we are also getting to know Rob better. Since he and John are coming too, I intend to give him the once over as much as I'll be looking at Justin. It's always good to have each other's back."

Meg threw up her hands, shaking her head. No one knew any of the details about her and Rob. They'd only gone out on an actual date two times. More if one counted the recital, the ball games, and the pizza victory parties. Meg thought something was igniting between them. She blushed a deep crimson and swiftly replied, "Oh, M, don't be silly. I'm not sure Rob is interested in me beyond our common love of history. Has John said something?" Meg actually hoped John had confided something to M. She couldn't stop thinking about Rob—his hands, his mouth. She felt confused by her response to him. She found him attractive and believed he felt the same about her. Well, tonight would be eye opening for everyone, it seemed.

Three cars and three gentlemen rolled into the driveway at 6 p.m. on the dot. Even though they came separately, they seemed to have synchronized their watches. Meg referred to the house as a David Winter Cottage and Rob could see why. Nestled on an acre of wooded land, the house sat close to the road's edge. Its saltbox architecture was typical of a home built in the 1770s. Traditionally, they would have sheathed a house of that period in wood clapboards, but the artist builder had covered this house with stacked ledge stone that refused to hold a straight line. It could have been an illustration right out of Alice in Wonderland. At the back of the house stood a later addition, long and low. The builder had dismantled an old log cabin and moved it to the site. A propane gas tank stood outside the fence line, testifying to the age of the building. The well-established neighborhood boasted several lovely and unique homes on large wooded lots. None, though, were like the Lawrence house. This one stood alone, as unique as the ladies themselves.

All three Lawrence ladies stood at the door, ready to receive them. Rob brought two bottles of cabernet. John bore an excellent whiskey. Justin carried a bouquet in his arms. He greeted M and Meg kindly but reserved a brilliant smile and a special greeting for Juju as he presented the flowers to her. Exchanging looks, M pursed her lips and Meg pressed hers together. Sensing the unintended tension in the room, Rob bumped Justin aside with a laugh.

"Make room, Whitman. We all want to greet Juju."

Justin stiffened, but stepped aside with a sheepish grin. Juju blushed, burying her face in the pink roses.

Conversation flowed over cocktails. Justin sat near the piano, watching Juju play a few of the pieces she planned to perform for her student recital. When she had everyone's attention, she told them she had just recently added one very special piece; it would be a piano reduction of her own composing for an excerpt from Beethoven's Allegretto from Symphony No. 7 in

A Major, Op. 92. As her hands flowed over the keys, Justin closed his eyes and let the music wash over him. The room sat in complete silence as Juju poured every ounce of her love and passion into the compelling piece of music. You could have heard a pin drop when she finished and looked over at Justin, who sat with his eyes still closed, a tender smile on his lips.

"Beautiful," he commented, fixing Juju with his amorous gaze.

John opened the wine, the ladies plated the meal and set it on the table, while Rob and Justin visited in the living room. "So, Justin, you've mentioned you own some used car lots. I know nothing about cars these days outside of the basics of maintenance. With computers controlling everything, it's beyond my high school shop class knowledge. Is that a profitable business to be in?"

"I've had some success with it, Rob. Of course, my lots are tote-the-note types so there is a certain amount of risk, selling to someone who might default on their loan. Not everyone can afford to go to the larger dealerships, get traditional financing or purchase a new vehicle. I've had to do my fair share of repossessions. Sometimes those can be dangerous. Buyers don't usually take kindly to having their car towed off. What about you, Rob? You're a homicide detective. That sounds pretty depressing. I've heard there have been some young women go missing, and turn up dead. The newspapers have mentioned a few things about each murder, but I know the police always hold back some critical piece of evidence. Are you working on those murders?" Rob looked at Justin and nodded in response. Justin leaned forward, his elbows resting on his knees.

"Are you making progress? Any hot leads?" Justin lowered his voice and took a confidential posture. "I like to think I'm an excellent judge of character. How can you tell someone is a killer? And how do you track them?" Justin's face had grown flushed and his voice took on an intensity with each question, while his eyes remained deadly cold and calculating.

Rob glanced over his shoulder toward the dining room to confirm their conversation would remain private. If Rob didn't know better, he'd think Justin was interrogating him. Keeping his voice equally low, he replied, "Well, it's not something I usually talk about. Yeah, it's depressing. Death is always an unhappy surprise, especially to the victim. It devastates the families. As for knowing when someone is a killer. It takes time. It's like putting together a thousand-piece puzzle that is all one color. You look at each piece and see if it fits. I like to think I'm pretty good at reading people too. Take you, for instance. You appear to be an upstanding citizen, successful businessman, friendly guy. But everything is not always as it appears to be, you know what I mean? I'm sure you have a similar challenge when you look at a used car. You just know if someone took care of it. It's curious, but I just seem to know." Rob watched Justin to gauge his reaction. His cop radar had been sounding since the night they'd met at john Q's. People didn't usually ask such blunt questions. Justin seemed too interested in the subject.

M stuck her head in the living room. "Dinner is served." The two men stood and Rob gestured for Justin to precede him to the table, thinking even if he wasn't guilty, he just might be one sick bastard.

The meal was wonderful. Justin hung on every word Juju spoke, adoration shining in his eyes while she talked about a visit she made to the two elementary schools where she'd be teaching.

"The children are very excited about a new teacher." Laughing, Juju's delicate hand covered her heart and her voice softened. "Oh, you should have seen their cute little faces. They are so innocent and open to new ideas. I can't help but love them. One little boy I overhead remarked how I was centuries younger than old Mrs. Hart, who I'll be replacing. I guess at seven years old, a twenty-year difference in age can seem like centuries." Juju glanced at Justin, waiting for the compliment she had been fishing for. He hit it on the mark, raising his glass in salute.

"Even when you are centuries older, you'll never be like old Mrs. Hart. Your inner beauty will shine through your lovely eyes and the children will see it."

Juju dimpled and had enough sense to blush at his comment.

Meg shook her head at the sappy exchange and smoothly changed the subject. "Teaching adoring children is not something a tired old college professor enjoys. The American History 101 class has a wide variety of students; many not taking history as their major. Besides the usual curriculum and tests, each student must write a paper on a historical figure. They usually choose one of the founding fathers. I expect they will quote every mundane fact about Washington, Jefferson, and Adams. Sorry, Rob. There are always two or three who choose Franklin. And with the popularity of Hamilton, I expect a few papers on him. Someone will probably incorporate Broadway lyrics as actual quotes. This year's batch, though, might prove interesting. There is one in particular I'm looking forward to reading." Meg held up her hand, palm out.

"Let me assure you, I tried to dissuade the student from following this train of thought but, well, you won't believe it…" When dessert and coffee had been served, Meg continued explaining the situation.

"I don't know why the student chose this topic. History isn't his major, and he seems to live in a world of fantasy and video game heroes. The title he proposed is 'American Traitor, the Infamy of Benedict Arnold: Was it in the Stars?'."

John and Rob turned stunned faces to Meg, then burst out laughing. John was the first to recover. Wiping tears from his eyes, he composed himself, offering a straight-faced observation. "In the stars? Well, now. That sounds like an asinine choice. Is the young man daft?"

"As a professor, I cannot comment on the student's mental balance. However, I am looking forward to reading his take on it. And I can't wait to see what sources he cites. I'm sure he will quote all the usual references but, and get this; he also alludes to Arnold's sign of the zodiac. His birth date is January fourteen, and that is the sign of Capricorn. The student's synopsis intimates that Arnold's birth date played a role in whom he was. His personality. He theorizes it might have contributed to his treason. He believes Capricorns, and in this instance, Arnold, possess qualities that make them suitable for being disloyal. Capricorns are supposed to be rational, pragmatic, and natural born leaders."

M nudged John with her elbow. "A point to Mr.

Arnold," causing another round of laughter.

"Indeed," Meg continued. "Another characteristic he notes is they travel a lot. And apparently Capricorns dislike commonness and ignorance. They have great self-control."

Rob topped off his coffee, stirring it meditatively. "If zodiac signs really work, my job will be a lot easier."

"Or you'll be out of one," John observed dryly.

Meg patted Rob's hand. "I don't think you have anything to worry about there. But convinced this will all prove Arnold's treachery; he adds Capricorn people are usually disciplined. He believes that could explain Arnold's confidence in the success of his schemes. Extremely focused on serious things; Capricorns are friendly and fun the rest of the time. Those born under this sign are educated and balanced. They thirst for knowledge and enjoy knowing as many things as possible, but they also know when and with whom to share their extended knowledge. This student also cites negative traits as being sometimes dictatorial and suspicious with persons they don't trust."

Juju almost spit out her coffee. "Ha. Are you sure he isn't referring to his professor?"

M shot a warning glance across the table at Juju while Meg feigned outrage. "I have high standards and expectations. I am not dictatorial."

"So, this student claims Capricorns are rarely impulsive, but when they are, they act hastily and are often erratic. They are sometimes conceited and narrow minded. I have to admit that it all sounds fascinating, but I fear it may be more a piece of fiction. It will be a challenge grading this one. I suggested he bring in actual facts to support his theory, or at least take an informative stance with the paper. Otherwise, I'll have to do research to know if any of his research is remotely accurate. I might develop the ability to read everyone's zodiac chart and predict their future." By the time she finished explaining the student's hypothesis, the incredulous looks of the group had morphed into outright horselaughs.

"You won't believe it," John comically observed, "but I was just reading in the Farmer's Almanac this morning that we have our own candy based on the Zodiac. Maybe he'll quote that. I'm a Cancer and my candy is the classic Hershey bar."

"Well, it all sounds pretty preposterous, but my birthday is November tenth, which I think makes me a Scorpio. You can start with me, Meg." Rob volunteered. Everyone shared their birthdates. When Justin's turn came, they eagerly turned to him.

Justin's gaze circled the table, taking in each individual, ending with Meg. His injured expression spoke volumes. "You just read mine. I was born on January fourteenth."

Meg leaned back in her chair, a muted 'oh' escaping her lips. She felt the heat of embarrassment flood her face as she realized her error. She instantly apologized. "Justin, I'm so sorry. I didn't think about you sharing a birthday with Benedict Arnold. That doesn't mean you are a traitor and who puts stock in the zodiac anyway…" Meg's voice died out as Justin folded his napkin with precision, placing it next to his dessert plate. He stood to leave. His voice sounded hurt; his face filled with wounded pride.

"I think perhaps I should go. It's been a lovely

evening and I hope I passed everyone's inspection. Meg, I know you are protecting Juju. I'd like to take her out, have some one-on-one time with her. Get to know her better. Juju, even if your family says no, you are an adult and I hope you decide in my favor." Justin walked stiffly out the door.

"Oh Meg, how could you? You ruined a wonderful evening!" Juju burst into tears, threw down her napkin, and ran out after Justin. Silence descended on the room.

"Wait, Justin, wait. I'm so sorry about what Meg did. She didn't mean anything by it. How could she know your birthday is on January fourteenth? I don't care what they think. I want to be with you. Let me get my purse and let's go someplace–any place."

Justin held Juju by her shoulders and looked into her eyes. She was so trusting. It would be so easy to thumb his nose at the barriers Meg and her aunt had put up; to just take Juju away.

"No, Juju. I know Meg didn't mean anything. It just took me off guard. I want to do this the right way. Give me a couple of days to figure out how I can win Meg over. I'll call you, I promise. Even in this short amount of time, I have come to care deeply for you." He took her in his arms and kissed her, letting his tongue touch her lips, eventually exploring her mouth as she yielded to his touch. His kiss left her breathless, holding her hand to her heaving breast. It had been their first kiss, but not their last. He climbed into his car and drove away, trying to channel his frustration. He headed to his shop to work on his car.

Chapter 22

Rob arrived at the tire shop ten minutes behind Pete, all the while thinking, 'no rest for the wicked', and no brains either. One glance at the scene had him thinking, what goes around comes around. The shooters from last week's drive-by appeared to be the target of a revenge killing. Three gang-bangers lay dead in the garage. Two had been caught unaware, taken out where they sat on the sorry couch, lines of coke on a small mirror on the make-shift coffee table. Rob checked but didn't see any baggie of goodies. Shooters may have taken it with them. The third managed to pull his weapon, but the pants around his ankles hindered his action and he died on the floor by the toilet.

Rob and Pete stepped aside as the Crime Scene Techs entered. They set up their station and processed the scene. The number of little yellow plastic tents marking evidence grew with each bullet casing discovered. Either the shooters had stock in munitions or were lousy shots. When their old friend Bud Gillet pulled up, Rob and Pete went outside to talk.

Leaning against the hood of his car, Pete rolled his neck and shoulders, stretching the muscles while Rob leaned against the dirty brick wall, arms crossed. The street lights failed to illuminate this side of the building and he stood in shadow. His eyes tracked a black Nissan sedan driving slowly by. Three young men gazed out at the tire shop. When they saw Rob and recognized 'cop', the driver sped rapidly away. Rob noted the license plate and called it in.

Ten minutes later, Rob and Pete discussed the recent visitors to the scene. They were fellow members of the gang. Knowing the stupidity of this segment of the population, they suspected trouble would soon follow. The challenge would be to intervene before it escalated into a full-fledged gang war. It didn't take long.

****

Rob and Pete parked behind the SWAT Humvee a block down from the suspect house. Officer Goldberg with SWAT, walked over to update them on the status. The original witness from the shooting, Mr. Moss, had called 911.

"According to dispatch, the vehicle, a light blue Mercury Milan, pulled up in front of the house. Mr. Moss reported he believed he saw the suspects pull weapons as they exited their vehicle and rush inside. He heard shouting, then silence. Patrol responded and cautiously approached the house. Receiving gun fire from inside, they called in SWAT. Right now, it appears to be a hostage situation."

SWAT followed a strict mandate for their actions. Priority of Life. First came the hostage, second the uninvolved persons, third officers and finally the suspects.

Rob looked at Goldberg. They'd known each other since Rob played with the Rangers. Goldberg's team ran protection for all the major events in Alton, including the ball games. Sporting events were soft targets, so SWAT monitored the parking lots and entrances. They would station themselves in sniper nests, watching for suspicious activity in the crowds. He and Goldberg shared cold brews and a few laughs. To say he was big would be an understatement. Any one serving with SWAT had to operate wearing equipment weighting up to seventy pounds. Each member passed a battery of physical tests involving running, dragging one-hundred seventy pounds of dead weight, burpees, climbing steps and ladders, dragging dead weight again, more burpees and then, accurately shooting their weapon. To do all this and more, within a specified number of minutes, required incredible stamina and strength–both physical and mental. This department didn't attract the faint of heart and Goldberg didn't have one. He knew his stuff and led a tight team. Rob was glad to have SWAT in the lead.

Rob let his gaze circle the area around the target house. Patrol cordoned off the streets and evacuated the neighbors. Swat positioned their armored vehicles in a semi-circle at the front. Snipers established their positions at the four compass points. They prepared drones for deployment. "Please tell me where you're at, Officer Goldberg," Rob asked. He wanted to know the details but knew the men and the operation fell under Goldberg's command.

"Tax rolls identify the owner of the house as Emaline Johnson. She has three children, ages nine, ten and sixteen. She is the night manager at the IHOP on I-30. Solid, no criminal. Her two younger kids; Deon and LeBron, are good students. The daughter, Aiesha, is the sixteen-years-old. She has been dating a known gang-banger by the name of Dante Driscol. According to the neighbors, all four are home and potential hostages.

They are our priority. We are set to contact the suspects. I understand you took the initial drive-by shooting call. You are welcome to observe."

Rob motioned to the SWAT commander. "Your show, Goldberg," he said, knowing he and Pete were spectators for this one.

Goldberg powered up the PA. "Attention in the house. This is Officer Goldberg with the Alton PD. No one needs to get hurt. Tell me your name. Let's talk." SWAT officers spent a significant amount of time training in hostage negotiations. Goldberg would try to reason with the suspect first.

"Screw you, cop! That M-F killed my big brother."

"You have every reason to be upset. The cops know who did this. They're gonna make an arrest and the shooters will go to prison. You don't have to do this. Come on, man. Think! Will hurting those people bring your brother back?" Goldberg held his breath as the silent seconds ticked off into minutes.

"Someone needs to get hurt. Someone needs to pay."

Goldberg heard a hitch in the speaker's voice. Goldberg prayed for the crack in the armor. "Okay, I hear you. Let's talk about this and see if I can work something out. Can you tell me your name?"

The laughter filtered out of the house. "What? You wanting to ask me out on a date?"

Goldberg rolled his eyes, and dropped the PA. "Cute, dude." Bringing the PA back to his mouth, he replied, "Actually, I'm trying to make our conversation go a little easier. Do you have a cell phone? We can talk on that rather than yelling back and forth?"

"Yeah, I've got a cell, but I ain't gonna give you

my number. Give me yours. I'll call you."

While Goldberg went through the steps to build rapport and negotiate a non-violent end to the hostage situation, Rob circled the cordoned off area to the house of James Moss. He found the older gentleman sitting in his rocker on the back porch, shotgun leaning against the back wall.

"Hello, Mr. Moss. You know the authorities have evacuated this area. You shouldn't be here and certainly not sitting on your back porch with a shotgun within arm's reach."

Jim Moss angled his head in Rob's direction but kept his eyes firmly set upon the back door of the hostage house. "Don't see no reason to leave. Those boys couldn't hit the side of the barn and I seen a lot more trouble when I was in Nam than I'll see here. As for that shotgun? Well, it's loaded with buckshot. I use it to keep rabbits out of the garden." He smiled in a way that let Rob know it was the story he told law enforcement on a regular basis.

Rob smiled himself. "Okay, just keep your nose clean, will you, Mr. Moss? The gangsters in that house may not know how to shoot, but the SWAT boys do and they might not consider that shotgun as only rabbit infestation prevention." With that, Rob walked around back, taking time to warn the two SWAT officers on this side of the perimeter about the old man and his shotgun. He returned to find Goldberg still trying to establish a dialogue with the hostage taker, growing more frustrated.

Goldberg held the cell phone six inches from his ear, the demands from the hostage taker reaching mega decibels.

"You tell Dante I got his skank in here. I'll hurt her. Cut her bad if I don't hear from him. You tell him!" The perp punctuated his comments with three gunshots. They pinged harmlessly off the trash cans at the curb. Goldberg muted the phone, leaning into his second in command. "Judas Priest. Another damn PhD candidate." Unmuting, Goldberg moved through the de-escalation techniques, while his communications tech used the caller id to bring up a history on the kid inside. Jaime Quintanna, fifteen. No serious raps but heading down the wrong path after his brother. Hoping to build rapport, Goldberg calmly continued. "So, it's Jaime, right? Look, while we're working out the details, do you need anything? Something to drink? Food, maybe?" Goldberg wanted to keep Jaime talking. If he was talking, he wasn't hurting anyone. The speakerphone picked up crying in the background. It sounded like it might be the younger boy. "Jaime, how is everyone? They holding up okay?"

An angry voice shouted "Shut-up" then blasted through the phone. "Look, Goldberg, we don't need nothing but Dante's ass. You get him here or I'll hurt someone." The crying ratcheted up a notch, joined by what sounded like the grandmother.

"Yeah, Jaime, I'm working on that. I got officers tracking him down. He's a chickenshit, hiding out." This garnered derisive laughter from inside.

"Damn right he is! Cocksucker has to have his bros back him up all the time. He don't have the guts to face anybody."

Goldberg heard comments of agreement over the crying in the background. "Jaime, you and your friends, they know Dante is chicken and we're going to bring him in, but I need something in return. Sounds like you got distractions going on with that crying. How about you let the two kids come out? You don't need them if Dante is hot for Aiesha." There came a significant pause and muffled voices on the other end. The crying had grown in volume. Goldberg waited. A small bead of sweat ran down his cheek. Pushing the crying could go two ways, but based on Jaime's age and criminal record to date, Goldberg's instincts were to push for release of the kids and grandmother. At least until Jaime severed the connection.

"Shit!" Goldberg set down the phone and rubbed his forehead. "Thought I had him for a second. Send in the drone. Let's see what we have working here." The operator of the drone stepped forward. He selected the smaller unit, sending it toward the house. He'd drop it down to look in the windows. They'd learn the layout of the property and where the hostages were being held. The team gathered around the monitor, watching the feed. Ten minutes later, they had more information and an impatient suspect in the house.

"Hey, Captain cop-shit. Where is Dante? I'm tired of waiting." Two shots rang out, followed by a scream.

"My baby, my baby."

The SWAT team didn't think, didn't hesitate. They charged toward the house, busting through the door. A surprised gang-banger turned, gun dropping, hands immediately in the air. The other bangers dropped their weapons and ran out the back door, only to be surprised by a butt load of buckshot from Mr. Moss, who had remained resolutely waiting for the right opportunity. One member of the SWAT team ran up to Moss, yelling for him to drop his weapon and get down on the ground. The others ran up and took the two wounded bangers into custody, calling for an ambulance.

Rob walked over to a handcuffed Mr. Moss. "You know, you're damn lucky they didn't shoot you. You'll have to surrender your shotgun and there will be forms to fill out. Maybe a fine for shooting a gun within the city limits."

Mr. Moss smiled a toothless grin. "Not a problem. Been a long time since I had this much fun. Thank you, detective."

Rob shrugged.

Pete headed home and Rob turned toward Antonio's. He had a dinner date.

****

Rob arrived earlier than planned and let Antonio know he was expecting Meg for their 7 p.m. reservation. Antonio smiled, raising his eyebrows knowingly, and inquired if Rob would like to wait in the bar. Moving in that direction, he saw Justin and Juju sitting at one of the small bistro tables, enjoying a cocktail. With eyes only for each other, they didn't notice his entrance. Rob had a fleeting thought of leaving discreetly when Justin, throwing his head back, laughing, saw him. Rob didn't miss the tightening of Justin's jaw and the shutters that dropped over his eyes. Without a way out, he walked to their table.

"Juju, Justin. This is a nice surprise. Are you here for dinner?" Rob inquired while shaking Justin's hand and kissing Juju on the cheek.

Juju's face lit up when she saw Rob, then her face fell. Exhibiting the look of a child caught playing hooky, she cast her glance behind him, checking for Meg. She shot a glance at Justin.

"Hi, Rob," he replied easily. "Yes, we're here for dinner. Are you alone? Would you like to join us?"

Pleased that Justin extended the invitation, Rob nodded. "Actually, I'm meeting Meg. We have reservations for seven. She should be here shortly. This might be that opportunity to do the double date thing we talked about before. Shall I change our table from two to four?" Rob asked, hoping the young couple would agree. He knew the importance Meg placed on getting to know Justin. Propitiously, Meg entered, waving to Rob, her expression giving away her puzzlement.

"Oh, my goodness. Hello. What are you two doing here? I know we talked about double dating. Rob, did you plan this? Juju, Justin?"

"A gift from the gods," Justin chimed in with a laugh. "JuJu mentioned Rob recommending Antonio's and thought we'd try it. I trust the manicotti is as good as you claim." He raised his brows, inquiring of Juju and getting her smiled 'yes' in return, added, "Sharing a table sounds like fun."

Meg sat with Juju and Justin, while Rob let Antonio know the change in reservations. Returning to the bar, he paused, watching the three talk, reading their body language. Justin used the term 'trust'. Rob didn't think Justin did that easily, but then, neither did he.

Antonio smoothly arranged for the two couples to share a table and took an order for an exceptional bottle of wine, selected by Justin. Rob thought the evening was indeed a gift from the gods, as it allowed him to delve deeper into Justin's background. Having approved the wine, Justin held Juju's hand while Rob launched into a friendly interrogation.

"You missed a great ball game. We've been trouncing the competition and playoffs loom large for the boys. Did you play any sports growing up?"

Toying with the stem of his wineglass, Justin considered the question. "I had a few friends. We tossed around a football, played a little sand lot baseball in grade school. I take it you played a lot of sports growing up?" he countered.

Well done, thought Rob. Justin effortlessly threw the ball back into Rob's court, avoiding giving any real details. Take two. Rob answered, giving a little of his own personal background, hoping to lull Justin into opening up. "Yes, I did and was pretty good at it. It became the center of my life until an injury sidelined me. Then I moved on to Plan B, which turned out to be a bachelor's degree in history and psychology. That led me to police work. If not sports, what did you do for fun when you were younger?"

Justin's eyes darted to the top left. He smirked, but gave Rob a little more information. "Ah, a four-year degree. Nice. I have an Associate's degree in Business Administration. Comes in handy with owning tote-the-note lots. I feel a little outdone on the educational front sitting here with you three." Justin craftily turned the spotlight on Meg. "You have your PhD in history, don't you, Meg?"

Meg shot a quick glance at Rob and responded, sending the ball back across the net. "Yes, I do and Juju will pursue her master's in music education while teaching. It won't be an easy load. Have you ever considered getting your bachelor's degree, Justin?"

"I'm afraid time is at a premium, as my business is a demanding taskmaster. My work keeps me traveling and the hours, well...Oh, here is dinner." Justin ended the conversation by raising his palms upward while the waiter served their salads and catered to everyone's requests for cracked pepper and parmesan cheese.

Rob let the conversation ebb and flow without specific direction. He found himself enjoying the evening and noticed even Meg warmed to the young man. Ending with coffee and a shared slice of cheesecake, he saw Meg's nod to Juju, giving her tacit approval of Justin. Rob took a deep breath of relief.

When the check arrived, Justin quickly handed off his credit card, preventing Rob from paying. "That's kind of you, Justin, but hardly fair. If you recall, I was the one that originally suggested we double date. May I at least cover the tip?"

"Absolutely. Next time, you can pay for the meal and I'll cover the tip. And I'll order the Osso Bucco," Justin agreed with good humor.

Rob smiled, then frowned at the vibration of his phone. "Excuse me. I need to take this." Stepping into the foyer, he answered, "Adams." He listened, a grim expression on his face. "On my way." Hanging up, he went back to the table.

"I apologize, but I caught a case. I'm sorry, Meg." Rob's lips curled into a smile, but his eyes remained untouched. "Kind of comes with the territory of dating a cop. Justin, will you make sure that Meg gets home safely?" Justin agreed. Rob leaned down to give Meg a kiss. She laid her hand over his.

"If you're my cop, I won't mind. Be safe and call me when you can." They held each other's eyes for a moment, hope and promise shining.

Chapter 23

Two days later, two days without being with Meg, had Rob impatient to see her, touch her, kiss her. He pulled into the driveway of the Lawrence house behind John's sedan. What he saw still amazed him. The neighborhood comprised several unique custom houses, but no other compared to the Lawrence home. Heck, Rob had never seen another like it anywhere, including his many trips to Williamsburg and along the east coast. Two large terra-cotta pots filled with trailing evergreens and ornamental grasses flanked the front door. The windows on the back portion of the home displayed window boxes filled with brightly colored flowers that added their perfume to the air. Rob recalled the warm and inviting atmosphere of the interior during the get-to-know-Justin dinner that turned into the Benedict Arnold disaster. He and John had stood speechless as Juju came charging back into the house, shooting daggers at Meg, who felt horrible at her gaff and unintended insult. M tried to reconcile the two young women without success. The men made a hasty retreat, hoping the women would resolve the situation without bloodshed.

Rob walked to the door with a spring in his step. He thought of the particular stamp each woman put on their inviting retreat, admiring the welcome hominess. A center door opened to a small entry with stairs. The living room on the left with two chintz sofas, a coffee table, and a stone fireplace offered a view to the front out of a large multi-paned window. Light poured in, making the room bright and cheery. Small octagonal windows flanked each side of the fireplace. This room opened to the dining room, which opened to the kitchen, casual dining and family room with the baby grand. The reclaimed log addition extended from the sitting room, accommodating a laundry room and two comfortable suites with private baths—one for Juju and one for M. Meg had the second floor all to herself. Her suite offered a small study and sitting room. French doors opened onto a private balcony with stairs leading down to the back garden. The two lower suites also had a private entrance off the colonial styled terrace with both a cutting and kitchen garden. Ringing the bell, he waited for the door to be answered. This would be the first time he'd picked up Meg rather than meet her and the first time the family knew they were officially dating. He'd made reservations at Edison's Chop House. He'd pulled his one suit out of the back of his closet and shined his shoes.

M answered the door and looked approvingly at Rob's attire. "You clean up pretty well, Adams. If I were twenty years younger, I'd give Meg a run for her money, but then I figure it would be a waste of time because I can tell you only have eyes for her." She stepped back and gestured for Rob to enter. "Make yourself comfortable. Meg will be down in a moment. You know that old saying about always keep the gentleman waiting. Don't want to seem too anxious. Oh la, I miss dating." M laughed and went up the stairs to let Meg know Rob had arrived. John came sauntering out of the back of the house, a scotch in his hand.

"Nice to see you, Rob. Thanks for getting Meg out of the house. Gives me some alone time with M. She's cooking me dinner and baked a rhubarb pie for dessert. I'm going to ask that woman to marry me," he confided.

Rob looked up in surprise. Surely his friend was joking. He hadn't realized John and M were quite that serious. If so, it seems he wasn't the only one falling for the Lawrence charm. Hearing footsteps on the stairs, Rob turned to see Meg descending, a delicate hand trailing down the banister, a wistful smile on her face. M followed two steps back, her hands clasped to her breast, her heart in her eyes. He felt the air rush out of him. Meg had selected a royal blue square necked princess cut dress with cap sleeves that hugged her curves and skimmed over her breasts to fall just above her knees. She wore dainty star sapphire earrings and a simple matching pendant. Rob couldn't identify the emotions aroused by the sight of her.

Rob felt Meg's eyes travel over him from head to toe. She had never seen him in anything other than casual clothes and stared, transfixed by his transformation. The guys at work chided him for his GQ model style. Tall, broad of shoulder and narrow of hip, he self-consciously ran a hand through his dark wavy hair, causing a stray lock to break free and fall over his forehead, looking dangerous and delicious. Frozen in the moment, they both knew if they didn't have an audience, they would have skipped dinner and gone back to Meg's room for dessert. M hustled them out the door, then turned with a smile for John that promised more than rhubarb pie.

****

Rob helped Meg from the car, tucking her hand into the crook of his arm. They walked into the plush elegance of Edison's. Muted conversation and laughter floated through the room. The maitre d' escorted them to a table at the window where the twinkling lights of Alton's entertainment district spread before them. They dined on a sumptuous meal of steak, garlic mashed potatoes and creamed spinach. Throughout dinner, their eyes feasted on each other as much as the food set before them. They barely did the ambiance of the restaurant or the quality of the food justice for their desire to leave and return to Meg's home.

Sneaking in like teenagers, they stole up the stairs to Meg's private retreat. Her small sitting room combined an office and library. When the door shut behind them, Rob drew her into his arms. He rested his cheek on soft curls and enjoyed the fit of her body to his. Breaking the embrace, Meg went to her mini-frig and pulled out two small bottles of water. Handing one to Rob, she took his hand, leading him to the small sofa. Sitting side by side, Rob struggled with the next step. He played with her hand as he looked around the room, taking in the muted floral patterns in the curtains and upholstery. The desk was solid oak. A drafting table and magnifying light stood in the corner by the window. Something covered in acid-free paper sat on its surface. The shelves along the wall were full of reference books that showed age and love.

Rob stood to get a closer look at a photo of two young people on the steps of a church smiling out of its frame. Meg's parents, Rob surmised. He circled the room to a second portrait hung on the wall. Her folks sat next to each other on a bench. Mom held Juju, then a toddler, in her lap. Meg must have been about seven years old. She stood next to her dad, smiling gap toothed at the camera. Masterfully done, the photographer captured the love shared by the family.

Returning to his place on the sofa, he playfully observed, "That's a cute picture of you. I'm glad to see your teeth grew in." He huffed when Meg gave him an elbow shot to the ribs. "This room reminds me of you. It's cozy and soft, yet full of energy. It's comforting. I could spend a lot of time here." He set down his bottle and turned to Meg. "I could spend a lot of time with you." Rob lowered his head, claiming Meg's mouth with his in a tentative kiss. Growing more bold, he let his tongue brush over her lips. He nibbled at them, then claimed her mouth once more, teasing hers to open. He feasted, tasting her, smelling her scent. Meg hummed her pleasure into his mouth as he deepened the kiss and kindled flames of desire. Reaching up, Meg tangled her hands in Rob's hair, drawing him and his kiss deeper. He felt himself grow drunk on her scent, her touch.

Pulling back, Rob gazed into Meg's languorous eyes, then stepped into the deep end of her sensuous pool. He nipped at her lips, traced them again with his tongue, then ran kisses across her cheeks and brow and into her hairline. Nibbling her ear, he moved his mouth down along her neck. She threw back her head, opening herself for his kisses and caresses. His hands were busy touching and teasing. His hands glided to her shoulders, drawing her closer. She pressed into him, wanting more. Rob brought his mouth back to Meg's once more. He reached for the zipper to her dress and lowered it, revealing her shoulders. Tracing his mouth over her soft skin, he burned a path along her neck and down to the warm spot between her perfect breasts, stopping to revel in the rapid beat of her heart as she surrendered to him. They sank back against the cushions of the sofa so he could lay claim to all of her.

No urgency drove them, just a slow, steady pulse of desire. Rob's fingers floated along her skin, exploring every inch from her arms to her legs, savoring every moment until they reached the lacy trim of Meg's bra. His fingertips brushed teasingly across her breasts. He returned his kisses to her face, eyes, cheeks and finally, her mouth. Rob shivered at the sensation of Meg's breath as she sighed his name against his mouth. Cupping her breast, he circled the tip of her taut nipple with his thumb, hands moving over her satin skin. Letting his mouth follow, he trailed feathery kisses along her upper arm to her hand. He paused at the delicate area of her inner elbow, nibbling and sucking while watching Meg's eyes dilate with passion.

Moving on, Rob took one finger, then the next, kissing each in turn. Passions mounted as Meg's soft moan drove through Rob's tenuous hold on control. He reined himself in and placed his hands on each side of Meg's face, looking into her eyes. Seeing the flame of desire burning higher and hotter, he ravished her face, her mouth.

"I want you, Meg. God, I want you." Moving away from her mouth, he brought his insistent lips to her breasts, nibbling at the tender flesh until Meg grabbed Rob's shoulders, and arched her back toward him, demanding he take more.

Meg's hands pulled frantically at Rob's shirt,

freeing it from his pants. She undid buttons and let her hands caress his shoulder, run over the planes of his muscular chest. His quick, indrawn breaths grew ragged as her nails grazed over his abdomen before she fumbled for his belt. Rob reached to assist when an inopportune knock on the door made him freeze. He and Meg exchanged looks like guilty teenagers as M's voice called through the door.

"Hello you two. I thought I heard a car. Home so soon? John and I are just going to have pie and coffee. Care to join us?" Rob heard a certain tone in M's voice that clearly showed she knew exactly what they were doing and what she was doing. Rob rolled off Meg ending up on the floor. He lay with his arms outstretched and eyes closed, trying to get control of his breathing and his arousal. Meg looked over, eyes wide, a hand covering her mouth.

Stifling a giggle, she whispered, "Busted," then called out, "Sounds wonderful, M. Umm, we're just looking at John's map. We had dessert at the restaurant, but we'll join you for coffee. Be right down." Composing themselves, they made their way to the kitchen.

M had confided to John earlier her semi-cruel plan for convincing the young couple they were in love. "Oh, John, you know human nature is to want what you can't have. I just made sure they couldn't have it in order to build the intensity of their feelings. Rob Adams is just what the doctor ordered for Meg's wounded heart. She just hasn't figured it out yet."

John leaned in to nuzzle M's neck, eliciting a hum of pleasure. "I'm glad you aren't keeping my feelings from intensifying," he said in a husky voice. "But I have to warn you, Rob's heart is wounded too. I think they are both gun shy about opening up to love. When should we tell them we're engaged?"

"Soon, my love, soon. In the meantime, I do have a private entrance to my suite of rooms in back. I'm looking forward to having that fuzzy caterpillar under your nose tickle a variety of parts of my anatomy," M said with a coquettish gleam in her eye.

Meg walked into the kitchen, flushed of face. Rob followed more slowly, a droll expression on his face. John had his arm around M and was grinning from ear to ear. He had a devilish twinkle in his eyes.

"Ah, here they are now. Why don't we take our coffee and pie into the library?" M suggested. She led the way with a tray holding pie, plates, and cups. John picked up the coffee carafe to follow, taking time to smirk and inform Rob he'd buttoned his shirt crooked.

Rob glanced down and fixed his clothing, then trailed behind. The library opened off to the right of the front door and best reflected the Lawrence personality and respect for education. It boasted a fireplace and multi-paned window to match the living room. The front window sat opposite a wall of books. An oval coffee table sat surrounded by four wingback chairs upholstered in muted jewel tones. Two low ottomans were tucked in the alcove by the the window. The floor lamp between each pair of chairs gave illumination for reading. An antique secretary stood against the wall at the cased entryway. It all spoke to a more genteel time when TV wasn't the primary form of entertainment. The only nod to modernity in the room was the gas insert in the fireplace. Rob felt right at home.

M persuaded Rob and Meg to try a small piece of

rhubarb pie, which Rob remarked was the best he'd ever tasted. They enjoyed the delicious treat and when John and M went to get more coffee, Rob stood to explore the space and the small secretary where Meg had placed her notes for the Flea Market Find or Forgery lecture. He let his hand casually roam over the stack of papers, shifting through some of Meg's photos and notes when he came upon a picture that struck a familiar chord.

"Meg, what is this?" he asked, handing her the photo. His stomach tightened, waiting for her answer.

Setting down her coffee, Meg reached for the photo. "Oh, that's a British half-penny coin minted around 1790. Why do you ask?"

"Can you tell me what the writing on it says?" he asked, growing more interested.

"It's hard to see because of the age of the coin, but it says 'End of Pain' and there is a hanging man. The British minted it because of their dislike of Thomas Paine's support for the French Revolution. It's very rare and I can't imagine where John found it, but he won't come clean regarding that. Rob, this photo seems important to you. What is it?"

"I can't tell you right now, Meg. It involves the murders. Do you have the coin?"

"No, Rob, she doesn't, but I do," John interrupted, standing in the doorway to the library. "It's in the safe at my place. Do you need it?"

"Yes, John, the sooner the better." Rob shot John an intense gaze, one John knew meant Rob had found another piece of his puzzle.

They left the two women wondering what had just occurred as the two men said a quick goodnight and drove off.

****

John and Rob drove straight to Q's where John pulled the old coin from his safe and handed it to Rob. "See here, Rob, the writing is fairly clear 'En f Pa n' and you can make out half the hanging man. It's a beauty. I'd seen nothing like it and asked Meg to take a look. She did the research. It would be quite valuable except if you look closely here and here," —John used the tip of a pencil to point out notches— "you'll see where someone attached prongs to hold it in some piece of jewelry, probably a ring. I've used it as a template for several recreated pieces. Had a nibble on selling one through my online business but the buyer was looking for the real thing, not a copy."

Rob turned the coin over, studying the engraving. It looked close, damn close, he thought. "Where did you find it, John?"

"In the last place I'd ever expect. You know, I sometimes take my metal detector and go exploring. Well, I was walking River Legacy Park and crossed into the old drying beds. You know the place where all those looney birders go? I followed one of their paths and lo-and-behold, there it was. I couldn't believe my luck. What's the fascination with this, anyway?"

"I haven't made this public, and I'd appreciate your discretion. The killer may have used this coin as a brand on the first victim, Kathy Erickson. We found her body in the drying beds. It's possible the killer dropped it. I guess I'd be dreaming to think you haven't thoroughly cleaned it, but may I take it and have it tested for any DNA?"

John nodded assent. "You may, but you're correct.

195

I cleaned it thoroughly. I hope you can find something to help with the case, but I wouldn't hold my breath for DNA. Sorry, Rob. I wish I'd known then what I know now. Let me put it in a plastic sleeve for you." John took the coin and inserted it into a protective sleeve and handed it to Rob.

"Thanks, John. I'll get you a receipt for it tomorrow. Even if we don't get DNA, your observation about it being part of a piece of jewelry will be useful. I'd also like additional information on any interest you've gotten for your recreations. Maybe our killer wants it or a similar piece back. You said someone had reached out to you online. I'd like the contact information you have on the individual."

"I'll give you everything I have on that. What else can I do?" John asked.

Rob stood staring at the coin for several seconds, thinking about the pieces of the puzzle. Now he had another piece, but right then it wasn't connected to anything else that gave it shape or substance. It stood, one lone piece in the middle of nothingness. He needed more to flesh out a killer.

"Let's meet in the morning so you can show me exactly where you found it."

The two shook hands and parted company for the evening. John poured himself a scotch and sat in front of his fire, contemplating the evil in the world; Rob headed home, thinking about a thousand-piece puzzle.

****

Rob added the information and a photograph of the antique coin to the case file. He stared at it for twenty minutes, turning over several ideas, theories, and questions. What the hell was the significance of an antique coin? Nothing came to him. Just like the necklace, the coin was another piece of the puzzle, but where and how it fit, he hadn't a clue.

Pete crossed the room with his easy gait and settled into his chair. Rocking back, he steepled his hands and stared at the same picture that absorbed Rob's attention. "I've got Penny Holmes working on the URLs of anyone that clicked on John's website. He has lots of stuff and gets lots of hits."

"Ah, thank you Dr. Watson. Holmes will ferret it out." Rob smiled, quoting their usual line when it involved Penny's IT expertise.

Rob rose, circling the workspace. He turned and poured himself a coffee, tipping the pot to ask if Pete wanted one. Getting a nod, he filled a second cup and carried it to Pete's desk. Sitting, Rob pulled a pad of paper and pen out of his drawer. Brainstorming, he and Pete made a list of everything connected with antique coins, no matter how remote. It might give them something to follow up on and lead them to the next piece of the puzzle or the killer. After filling the page, Rob realized how tenuous a lead the coin was.

"Judas, where to begin? We're already chasing every custom jeweler in the area to track the necklace. Add to that the coin and the possibilities expand tenfold. There are antique coins, the time minted, Thomas Paine, French Revolution. The list goes on and on." Rob rubbed his hands over his face, blowing out a stream of frustrated air. They eventually came up with eighteen possibilities. Revolutionary War enthusiasts, collectors, and re-enactors being the most logical starting point. Last on the list was Meg and her upcoming lecture on Flea Market Find or Forgery.

Rob kept a ball and pitcher's mitt in his desk drawer. It helped him think through a problem. He pulled it out now and, pacing the small space in front of his and Pete's desk, he let his fingers grip the ball, feel the threads of the seams. Throwing it into the glove over and over, the gears turned in his head.

Chapter 24

Trooping triumphantly into john Q's, the boys held
the trophy aloft for all to see. John called ahead,
informing the kitchen they were on their way. The soft
drinks flowed freely, and each player and his parents
relived the highlights of the game. Excited words
tumbled over each other as the boys recounted
successful plays and buoyed up the spirits of those that
dropped the ball, literally.

With victory pizza and soft drinks loading down
the table, the full ceremony began, culminating with
putting the trophy in its place of honor by the front
door. A frame below the shelf sat empty, waiting for the
team picture, which would include Pete and Rob.
Smaller snapshots of Meg as team scorer, the cheering
crowd, moms and dads, Eileen, Bella, M and Juju,
would surround it. Justin had made a couple of games
but missed the picture day. He joked about the witness
protection program and Benedict Arnold. He'd forgiven
Meg her gaff and embraced the irony. Ha-ha.

"Gentlemen, hats off please and inside voices,"
Pete cautioned them. "We don't want anyone calling
the police for code 10-101." Ben and Alex rolled their
eyes.

"Dad, you are such a goober."

"Am I? Ha, no pineapple pizza for you!!!" Pete
exclaimed, pinning both boys in head locks, to which

they giggled furiously.

Laughter and teasing filled the room as each family enjoyed themselves around the table. Rob sat off to the side, a cheerful smile curving the corners of his mouth as he watched. He felt her intent gaze without even looking and turned his head. Quirking his brow, he silently asked the question. Meg smiled in return and moved to the chair next to him.

"You look content, Rob. This is cathartic, isn't it?" Meg placed a hand on his forearm. Her touch sent electric shocks pulsing through his body.

Rob looked at her hand, then into her eyes. He felt himself drawn into the slow circle of a whirlpool of emotions. How could one woman do that to him? It had never been like that with Carrie. Even though he thought he loved Carrie, it had never been like that. He raised his hand to her face and, cupping her cheek, brought his lips down on hers in a soft kiss. Pulling back, he looked at her, searching her eyes. "I am more than content, Meg. I might even be happy."

Just then, Ben bounced over. "Hey, no kissing at the table. That's gross!" Meg blushed and Rob realized an eleven-year-old could feel jealousy. Wisely, Meg hastened to smooth ruffled feathers.

"Oh, really, little mister! How about if I'm kissing you!?" Meg grabbed Ben and showered his face with loud smacks, tickling him till he couldn't stand for laughing.

"Uncle. I give, I give!" Ben, red faced and loving every bit of Meg's attention, pulled away but stayed within the circle of her arms. She had saved his heart from being broken, but Rob knew he'd have to have a man-to-man talk with Ben if he planned to move in on his girl. Rob's cell phone tinged. He read the message. The happy in his eyes dimmed.

Rob stepped over to Pete and informed him of the Hanson's call. He told him to stay with the celebration. If something required Pete's attention, he could meet Rob. Giving Meg an apologetic farewell, he headed to the station to return the call from Mia's parents.

****

Rob grabbed a cup of the squad room coffee, took a sip, turning up his nose. A more accurate name and better description would be sludge. He set it aside and dialed Mr. Hanson's cell phone.

"Hello?" a muted voice answered on the second ring.

"Mr. Hansen? This is Detective Adams, returning your call. How may I help you?" Rob heard the sob in Hansen's voice as he answered.

"Detective." The relief in his voice was palpable. "They found Mia. Thanks be to God. We are so blessed. They found her along the side of a road, in a ditch. She's hurt, but she is alive. Thank God, she is alive!" Rob heard a door open, then close, followed by Hansen's voice growing louder, more sure.

"She has been in an accident of some sort, they say. A motorist saw her lying on the side of Davidson Street, near Handley Road. It was late at night. They didn't know what to do, so they called the police and an ambulance." Hansen's voice broke with emotion. He fought to gain control. "Mia had no identification on her. She must have lost her purse. The paramedics took her to JPS, where they treated her injuries and admitted her as a Jane Doe." Hansen paused, then the sound of him blowing his nose came across the line.

Rob took advantage of the break in Hansen's monologue and asked, "Is she conscious? Did she make a statement?"

"God, no. Mia has been here for the last four days in a semi-comatose state. When they found her, her clothes were torn and covered in dirt. She has severe lacerations, abrasions, a broken leg, serious head gash, and a concussion. The doctors couldn't get any information out of her until this morning when she woke screaming about a man taking her."

"Where are you now? Still at JPS?" Rob asked, feeling an urgency building in his gut.

"Yes, we're still here at JPS. She told them her name, and the hospital called the Fort Worth PD, who called us. I thought you needed to know as soon as possible." Hansen exhaled like he'd been holding his breath since Mia had gone missing.

Rob closed his eyes and prayed. If the killer took Mia and she escaped, this was another lead, another piece of the puzzle. Sometimes justice worked poorly and slowly, but in this case, at least it worked. "May I come visit, Mr. Hansen?"

Mr. Hasen wavered before replying. "Yes, yes. Of course. We want you to catch who ever hurt our little girl."

Rob hung up, taking a few minutes to say a silent prayer of thanksgiving. Not only was Mia safe and alive, but this might lead them to the killer before he could take another young woman. Having texted Pete, he drove to john Q's, picking him up on the way to JPS.

****

Meg had listened to Rob's brief explanation for leaving. Her gaze followed him as he left, the worry in her eyes mirroring his, but for an entirely different reason. Turning back to the table, she tried to hide her concern, but Eileen's sharp eyes picked up on Meg's distress. Knowing that loving a cop wasn't easy, she squeezed Pete's hand and moved to sit next to Meg.

"It's not the first time duty has called Rob away. Pete will soon have to follow. Their dedication and passion for justice, protecting the victim and their family, is one of the most important things they do. They eschew the danger, putting their lives before all others. It's often frightening."

Meg blinked back her tears, turning shining eyes to Eileen. "How do you do it? How do you let them walk out the door knowing that some idiot could shoot them? That they could die?"

Eileen leaned a shoulder against Meg's, tilting her head. They watched as Ben and Alex teased Bella, and Pete rescued his baby girl, cuddling her in his arms.

"Oh, Meg. Look at the three wonderful gifts I have because I chose Pete. He is everything to me and I'd die if I lost him. You learn to cherish every moment, every day. Never go to bed angry, make love with every glance and touch and kiss goodbye like it could be the last time. It's who he is, this man I love. It's who Rob is. Meg, I believe you love Rob. And I believe he loves you."

Meg would have admitted her feelings, but the moment was interrupted when both women noticed Pete reaching into his pocket to pull out his phone and read a text. The exchange of looks between him and Eileen told both women the truth of the situation. Pete took time to tousle the hair of his sons, giving each a fierce hug. He scooped Bella up into his arms and nuzzled her neck, growling like he'd gobble her up. Bella pushed back with wiggles and giggles, trying to escape. Pete tightened his grip and rocked her back and forth, then planted a loud smack of a kiss on her cheek before setting her down. He reserved his last farewell for Eileen, pulling her toward the door for some privacy.

Meg watched the love and devotion exchanged between each Bonnert family member. She noted the time Pete gave them. Time. A precious and valued commodity. Pete took it and generously gave it back. Watching the interactions between the family, Meg realized that what she thought she had with Conrad paled in comparison. Conrad had been selfish with his time and with his feelings. Childish blindness had prevented Meg from seeing the truth. What she saw now was love. This was life.

****

When Rob and Pete arrived, they found Mr. and Mrs. Hansen flanking Mia's bed, holding her hands and telling her everything was going to be all right. She was safe now. Mia looked small and helpless, and still traumatized.

"Mr. Hansen?" Rob quietly queried. "The doctor says Mia is stable. Do you mind if we talk to her? Alone?" He didn't want the parents in the room, knowing they would jump in, hoping to shelter their daughter from further distress. With the best intentions, her parents could inadvertently distort Mia's recollection, altering her statement. Rob needed her purest memories. Mr. Hansen reluctantly agreed, introducing Rob to Mia and stepping out of the room with his wife.

"Hi, Mia. Please, call me Rob. This is my partner, Detective Pete Bonnert." He sat in the chair her father had just vacated, giving her a kind smile. He patted her hand and sat back, taking out a small notepad. "I'm glad to see you are feeling better. Do you mind if I take some notes?" Seeing her assent, he continued. "You dad said you remember being taken by a man. Can you tell me what happened?"

Mia nodded, her eyes wide and still a little glassy. Rob glanced up at the morphine pump. Mia could press a button when she felt pain building. It would only dose a specific amount of medicine, but he knew the placebo effect of being in control helped patients deal more effectively with the pain. He watched her fingers fumble for the button even now, though she'd just pressed it only moments ago.

Mia licked her lips, pressing them together with the same intensity that she clasped her hands. "I was walking to my car. I park in the south lot and it was drizzling, so I cut across the park. This guy came up to me and offered to share his umbrella. At first, I was concerned because of, you know, that wacko, but he said he was a student escort. He was done with his volunteer shift and heading home. Well, I thought he was safe. He was really cute and seemed nice, so we walked together. He invited me for coffee. It was just down the street. Since it was raining harder, he said he'd drive. As we were leaving the parking lot, he told me he had a new puppy. He showed me a picture on his phone. He said the little guy wasn't quite house broken yet and asked if he could swing by real quick and let him out. I was still looking at the picture of the dog and wasn't really paying attention, then I saw he had turned away from the coffee shop and campus. It scared me. I told him I changed my mind and didn't want to have coffee. I asked him to take me back to my car, but he kept driving." Mia anxiously creased the bedsheet, her eyes twitching back and forth as she recounted the abduction. "I yelled at him and tried to get out of the car. That was when he hit me. I don't remember much after that. Things went dark. Maybe I blacked out. I don't know." She glanced at the door, looking for her parents' comfort.

Rob squeezed her hand. "It's okay, Mia. No one can hurt you here. You are safe. My partner, Pete and I will make sure of it and if I read your dad right, he won't let anyone hurt you, either."

She squeezed her eyes shut, took a calming breath. "When I came to, it was dark. We weren't near anyplace I recognized. He was humming to himself, tapping the wheel with one hand and rubbing the other over my head, playing with my hair. I was so scared." Mia's voice faltered. She cleared her throat and looked at Rob. "I pushed away from him and jumped out of the car. I don't know how fast he was driving. I didn't think of anything but getting away. Next thing I knew, I was here in the hospital." She was crying now. Pete went to the door asking the Hansens to come back in. Mrs. Hansen went to her daughter. Sitting on the side of the bed, she held her as Mia let go heaving sobs. Rob watched Mrs. Hansen stroke her daughter's hair, shushing and rocking her. He gave them time to comfort and calm.

"Mia, I know this is difficult, but I have a few more questions. Do you think you could answer them? You might help us find this person and save someone who isn't as strong as you." Rob leaned forward and touched Mia's arm. He wanted her full attention and focus. "Can you tell me what the man looked like? Can you tell me how tall he was?"

"Umm, he was taller than me, but everyone is." Mia closed her eyes to remember. She smiled thinly at her joke. Petite, Mia stood at only 5 feet, 2 inches. Most everyone would be taller.

"You said he was cute. Did you notice the color of his hair or his eyes?"

"Yes. The man had short brown hair and green eyes, I think. He had that scruffy look, like he hadn't shaved for a couple of days. He kind of reminded me of that guy on that TV show about a doctor ...*Amsterdam?* Real dreamy. Ryan...Ryan something. Does that help, detective?"

"It certainly does, Mia." Rob nodded and smiled encouragingly at her. "Do you remember anything about his car? A make or color?" Rob held his breath, as this would be a key piece of information.

Mia sighed, exasperated. "I'm sorry. One car looks a lot like another to me. It was nice, clean. Maybe silver? I just don't remember. By that time, it was coming down in buckets. I just wanted to get in and out of the rain." Mia swallowed a sob and turned into her mother's arms.

"It's okay, Mia. You rest now. I'm going to give your dad my card. If you remember anything else, you can call me, okay?" Rob gave her hand another squeeze and he and Pete walked out. They exchanged looks. Rob shoved a hand through his hair in frustration.

"Not much to go on, I'm afraid. Her eye witness account, as good as it is, isn't all that helpful," Pete observed. "They'd have cleaned her up when she came in and she's been in the hospital for a few days. Unless her clothes contain forensic evidence, we're nowhere."

Rob starred at his shoes. "Yeah, except, I know someone that reminds me of that *Amsterdam* guy too. Damn."

Chapter 25

Rob looked at the charcuterie board. Charcuterie? Hell, who was he kidding? Crackers, cheese, sliced salami, a handful of grapes, and some strawberries. He'd popped for what appeared to be a fancier cracker, hoping that would dress it up, wondering what a water cracker wafer was. When he opened the box and tasted one, he wasn't sure it justified the extra dollar and a half. Thankfully, he had some Ritz in the pantry.

The knock on the door had his heart knocking against his ribs. Rob opened it to the woman that had somehow crawled inside his brain. He went to sleep thinking of her and woke, wanting to be with her. Besides joining the ladies at john Q's on their girl's night out, he and Meg had enjoyed dinner out a few times. And then that time at Meg's when they'd come so close. She had wanted him as much as he wanted her. It all added to his frustration and desire. Rob took a leap of faith and invited Meg to come over for a light meal and a movie. This would be the first time alone together since M had interrupted them in Meg's room. The entire episode made them feel like guilty teenagers, but as adults, both felt the pull of a deeper, more meaningful relationship.

Rob's eyes roamed over Meg. Instead of her usual professor attire, she wore skinny jeans and a loose light-weight sweater that threatened to slide off her creamy white shoulder, inviting his kisses. He felt a stirring in his gut, pure, unadulterated lust.

"Hi. I'm not early, am I?" she asked. Her fingers fidgeted with the snap on her purse, clicking and unclicking it until Rob reached out and took her hand, bringing it to his lips. The intent was to calm, but the action brought a flush to her face and a sharp indrawn breath.

"Not at all." He sensed a brief hesitation when he opened the door wider. She slipped past him, leaving behind the slightest hint of nutmeg. The scent, subtle and exotic, floated in the room's air. Closing the door, Rob reached out and took Meg by the arm, turning her into his arms. He kissed her gently. Standing back, he gazed into her liquid eyes. He pushed her to arm's distance and let his eyes roam over her from head to toe. "God, you're so beautiful."

Rob watched her struggling to breathe; her thoughts racing behind those blue, expressive eyes. He took Meg's hand and led her to the sofa. Pushing her down to sit, Rob went to the kitchen, where he poured two glasses of wine. He had already placed the 'charcuterie' board or, in Rob's world, *snacks*, on the coffee table for them to enjoy during the movie. Returning to the living room, he handed a glass to Meg and raised his in salute. Meg took a sip, then licked her lips. He stared at the rim of the glass where they'd touched. Rob yearned to be the glass as Meg brought it once again to her mouth. He didn't have to be a detective to know she was afraid. She wasn't alone in that feeling. So was he. They had fallen so far, so fast. It unbalanced them. Both had past disappointments. They didn't want what they had now to fail.

Rob had cued the movie up earlier and, settling on the sofa next to Meg, cast an expectant gaze in her direction. "I selected this specific movie with you in mind. I can't wait to hear your take on it." A sparkle of mischief danced in his eyes.

Meg returned his gaze suspiciously. Rob chuckled inwardly, thinking she needed to relax and enjoy things as they presented themselves. Pulling her into the crook of his arm, he felt her take a breath and settle in. He hit play.

Leaning forward to grab a slice of cheese and cracker, Meg paused as the familiar tattoo of the drums sounded, growing in volume and intensity. Without even looking at the screen, she knew and started laughing. She turned and punched Rob playfully on the shoulder. "Seriously? *1776*? You will not sing the love songs to me, will you? You are such a nut." The two laughed at the absurdity of the situation. Then Rob sobered. He looked at Meg. He felt a sense of awe and wonder as he took her glass and set it on the table. She was so perfect. Sometimes he felt she might be too perfect for him. He wanted to love her and to be loved by her.

The hell with the movie.

He took her hand, and they stood. As the opening song began playing, Meg made the first and amazing move. Stepping into his arms, she ran her fingers along his cheek and across his lips. She had always marveled over his thick dark hair and tall forehead, his straight nose and full sensuous mouth. She had joked that his fore bearers must have been more Welsh than English with a bit of Viking marauder thrown in. Meg stood on her tiptoes. At 5 foot 5 inches, she could just reach his chin with her lips, so that was where she began. Placing light feathery kisses along his jawline, she moved down the strong column of his neck and across his collarbone, releasing the buttons of his shirt. As her mouth took possession of his body, Rob stood immobile, hands resting lightly on her hips. He'd never had a woman take the lead in this way. Her hands pulled the shirt from his jeans. She pushed it open, baring his chest. Her mouth played across it, kissing and nibbling while her fingers feathered through the hair. She followed it to the V-shaped pattern that led her lower. He found himself responding to her touch, enjoying the journey. When he couldn't stand it any longer, Rob scooped her up and carried her to the bedroom.

Laying her on the bed, he knelt at her feet and removed her shoes. He placed a kiss on the insole of each tiny foot, eliciting a stifled giggle and bringing a smile to his face. His hands trailed up her legs and grazed her breasts. Though still fully clothed, their bodies pressed together and touched from top to bottom. Rob's hands tangled in her hair as he held her head prisoner and assaulted her mouth, face, neck, and ears with kisses. He pulled her sweater over her head and gazed at her perfect body, encased in a lacy bra that barely covered her heaving breasts. Her flesh quivered as his hands and mouth worked unimaginable magic. Tracing a pattern from her face to her neck, he paused to taste and tease her pulse point, reveling in the pounding of her heart. Meg arched against him, pulling his head in tighter and moaning with pleasure. He returned to her mouth, brushing his tongue seductively over her lips until their tongues mated and moved together in an erotic tango of temptation.

Pulling back, Rob gazed into her wide, trusting eyes. "My God, Meg. You are so beautiful. Everything I could ever want."

"Then, have me, Rob. Have me. For you are everything I could ever want as well."

Rob kissed her then, slowly and tenderly, savoring the taste and feel of her. He let his lips trace a path to her shoulder, nipping lightly while his hand pushed down her bra strap, exposing her perfect breasts begging for his mouth.

A sudden feeling of awe came over him. He hesitated. His dear sweet Meg. How could a woman make him feel so full of love? Rob brought his mouth in worship to hers and breathed her name. He swept his lips over every inch of her as he slowly removed each piece of clothing with reverence until she lay before him, naked and inviting. Standing, Rob quickly shed his clothing, never taking his eyes from hers. He stood over her, much like the Viking marauder she'd talked of. She was his and he would have her. The world spun away as he abandoned himself to his feelings.

Ravenous for her soft, warm and inviting flesh, Rob's touch sent Meg soaring toward the cliffs. As she rushed over their edge, she cried out; and falling, falling, sank into the warm waves crashing over and through her.

Moving together, they rose again toward the crest of a wave that lifted them, floating like driftwood on the curl of the water just before it crashes down. Rob gave a cry of release, collapsing on top of her. His face buried in her neck, he unraveled into body melting murmurs.

It took a few minutes for their ragged breathing and

heart rates to slow. Rob rolled to the side and covered them both with the sheet. Kissing the top of her head, he pulled her tight into the crook of his body, and lay a possessive hand over her hip, letting his fingers splay across her abdomen. Meg nestled in closer, and they both sighed in contentment.

Afraid to speak and risk ruining what was possibly the best sex he'd ever had; Rob snuck a look at Meg. Her eyes were closed and her mouth was parted. Her complexion was flushed, and she looked like a cat that had just consumed a whole saucer of cream. She stretched like one and rolled toward him. Laying her hand on his chest, she tickled his hair. Her mouth curved in a most satisfied smile.

"Hmmm, that was wonderful, Rob. To paraphrase John Adams in the movie, I think we just romped through Cupid's grove together and surveyed the promised land. We certainly crossed the Rubicon."

Rob laughed, hugging Meg to him, and felt himself rising again to the occasion. He rolled her onto her back and looked at her and then at his growing erection with a playful glint to his eye. "Not to steal John Hancock's line but, 'McNair, go ring the bell.'" And that was what they did, two more times before drifting off to sleep.

****

Meg woke to the pleasant sensation of Rob's arm holding her close to his body. They were spooning, and she thought the fit was perfect. He must have sensed a change in her breathing, because she felt his velvety lips kissing the back of her neck and shoulders. His hand found its way to her center, sending a series of sensations cascading through her body until he brought her to an all-consuming and satiating climax. She purred with pleasure and prepared to return the favor when his cell phone buzzed.

Sitting up, he picked up the phone. "Adams," he answered, running a hand through his hair. "That's good news, Mr. Hansen. I'll be there in forty minutes." He turned and kissed her languorous body. "I'm sorry. I have to go. Make yourself at home. I'll put an extra key on the table so you can lock up when you leave." He kissed her again and went to take a shower.

****

After the unforgettable night with Meg, Hugh Hansen's call gave Rob another reason to smile. The hospital discharged Mia. They were taking her home. He asked Rob to swing by the house as Mia remembered something else.

Hansen escorted Rob into the living room where Mia sat on the couch, her broken leg resting on a pillow, a handmade quilt tucked around her. Mia's mother had styled her hair in twin braids, making her look more childlike than her nineteen years. He observed the dark shadows under her eyes; saw she had lost weight. Trauma did that to a person. As Rob approached, Mia instinctively reached for her mother's hand, fear alighting in her eyes for the briefest moment.

"Hello, Mia. You're looking much better. These are for you." Rob had stopped to buy some flowers. It did wonders to ease her anxiety.

"Hello, Detective Adams. Thank you. It's very kind of you." Mia smiled and buried her face in the daisies. Their simplicity only made her seem that much younger and innocent. "I am much better. The dreams don't come as often now and mom says they'll come even less, now that I'm home."

Rob settled into the chair by the couch and took out his notepad. Mr. Hansen brought him a cup of coffee and sat next to Mia, holding her hand. Rob made small talk with Mia and her folks, eventually getting to the question he wanted to ask. "Your dad said you remembered something. Tell me, please."

"Sometimes I wish the dreams would stop, but then I want them to come because I remember things when I dream." Mrs. Hansen gave Mia a nod of encouragement. "I asked Mom. She said she didn't know if it was important, but that I wouldn't know unless I told you. I remember what he hummed that night; that night when he took me and he was stroking my hair. It was a Billy Joel song, 'Uptown Girl.'"

Rob's gaze never wavered. "Are you sure? 'Uptown Girl'?" Mia nodded. Mrs. Hansen squeezed her hand. She could tell the importance of Mia's revelation. But Rob wondered what the hell he was going to do with it now?

****

Rob and Pete stood staring at their collective scribbles, notes and doodles on the legal pads sitting among the detritus of fast-food wrappers on the desk. They had lots of little pieces to the puzzle. A necklace, a coin, encounters with cops, Billy Joel, a silver car, going for coffee and a puppy. Rob liked to diagram the clues and random thoughts, drawing lines from one obscure idea to another, trying to see if something made sense. But nothing tied it all together to give them the killer. Rob wrote each known fact on a post-it and stuck them to the blown-up map of Alton. He was hoping something would gel.

"Okay. What have we got? Two victims, one

attempted abduction. All university students. All long blonde hair." Rob ran down the list of clues. "COD strangulation, necklaces with their names indicates he had time with them."

"Or, knew them before he took them so he could buy the necklaces. I'm still running down custom jewelry shops to see if I can identify where he had them made. Threw in a custom ring, but hell, that's out there." Pete checked his list. "There are only about forty local. No hits so far. I'm almost through with the list, but he could have ordered them online."

Rob nodded. Sitting at the desk, he drummed his fingers, staring into space. He stood. Walking behind his chair, he rested his forearms on the back and sucked his bottom lip in concentration. "He washed their hair and combed it, probably after he'd killed them. It shows he cares about them in a twisted way. Dumped in a rural setting. They found Mia in a rural area." Rob looked at the map on the board. He'd put a black X on the dump sites. Using a yellow highlighter, he circled all the rural areas between the dump sites and the university.

"Alton has several areas that haven't been built up yet. Hell, there is a whole area off Pleasant Ridge, one over by the Baptist College, one by the airport. South Canton is loaded with potential dump sites. He hasn't gone that far from the university." Rob wrote another post-it and stuck it off to the side of the board, followed by a second one. "There aren't many rural or wooded areas around the university. These are the best bets, assuming he stays true to form for dump sites. Where does he live? Where does he kill? Are they two different locations?"

217

Pete was studying the map with Rob's highlighted areas. "Well, we know at least one time he picked up his victim in a silver car, no make or model, and he whistles Billy Joel songs. What about the puppy angle? I can't see it. Oh, and don't forget, he looks like Ryan Eggold. I'm not sure where that gets us. And what about the brand? I know we're looking at the coin John found. Is that what he used?"

"Hell, there is no conclusive proof it's the same coin, but I'd bet my bottom dollar it is. But what is the connection?"

Rob rubbed his hand over his face in frustration. After talking to Mia, he'd met Pete at the station and they were into their third hour of playing pin the clue on the donkey. No matter how they organized the post-it notes, nothing made sense or connected the dots. They needed more pieces.

Rob picked up the baseball on his desk, placing his fingers for a curve ball and felt the start of a plan take form.

Chapter 26

The women were off on their annual Thanksgiving holiday trip to Destin, Florida. They planned to enjoy the beach and sunshine while the three guys stayed home, missing them. When Meg originally told Rob about the trip, she'd laughed. *It's not really a vacation for me*, she had confessed. She usually spent her time reading and grading her student's papers. Each year, the Lawrence ladies rented a little gulf side cottage. They looked forward to sitting on the beach, reading books and enjoying the sun and surf. No turkey for them.

Rob's folks had flown to Chicago to spend the holiday with his brother's family, so when Pete invited Rob to his place for Thanksgiving Day, he gratefully accepted. But that was only one of the four days and now he found himself thinking of Meg and feeling lonely. Rob still had his doubts about Justin. The Ryan Eggold resemblance made Rob uneasy. The relationship between the two men remained guarded. One point Justin had in his favor for him was that he worshipped Juju. He made her happy, which made Meg happy and ultimately, made Rob happy. The whole situation seemed only a bit convoluted. Justin acted a little odd and distrustful. Well, that was a two-way street, as Rob continued to observe him, listen for the meaning behind the words. Ironically, with the women out of town, the two men found solace in each other's company. They joined John at the tavern to hang out, watch sports and talk cars.

On the Friday following Thanksgiving, Justin came into john Q's. He'd put in a full day at his shop, next door. The Vandenburg business had developed into a money-making machine. The business was up and running. He extended an invitation for Rob to stop by Saturday afternoon and take a tour before heading over to john Q's for a burger and the game. Rob took him up on the offer. It would give him another angle on the man, maybe one that would turn the key in the lock to who Justin Whitman was.

Arriving a little earlier than the suggested 4:30 time, Rob took a moment to check out the exterior of the building. Justin had hired a lawn maintenance company to clean up the landscaping, replacing the half dead shrubs with new ones and adding an ornamental tree. A sign reading 'Whitman Automotive' hung on power washed brick. Everything looked clean and respectable. Rob hoped Justin proved to be, too. He entered through sparkling clean glass doors into a small reception area. A soft chime announced his arrival, but no one was there to greet him. He poked his head into a private office, finding it empty, then followed a short corridor to the garage space. It held double bays for eight cars. Seeing Justin, Rob called out.

"Hi, Rob. I'm just finishing up. Give me a second, would you?" Justin turned back to a young man. They both stuck their heads under the hood of a Dodge Charger. "You're going to have to rebuild the carburetor and check the gaskets. That will certainly help with the mix. We can look at that Monday. You should head on home. Your mom is probably wondering where you are. Oh, and by the way–don't forget to finish reading that book assignment. Your teacher told me you have a test on Wednesday." Justin clapped the young man on the back and they went to wash up, sharing the faucet and lava soap.

Justin returned, drying his hands on a towel, walking across the workshop. Rob's eyes tracked the teenager going out the door, a perplexed expression on his face. He turned a questioning look to Justin.

"That's Mark." Justin gestured over his shoulder with his chin. "He takes a shop class at Lamont High and has been having a little trouble lately. Staying out late, letting his grades fall. I talked to the teacher and, with his help, I'm starting an apprentice program for some of his students. I've found that a lot of the kids that gravitate toward mechanics come from single-parent or troubled homes. Sometimes a mentor helps them make better choices. I hope I can make a difference in their lives. Never too early to start them on the right path." Justin smiled uncertainly. Rob sensed a growing respect from Justin, a yearning for acceptance and friendship. Being a cop, he wondered about the sincerity.

"That's very admirable, Justin. I'm sure the young men will benefit from your guidance." Rob took a moment to inspect the tools on the worktables; each meticulously cleaned and organized in their holders. Justin evidently taught the 'how to' as well as respect for the tools of the trade. *This guy is amazing. Is he everything he appears to be, or is it just a convincing act?*

"I am impressed. What are you teaching the kids?" he asked, looking around at the disassembled engine parts and a couple of cars undergoing body work.

"Pretty much how to take an old junker, triage it, repair it and make it good as new. That's how my dad taught me. We'd pick up the best-looking car at the salvage yard and rebuild it from the ground up. If someone can do that, they can make a good living. Heck, might even end up owning Tote-the-note lots." Justin shrugged.

"Are those Dodge Chargers?" Rob asked, taking in the two cars undergoing repair work. "That's what our PD use."

"Do they? Yeah, I found those two cars at an auction I went to. Both need work, but that's the beauty in rebuilding cars. There were four, but someone outbid me for the other two. You can take two cars with problems and with a little work, create one car that runs like a champ. Just like you can take a person with problems, give them help and support, and create a better person. That's a lesson in life that I want to pass on to these kids."

Rob couldn't argue with Justin's dedication to helping young men. Over the past weeks, he and John accepted Justin as part of the group, although Rob remained suspicious. He felt certain Justin was hiding something. But what and why he held back was still a mystery.

The tour and enlightenment of Justin's work with the high school students added to the mystery. Rob didn't think of Justin as a bad guy and hoped for everyone's sake that the mysteriousness in his background would come to nothing.

****

Pete was up with the sun. Coffee perked and bacon

222

sizzled as Eileen came in from her overnight shift.

"Ooh, that smells wonderful. Pancakes! I'm starved. Didn't get much of a break last night. Three car pileup on I-30 following the game. Wrong way driver. One fatality." She leaned in for a kiss as Pete handed her a cup of coffee doctored with cream and three sugars. She liked it sweet.

"Thanks, babe." Taking a sip, she closed her eyes in bliss. "Kids up yet?" she asked and then heard the commotion of two sets of size ten shoes clamoring down the stairs.

Pete laughed. "Asked and answered."

Two ravenous boys bounded into the kitchen, snatched a strip of bacon from the plate, and greeted their mom and dad around stuffed mouths. Knowing their assigned duties, Ben made for the refrigerator for milk and juice, while Alex set the table. Two minutes later, Bella appeared at the kitchen door. She executed a perfect pirouette then chasséd across the floor to her father where she swept into an arabesque, her hand reaching for her strip of bacon.

"Ha, ha. Not without a kiss, my little princess!" Pete cried, grabbing his little girl and slobbering kisses all over her face.

"Oh, daddy! You'll muss my hair!" Bella protested.

Pete chuckled and took the cup Eileen had refilled for him. "Pancakes in two minutes. Take your mark, get ready and soon to go!" Pete crowed.

Sitting down with his family, he led grace and while everyone tucked in, his eyes sought Eileen's and smiled. There was nothing as precious as family.

Following the meal, the boys cleared the table

while Pete and Eileen enjoyed one more cup of coffee and each other's company before Pete had to leave for work. Bella gathered his things, bringing them into the kitchen nook. As she placed his work notebook on the table, a photo dropped to the floor. It was an IMDB picture of Ryan Eggold, the best lead they had on what the killer looked like.

"Hey, I know this man." Bella tilted her head, gazing at the photo. "He was at the ballgame. He's very handsome in this picture, but he didn't get dressed up that day. I remember he didn't shave and wore a hat. You know, not a baseball hat, but one of those weird ones? Like grandpa wears when he cuts the grass. Do you know him, Daddy? He's a movie star, isn't he?" Bella asked, brown eyes innocent and unaware.

Pete turned to Bella, a confused look in his eyes. "What did you say, Bella? Which ball game?"

"Oh, the first one Meg came to. That's why I remember. We got there early, so Mom said I could have a sno-cone. When I was walking back from Cool Ice, I saw him. He was staring at Ms. M and Juju, so I thought he might know them. I smiled and waved, but he ignored me. Then Mary came to say hello, and I forgot all about him."

The boys had heard just enough to draw the wrong conclusion. Alternating between the two, they teased their sister, while Bella added excited comments about celebrities attending her dance recitals to her brother's speculations. "Are movie stars coming to see our games? That is way cool. How did they hear about us? I bet it's because of Mr. Rob. He used to play for the Rangers. He's a sports star!"

Pete shushed the trio. "Rein it in, you three. It's

just a picture of an actor, not someone going to your games or wanting to see you dance, Bella, even though they'd be crazy to miss either one. It's nothing for you guys to be concerned about." He calmed down the kids, but felt the nudge of Eileen's foot under the table. "Well, time for me to head to work and you three to school. Give me a kiss goodbye and get your stuff."

When the kids headed upstairs for their backpacks, Pete turned to Eileen. "Jesus. He might have been there. Did you notice him?"

She shook her head, a frown marking her brow.

"He's the best lead we have on the coed killer. God, if he was that close? And Bella said he seemed to know M and Juju. I need to tell Rob. It's another piece of the puzzle he carries around in his head." Pulling on his jacket, Pete hightailed it to the station.

****

Rob worked hard not to get too excited. A sighting by an eight-year-old might or might not be accurate or relevant. But he was sure of one thing. It became another piece of that thousand piece puzzle and hearing it, he wanted to ask Justin exactly where he'd been that morning.

Chapter 27

Dabbing some first aid ointment on the scratches Amy had made on his face, he examined the damage. It still pissed him off that the pink sweater girl got away. He took Amy two days later. She was a feisty one, different from his usual type. She'd caught him with enough force to leave a couple of deep gouges along his lower jawline. Well, in return, he'd slapped her around more than usual and made a few more cuts on her, deeper and more painful. He found it interesting to have one that fought back. He'd kept her around for a few extra days because of that. But after he brought her the pizza, and she'd wolfed it down, she spit in his face. That was it. He'd had enough.

Not since Vickie had anyone dared treat him like that. He felt the anger build, his mouth twitch with disgust, remembering how that bitch taunted him whenever his dad wasn't around. She'd walk around the house half-naked and even let him touch her, cooing like she liked it and wanted more. She'd take his hand and guide it to her breasts, telling him to squeeze and pinch her. He'd get a boner, panting for more. Then she'd push his hands away, laughing at him. He hated her and all the women like her, but he wanted her. He learned over the years, others were just like Vickie. But when that little cheerleader Becky came along, he hoped she was different, that she liked him. He enjoyed watching her play with her long blonde hair, brushing it back from her face flirtatiously. He imagined running his hand through her silky hair, brushing it until it shone.

Wearing a short skirt and tight t-shirt without a bra, she'd strut past the garage where he was working on the car. He'd read that sometimes shy girls acted like they were too good for a guy. He hoped she wasn't like Vickie, teasing and mocking him. When Becky finally worked up the courage to walk into the garage, she made a point of leaning over the front quarter panel of the car so he had a clear view down her shirt at her tiny tits. He acted cool. He really liked Becky and hoped she finally realized how good it would be if they were together. This is it, he thought. Becky wasn't like Vickie. She liked him. It was her shyness that made her take so long to come see him. Slowly putting down the wrench he had been working with, he wiped his hands on the shop towel, then tucked it into his back pocket. Smiling, he approached sweet Becky. Determined to prove to Vickie and himself he could satisfy a woman; he made his move. Hands darting out, he grabbed Becky, pinning her against the wall of the garage. Shocked by the speed of his attack, Becky pushed against him, struggling to break free. Trapping her, he groped, squeezing her boobs painfully while pressing himself against her hips and slobbering kisses all over her face. Repeating in a ragged voice how much he loved her.

Becky pushed back and when they sprang apart, she looked at her white t-shirt, now covered with greasy hand prints. Angry, she pointed at him, saying; "You greasy, no brain jerk! What do you think you're doing?

Look what you did to my t-shirt? I'll never get this stain out! And did you really think I would be interested in someone like you? Someone that always has grease under their fingernails and wears overalls covered in dirt and grime? Do you ever shower? Or wash your greasy hair? God, you are so gross." No longer angry, Becky started laughing.

That had done it for him. Just like that bitch, Vickie. She dissed him, laughing at him. No one laughed at him! He stepped forward and slapped Becky across the face. He'd cut her lip with the ring his dad had given him. The one with the old coin on it. His hand left a greasy print on her cheek. She looked at him in shock and fear. She tried to run, but he grabbed her arm and pulled her back into the garage, pressing the button on the wall to bring down the door as he hit her again, knocking her to the floor. He was on her then. She fought, kicking and scratching, trying to stop him from touching her and doing to her all the things he'd dreamed of. He felt her nails rake across his cheek, along his jaw. When he felt the warmth of the blood she drew running down his neck, he hit her again. She was crying and pleading with him by then, and he felt himself getting harder with each minute. As he tore off her panties and pushed into her, his hands circled her neck. He pumped harder and harder, as he squeezed her throat tighter and tighter. He came just as she drew her last breath. It felt glorious. After being called a loser and a below-average student, he'd found his calling.

He'd never felt this kind of power before, the power over life and death. It filled him with a profound sense of destiny. Getting rid of the body was easy. Dumping Becky into his trunk, he drove out to

Weeder's Pond. He shoved her through the center of an old tire and tied two car batteries to her, one at her neck and the other at her ankles. Dragging her out to the center of the pond, he pushed her under. He watched, fascinated, as her long blonde hair floated around her face. It moved him like poetry. Then she sank like a rock. He ran his hand through the little bubbles rising to the surface, making a pretty pattern.

He returned home in time to say goodbye to his dad, leaving for the Vegas Auto Auction and a long weekend of gambling. As he stood waving, he smiled secretly. He decided this weekend, Vickie would beg him to take her. No more just touching. He'd have her, show her he was more than man enough to satisfy her. He had two glorious days. Vickie stopped laughing at him, then eventually begged him to stop hurting her. When he finished, Weeder's Pond had another guest. He packed up Vickie's stuff and dumped it at the homeless shelter donation box across town. His old man would think the bitch took off like the others had before her. His dad would get drunk, think good riddance, and find another blonde bimbo. The old man would move on like he always did.

Over the next couple of weeks, he watched his dad drink himself into a stupor. Growing more disgusted with the old fart, he asked for his share of the money they'd made from the sale of the rebuilt cars. The old man slapped him upside the head, telling him to get the hell out. Well, screw him, he thought. Having found the stash of cash, he took it all and left. He learned he had a calling and the urge to answer it.

Chapter 28

The trip to Destin had been just what the doctor ordered, according to M. All three ladies came home relaxed and tan. The six of them gathered for their usual night out. John and Meg discussed going to the library in Dallas to see an original copy of the Declaration of Independence on permanent display there. It would be a fun and educational outing for all of them, they insisted. Everyone just nodded and rolled their eyes.

Rob hadn't forgotten Bella's observations. He worked his interrogation into the group's casual conversation. "Okay, so no one wants to expand their mind. How about something else? The Mavericks are playing. We could go to a basketball game. You know, come to think of it, Justin, you might not be interested in sports. You never made it to any of our little league games. By the way, where were you again on the weekend of the first game the ladies attended?"

Justin tore his attention from Juju long enough to answer. His brow furled, recalling the excuse he'd given them. "Oh, that was the auto auction in Lubbock. I flew in Friday night and didn't get back until Sunday late." Justin's tone turned defensive. "Problem?"

"Nah. Just thinking we created a monster that day. Juju is still nagging me about season tickets to the Rangers." Rob glossed over the entire exchange, tucking the information away to check on later. Even though Justin had shown himself to be likeable and even incredibly upstanding, there were still moments that things didn't jibe.

As each couple focused on each other, Rob kept half an ear and eye tuned into Justin. He sat next to Juju with his arm draped across the back of her chair. Justin's joy was unmistakable as he played with her hair, happy to have her home and be with her. Rob noticed Justin's fingers brushing over the small hairs on the back of Juju's neck, laughing at her giggles of delight. His fingers toyed with the chain around her neck.

"What's this, a souvenir from Destin?" he asked as he pulled on it to examine the pendant.

Juju laughed and batted Justin's hands away before he could get a look. "Don't be silly, Justin. You are such a goober. Even though there wasn't a card, I knew it was from you. It's so unique. I love it."

Rob noticed the look of confusion on Justin's face. Juju went on. "Don't play innocent with me, mister. It's the necklace you enclosed with your last delivery of flowers." Justin stiffened and swallowed hard. "And by the way, they really should call off the squad car assigned to shadow Meg and me. The campus police say that things have settled down. We're fine."

Rob hadn't heard all of what Juju said, so it did not alarm him, but judging from the look on Justin's face, he was terrified.

Chapter 29

Rob snuggled Meg into his arms. Her skin, silky under his hands, was damp with the sheen of sweat from their lovemaking. He knew he loved this woman, believed he might be ready to tell her. As he laid, dozing, he saw the duet between John and Abigail Adams in the movie *1776* play out in his mind. A smile curved his lips. Odd that his mind would go there. He subconsciously hummed the last few bars, "Yours, yours, yours." Then fell asleep.

Meg's side of the bed was empty when Rob woke the next morning. Pulling on his sleep pants, he walked out of the bedroom to find her wearing one of his ball jerseys and nothing else. She sat at the kitchen island, coffee in hand and laptop booted up, reviewing her lecture.

Rob ran a hand through his sleep tousled hair, admiring the view, said good morning, and poured a cup of coffee. Moving to stand behind her, he kissed the top of her head and nibbled the creamy shoulder left exposed by his shirt.

She turned her incredible blue eyes to him, love warming her gaze. "Good morning to you, too. You rarely get to sleep in and you looked so content. I didn't want to disturb you."

"Thanks, but the bed was very lonely without you." He placed his hands on her waist and nuzzled her neck.

"I think we would both benefit from more time in it," he whispered seductively. Meg turned and slid her arms around Rob's neck, leaning into the kiss he gave her as he scooped her up and carried her back to bed.

Fireworks exploded in his brain as Meg came, carrying Rob with her. With his heart pounding, he gradually returned to earth. When Rob could put together a coherent thought, he remembered his mother's invitation to dinner. She insisted he bring Meg. But before he spoke about that, he needed to ask something else.

Rising and moving into the kitchen, Rob split a bagel, dropping it into the toaster while Meg pulled the cream cheese from the refrigerator. They tucked into breakfast while Rob laid out his plan to a skeptical Meg. "I assure you the police presence will be invisible to the audience and you won't be in any danger."

Rob had thought long and hard about exposing Meg to any potential danger. He'd have four men in plainclothes in the audience. Pete would be backstage to cover Meg, and Rob would circle. A killer resembling a movie star based on Mia Hansen's vague description seemed unlikely, but Rob was determined to leave no stone unturned. The interest in the coin John found was too coincidental to be insignificant. And as Rob had learned, coincident did not exist in his line of work. Rob hoped this would be the honey that drew the fly.

Meg rose, nerves clear. She paced, wringing her hands, and considered Rob's idea. She started to ask a question, then retreated into more thought. A second pause and a raised finger turned into a head shake and dismissive hand wave. Finally, she turned troubled eyes to him. "What makes you think this person will attend the lecture?"

Rob recognized the tension building in Meg. "The additional publicity and newspaper article I'll arrange will throw a spotlight on the coin. And John agreed to post the lecture and the coin on his website. It's the one solid connection we have to the killer. Someone reached out to John about purchasing it. We haven't been able to identify the individual through his URL. This is the next best thing."

Meg resumed pacing, her fingers tapping on her thighs, her teeth worrying her lower lip. After taking two more turns across the small living room, she turned to face Rob. Fear mixed with anger simmered in her eyes. "Rob, if this person wants the coin and believes I have it in my possession, he may try to go through me to get it. Am I the sacrificial goat?"

Rob closed his eyes, bowing his head. He wanted to go to her, hold her and tell her he changed his mind, didn't want her to do it, but catching a killer required sacrifice. "Sacrificial goat is extreme. But, yes, Meg. The killer may see you as the way to get his coin back."

Meg ran hands through her hair. Knitting her fingers together, she cupped the back of her head, staring at the ceiling. Pressing her lips together, she exhaled meditatively, buzzing her lips in frustration, thinking. Then she thought about the risk versus the reward if they could catch the monster killing these young women. She knew Rob would be watching. She'd never be in danger at the event.

"Rob, I am not as much concerned for my personal safety as the safety of M and Juju. With the additional publicity, the killer may track down where we live. Can you guarantee all our safety?"

Meg was right. With her name associated with the coin splashed across every social media outlet, the killer might discover where she lives. "If he shows his face at the lecture, that won't be an issue."

****

When Justin heard the plan, he went ballistic. "What the hell are you thinking, Rob? You can't put Meg, Juju or M in the cross-hairs like this. This guy is smart, or you'd have caught him by now."

"It's the best chance we've got. Remember, Meg is front and center of the threat. I know that. So does she. It's a risk she is willing to take. And I won't let anyone touch her."

****

Rob watched Meg arrive at University Center. Even though she parked close to the door, she still glanced around, showing a zing of nerves. It didn't strike Rob as stage fright but apprehension with being alone, walking by herself to the hall. They'd talked about this. What if he came for the coin? For her? Rob has assured her he would have the garage and her under surveillance, even if she didn't see him.

Rob saw Meg shut off the engine, wipe her palm on her coat, and stop to press it firmly to her pounding heart before donning her gloves. Grabbing her purse and laptop, she opened the door and climbed out of the car. The wind whistled through the structure. She yanked her collar tighter around her neck, dipped her head, and strode briskly to the entrance.

He continued to scan the parking garage until Meg was safely in the building. Pete waited for her just inside the door. He'd dressed like a college professor and would act as host and escort for the evening. Leading Meg to the backstage area, he helped her set up her equipment and stood by as she and the AV guys completed sound and PowerPoint checks. When all was ready, Meg sat down in a quiet corner to review her notes. The hall was filling. John escorted M and Juju to their seats. Juju had insisted on attending the lecture over Justin's protests. She'd complained about being suffocated, claiming she couldn't go anywhere without a police car following her. Justin's seat remained empty.

Rob selected four officers to sit in the audience. Two posed as an older couple and arrived early. They sat in their assigned seats and scanned the audience for a TV star lookalike killer. The female officer took time to visit the ladies' room and scan the lobby. Two others dressed like college students; one Asian and one Caucasian. They arrived separately, eight minutes apart. Hanging around in the lobby, ostensibly checking out other students, each watched for the killer. Rob watched from the parking garage, slipping backstage to stand in the shadows.

A quick scan of the crowd failed to reveal anyone that fit the description Mia Hansen had provided. Shifting to a different angle, Rob's gaze moved methodically from face to face. The audience murmured or read the program. Each had received a copy of the PowerPoint and several were making notes. Even though Meg practiced her presentation and shared the PowerPoint with him, Rob found himself distracted the moment Meg stepped from behind the curtains. A change came over her as she walked to the front of the stage. Her gaze, entire body language, communicated authority and expertise. Her smile captivated the audience and when she spoke, her eyes swept the room, making eye contact with each individual, causing them to feel she was speaking only to them.

Meg used clips from public television's popular antique show and other graphics to break up her presentation, each segueing into the specific item on display. She spoke about each example, sharing the authentication process and her determination of 'find or forgery'. Meg educated the audience on the importance of research.

When the time came in the program to discuss the coin, Meg provided a concise overview of the period's history and displayed slides of the coin and similar ones. Using her laser pointer, Meg noted the differences in quality, the areas where one would expect to see wear, as well as typical metals used in making them. Meg spoke to the value of such a remarkable piece of history, assuring the audience that they held an item of this significance in a secure location.

Concluding her part of the program, she stood at the edge of the stage and, once again, swept the audience with her intense gaze. "A discerning collector's knowledge includes materials used, fabrication techniques, the style or fashion of the time, and normal wear, knowing what would or would not survive. They understand the art of artificial aging. A wise collector doesn't let emotion cloud their judgement. And a happy collector always enjoys the journey."

Meg opened the floor for questions. Rob moved to a new angle and watched the crowd. If the killer was going to expose himself, this could be the time. Fifteen minutes later, Meg answered the last question.

"Thank you, ladies and gentlemen. You have been a wonderful audience. Good night." She stepped offstage, and the crowd filed out.

Rob's people mixed in, watching, only to come up empty-handed. Frustrated the coin hadn't been bait enough to draw out the killer, he relaxed. Meg wasn't a target.

****

Parked in a darkened corner of the lot, he had searched for a familiar face. Having seen who he was looking for, he entered the building, then sneered contemptuously. Did the cops think he was that stupid? He made the Asian guy right off the bat. The couple acted too attentive to each other to be real. The fourth guy stood out like a sore thumb with his sweater knotted over his shoulders like some gay dance club slut. No, he was smarter than that. Looking around, he tried to spot the last of the unit covering the event. He didn't see them and figured they hid in the shadows. Well, he could hide in the shadows too, but did his best work in plain sight.

Taking his seat, he let his gaze roam over the crowd. No one of interest tonight. Just Juju. She had his undivided attention.

The lecture bored him until Meg arrived at his precious coin. He couldn't believe he'd lost it and wanted it back. As she talked about the historical significance and the quality of the coin, its condition and how that ultimately impacted its value, he grew angrier. The bitch didn't understand the significance; the importance of ending pain. At the end of the lecture, she thanked the original owners for allowing her to borrow her examples to photograph for the presentation. He swore under his breath, earning a disdainful glance from the elderly gentleman to his right. That meant she didn't have the coin in her possession.

Even though the police had been holding back salient points of the murders, he knew what they knew. What a rush to push the envelope. He wanted to taunt them. To rub their noses in it. He wasn't sure about the guy backstage, but recognized Rob Adams. It gave him a blast to stroll right past the lead detective without being seen. No one gave him a second look. As he stood to exit with the throng, he slipped the small white box under his seat. Someone would find it and when they did, Rob Adams would know the meaning and freak.

He walked out with the rest of the audience, right under the noses of the cops.

****

Rob followed Meg home to ensure her safety. When they arrived, he came around her car, helping her out, walking her to the door. While she fished her key from her purse, she paused, laying her hand on Rob's cheek.

"I'm sorry it didn't turn out like you hoped."

Rob took her hand and pressed a kiss into her palm. "Sometimes things don't go as planned. It lets us know the coin may not be as important as we believe. We'll keep working the case. We'll get him." Rob took the key from Meg's hand and opened her door. "Be sure to lock the door behind you. Goodnight, Meg." He kissed her, letting his mouth linger, breathing in her scent.

Meg stepped inside and when Rob heard the throw

of the deadbolt, he felt his phone buzz with a text. Waiting until he got behind the wheel, he pulled it out and read the message. It came from the university police department stating the cleaning crew at the College Center found something of interest.

Rob drove swiftly back to the university, parking in the fire lane, and rushed inside. The officer stood with the janitorial staff supervisor, waiting for him. A small white box wrapped in a plastic bag sat on the counter. With a nod, the supervisor explained.

"My crew found it after the program tonight. Section 7, row 9, seat 14." Leading Rob into the auditorium, he continued. "They found it here, under the seat, tucked out of sight. I'm afraid a couple of them handled it, passing it back and forth to look at it. Seems odd someone would leave a necklace. What does it mean, that inscription? 'Who's next?'"

It meant Rob had monumentally screwed up. The killer had been there. Had he noticed him and passed right over him? Did they catch him on camera? Rob asked for the tapes and headed into the station. It would be a long night. He let Pete sleep.

Chapter 30

Royce Roberson turned on to the gravel road that led to his deer lease. The old pickup with the faded paint rocked and shuddered across the cattle guard before hitting the rough gravel road. The last rains had left deep ruts. Royce was thinking he'd have to bring out his mini-dozer and level it back out before too long. His hunting buddy, Steve, looked out the window. Steve always had a joke or a wisecrack. They spent hours tossing barbs at each other over cold brews. Friends didn't get much better than Steve.

The sun topped the horizon and promised another mild day. They planned to set up in the hunting blind, hoping to bag some of the troublesome wild hogs before Christmas. "Damn vultures circling. I bet some jerks tried their luck taking down a hog and left it to rot. I wish those guys would stop doing that stuff. Don't they realize how dangerous it can be? A boar can kill you in a New York minute with their tusks. Besides, it's a waste of our time having to clean up the carcass."

They pulled to the end of the road about 100 feet from their blind and climbed out of the truck. Royce grabbed their gear out of the back of the truck while Steve slowly stood and stretched his back. It bothered him something fierce today. He popped two Gabapentin, dry swallowing them. Glancing up, Steve noticed four gigantic vultures circling overhead.

"Must be a decent size kill to attract that many. Hey, Royce, did I ever tell you about them using vultures to find the remains of them astronauts after the shuttle Columbia explosion? Those birds have incredible olfactory nerves and can smell a piece of rotting flesh the size of a quarter." Royce nodded, scarcely paying attention while Steve droned on about the gruesome vulture stories he knew. The man could sometimes drive a man nuts, but he still made Royce laugh.

When they came around the copse of trees just behind the blind, they disturbed a trio of the ugly creatures. With a great flapping of wings and a lot of low guttural hisses, the three flew off to land on nearby treetops, watching over their feast. Royce walked over to look at what they had been pecking at and pivoted away to throw-up. Steve was right behind him and almost fell over as he rapidly backpedaled away from the sight of a young woman with putrid purple and yellow flesh and her eyes pecked out. He fumbled for his cell phone and dialed 911.

****

Rob and Pete pulled onto the gravel road and met the local law enforcement officer. Someone had dumped the body in a rural part of Belton County and it wasn't in his jurisdiction, but when Sheriff Hawkins called and told him about the body, he figured it was his killer and the body of missing Amy Tucker. Amy had been a student at the local junior college, getting her basics out of the way. She had hoped to transfer to the university. Amy was a popular student with a serious boyfriend. He had reported her missing after she ghosted him for their standing Friday night pizza date.

Rob felt sick to his stomach. He snatched one of Pete's antacids. Extending his hand, Rob greeted the guy that looked like he was in charge.

"Sheriff Hawkins? Rob Adams, APD, my partner, Pete Bonnert. Thanks for calling. We got here as quick as we could. We've been working on this case. Anything you can share with us?"

Sheriff Hawkins greeted them and gestured to the county coroner doing his work. "Not much to tell you yet. Coroner just arrived. He was the one that clued me into your cases since you use the county medical examiner, just like we do. But from the info y'all emailed over and the missing person report on Amy Tucker, I'd say it's her. Young, blonde, from what we can tell. Since the animals have been at her, it's hard to tell if the killer combed her hair; but just as you mentioned when I called, she is wearing a necklace with her name. It's a pretty gruesome sight. Looks like she was out here at least a day. The vultures were just getting started when the two hunters found her. Luckily, the coyotes and hogs didn't get to her or there wouldn't be a lot left. But I can tell you, it won't be an open coffin. You're welcome to stick around. If you need anything, please let me know." Sheriff Hawkins touched the brim of his cowboy hat and strode off.

Pete stood back. Fewer feet meant less crime scene contamination, but Rob, being careful not to tramp on any evidence, walked over to where Amy lay. God, what a mess, he thought. This image wouldn't fade quickly.

Pete drove back to the station, letting Rob focus on the crimes. Staring out the window at the passing landscape, Rob shifted through everything. Some things one could never unsee. Amy was one of them. But he'd stand for her, be her voice and find her justice. They didn't bother to stop for lunch. Didn't have much of an appetite. Walking into the station a little after one o'clock, Rob made a beeline for the boss' office.

Rob knocked on Lieutenant Griffin's door, getting the nod to enter and sit. He crossed to the windows and looked out into the rain-soaked parking lot before turning toward the chair across from his boss.

"Lieutenant, this is the third young woman we have found with the same MO in the last four months. You know I'm not one to throw in the towel and I'm certainly not doing that with this case, but, if it walks like a duck, quacks like a duck…Look, what I'm saying is, whether we want to admit it, we all know it's a serial killer. I did some outside research. We're not the only jurisdiction to have this type of homicide. There have been several similar cases from here to Los Angeles. I think our killer is a traveler. It's a pain in the ass, but I'd like to call in the feds. I'll read them in, but wanted your approval before doing it." As Rob recounted the facts of the cases, Kathy, Debbie, and now Amy, he felt sick to his stomach.

Lieutenant Griffin brought steepled fingers to his lips and breathed in resolutely. "I agree. Make the call." Rob thanked the Lieutenant and went to his desk, dreading his next call. While he waited for an agent to respond, he pulled all the missing person reports in the county and built a spreadsheet with each one's physical characteristics–gender, age, hair color, occupation. An hour later, he had found two additional names of women reported missing since last March that fit the profile.

****

Rob looked up at the knock on his partition. Special Agent Thomas Hardy flashed his badge and sat down. He looked over at the half-empty pot of coffee. Rob took the hint and poured Hardy a cup, taking time to add a warmer to his own. Hardy put a 2-inch-thick file on Rob's desk and sipped his coffee.

"I took the liberty of printing up all the unsolved homicides in the southwest we've been working on, the ones where the victim profiles match yours. You're spot-on suspecting this is a traveler. I'm embarrassed to say, you're not the first to reach out to us. You know the saying, about how the left hand…well, no one else in the bureau put two and two together until recently. First one was ten years ago, Los Angeles. It was a hooker and, well hell, murders like this are common in LA, so no one paid much attention. The next ones are moving east. Mohave County had a few, Henderson, Nevada; Kingman, Arizona; Lake Havasu City, Arizona. The perp expanded his territory, and we had some in the Phoenix area. It goes quiet for a few months and then he crops up in Albuquerque. Another break in the action and the next hot spot is San Antonio. That's when I picked it up. Now you're seeing them here."

Rob almost jumped out of his seat when he heard Hardy's summary of the file, remembering the background report on Justin. The moves Whitman made coincided with the trail of the traveler. Tamping down his suspicion, he gave Hardy time to finish his report. Without further investigation, Rob's background search and the subsequent moves Justin had made, only made him a person of interest, not the killer.

Hardy continued. "All are college towns and the victims are young and blonde. I've included pictures. They're pretty grim but, well, you'll see. They found every one of them wearing a piece of jewelry with their name and, when decomposition didn't mask it, clean, combed hair. What the hell does the sicko get out of washing and brushing their hair? The killer branded all the victims too, but it sounds like he only did your first one. He might be evolving. When you've looked these over, let me know if you find anything else different from your killings. We figure when the media gets wind of this, they'll come up with a name for him. Something catchy–like 'The Traveler' for lack of anything better. Hell, that's what we're calling him."

Rob nodded in agreement and took the file from Hardy. He sifted through the photos, zeroing in on the brands burned into the other girls. "This answers my question about the branding. It baffled me until I snagged a clue recently. A historian found an antique coin that had markings on it, showing he might have mounted it in a ring. The brand on our first victim, Kathy Erickson, appears to be a match." Pulling the End of Pain coin from his file, he handed it to Hardy for his inspection.

Hardy had been working this case long enough that he didn't have to review the file photos to know he was looking at the pattern of the brands. He lifted his eyes to Rob. They held sadness for the waste of human life and a fire of determination to find the killer of these young women. He wore the deep grooves of worry between his bushy eyebrows and flanking his mouth from a perpetual frown. Hardy pushed the file toward Rob, who added copies of his case files from his investigations. Rob would take time to review it in its entirety, add what he could, and they'd have a complete dossier to give to the profiler. He also added Justin Whitman to the top of his list as a person of interest. Until he knew more, he didn't want to consider Whitman a suspect, even though everything seemed to point that way.

****

Twenty-four hours later, Justin was sitting in an interrogation room. Two uniformed officers had approached him when he arrived at the car lot and asked him to accompany them to the station. Detective Adams had some questions, the officers informed him. His first thought had been that something had happened to Juju. Last night on the way home after dropping her off at the house, a patrol car had pulled him over. The officer had been polite; respectful even. He asked for his license and registration and went to sit in his blue and white. Justin knew he hadn't been speeding and wondered what was up. He waited with his hands at 10 and 2 like they had taught him, impatiently drumming his thumbs on the steering wheel. After about five minutes, the officer returned, handed Justin his ID, and gave him a warning. He hadn't given it any thought at the time. Now he sat, waiting for the next act in this little charade they were playing.

The 'good cop' brought him a cup of what they evidently thought passed for coffee. He stared at the one-way mirror, wondering who stood on the other side. When the clock ticked over to 9 a.m., Rob walked in and opened the dialogue.

"Good morning, Justin. Sorry we had to inconvenience you this way. Some new information came to light in the recent murders. I wanted to see if you could give us any information that might help clarify it. Do you need another coffee?" he asked solicitously.

Justin looked at Rob like he didn't know what he was talking about. "Hi, Rob. Yes, I would appreciate another coffee. Can I get it from the same pot as yours? It looks a little fresher." Rob laughed. Justin was right. He'd gotten the vending machine version of coffee. Rob had the Keurig. Rob nodded and gestured to the glass. Pete came in after a minute with a fresh cup. Some detectives thought terrible coffee worked like sodium pentothal. Justin took a sip and thanked Rob. He figured Rob had finally made the connection between the murders and his moving around over the last ten years. He waited silently for Rob to make his opening move.

Rob reminded himself so far, everything he'd checked on Whitman came out clean. This guy helped young men in trouble, ran a successful business, and cared for the sister of the woman he loved. But Ted Bundy looked good on the surface, too. "Look, Justin. First off, you aren't under arrest. I'll be honest with you. We have discovered some disquieting coincidences. I'd like to give you the chance to explain them."

"Really, Rob? Do I need to call an attorney? Perhaps you should read me my rights." Rob looked at him. He could tell Justin was royally pissed when he continued. "Well, isn't this just great! So, you say I'm not under arrest. Then what exactly am I?"

"Justin, for God's sake, you act like the boogie man is hiding around every corner. Add to that, you're someone that has moved a lot over the last ten years and lived in the same cities where a series of killings occurred. This makes you a person of interest." Rob placed the list of all the cities in front of Justin. It matched the path of the killer. "Perhaps you can explain how you and the killer came to live and move along similar routes."

Justin pursed his lips and looked at the list, nodding. He sat back in his chair and hooked his thumbs into his pockets. "I can see where you'd find this curious. Have you bothered to look at the dates of my moves and the murders? I think you'll find I didn't show up there until after the first killing. Unless you think I can teleport, this is pretty thin evidence. Look, Rob, I've been here and done this before. You played ball. A batter gets three strikes and then he's out. When a player doesn't perform, they pull him from the rotation. I'm sick of watching the home team screw it up."

Rob sat there wondering where Justin was going with the baseball analogy. Justin knew something. The question was, what was it?

"Justin, this is me, and I think we both know what is at stake here. A good coach knows when to call it. Maybe it's time for a change in pitchers."

Justin blew out a breath with disgust and shook his head as if to say, 'no, I don't think so.' After all, he'd heard similar BS in the past and everyone struck out. "Are we done here? Because even though you say I'm only a person of interest, I don't intend to waste my time doing your job or answer any more questions without an attorney." Justin stood and looked down at Rob with distaste. "You know, they say he poses as a cop when he makes first contact. Do you wonder why I don't trust you?" Justin walked to the door and waited until the 'good cop' came to let him out.

Pete watched Justin exit the building and turned to Rob. "Okay, well, that could have gone better."

****

Justin had it. He was through hunting. He wanted it all to end. Let the police continue to stumble around in the dark. They were worthless. He and Juju would leave and start life fresh without the specter of a deranged killer hanging over their heads. Justin spent the day putting his plan into action. He pulled as much cash as he could out of his accounts, then he called his accountant. They planned for his investments to be funneled to a new separate account in the event the feds tried to freeze his assets. Next, he contacted a realtor and found a short-term rental they could use as a safe house until he could find somewhere he and Juju could disappear and be happy. He needed to take Juju away now. Justin caught up with her at school after her last class. After assuring her he loved her and everything would be all right, he asked her to go away with him. "Go home and pack a bag. I'll pick you up at six."

Chapter 31

Meg and M had run several errands already this afternoon. They stopped at the cleaners, then the wine store, and now they were standing in a ridiculously long checkout line at the grocery store. It felt like everyone was doing their shopping on the way home today and the store was shorthanded. People with full carts were using the self-checkouts. Time ticked by. It seemed to take forever. Meg checked her messages again to see if Juju had responded to her text about running late. She looked on impatiently as the technology challenged woman in front of them searched each item for the bar code, then carefully placed it in front of the scanner, waiting for the telltale beep before placing it in a bag. The woman insisted on talking to the machine each time it gave her trouble. She called the attendant several times for help and bagged everything, Meg swore, alphabetically.

When she'd finally completed her transaction, she turned an apologetic expression to Meg and M. "Sorry, ladies. I hate these things and can't wait till we get back to normal around here."

Then, as luck would have it, when she went to put her last bag in her cart, a big jar of spaghetti sauce broke through the plastic bag and shattered all over the floor. A pimply faced teenager came over, looking dismayed.

"Oh, geez. Clean up on checkout four, please," he said into his lapel radio, then stood by doing nothing.

As all other self-checkout machines were occupied, Meg and M had no other choice but to wait, watching their ice cream melt. Finally finished, they hurried to the car and drove home. Juju still hadn't responded to Meg's text. Well, they'd be home soon enough. By the time they arrived at the house, dusk had come and gone. Pulling into the carport, Meg turned off the ignition, popped the trunk and blew out an exasperated breath. "Lord. That's an hour of our life we'll never get back." She laughed, taking a couple of shopping bags from the trunk and walking into the house, followed by M.

"Hey, Juju, we're home. Sorry we're late. Errands took forever." Meg saw Juju standing in the door to the kitchen wringing her hands. Meg was the first to notice the small suitcase standing by the front door. "Juju, why is there a suitcase by the front door? Are you going somewhere?"

Juju had hoped to be gone by the time Meg and M got home. She wrote a letter explaining everything to them. It sat propped against a small vase of flowers on the kitchen table. "Meg, M, Justin is coming. He says I'm in danger. He said he is taking me someplace where I'll be safe and he will explain everything. I left you a letter, but now that you're here, well, I'm telling you in person. He asked me to marry him."

Meg set her bags of groceries on the counter. M slumped down on a kitchen chair, rubbing her forehead in disbelief. Meg was the first to recover. "Juju, this is insanity. You hardly know him. And what danger is he talking about? You can't just up and leave with him without details. It might just be a ruse to get you someplace where he can harm you. Maybe *he* is the danger. I won't let you go."

Juju bowed her back and M could see a whopper of an argument brewing when the door from the carport opened and a strange man stepped in.

"Ladies, ladies, ladies. You really shouldn't leave your door open like this. It's not safe. Anyone could walk in. And guess what? I just did." M, recognizing the threat, jumped up and rushed at the killer. He sneered and shoved her hard, knocking her against the counter where she hit her head and crumpled to the floor. Meg was on him in a second, but he backhanded her, knocking her senseless. Juju stood frozen in terror. He walked up and grabbed her by the hair. Pulling her to him, he placed a cloth saturated with chloroform over her mouth. It only took a couple of breaths for her to lose consciousness. He picked her up and carried her to the car, putting her into the back seat. Then he returned to Meg. Yes, he thought, he'd hit the jackpot this time. He'd take them both. Meg was heavier than he'd expected. Trussed up and being dead weight, it took a while to get her stuffed into the trunk of his car. He covered her with an old army blanket. Checking to make sure Juju was still unconscious, he bound her hands with duct tape, running the seat belt through her arms. It would keep her pinned to the back seat should she come around. He backed out of the driveway and was down the block at the stop sign when Justin turned onto their street and headed to the Lawrence house.

Justin felt good about everything arranged for their departure. He had hit a couple of snags and was running late. When he finally arrived at Juju's house, his watch read 6:30. The sparse street lights blinked on. Seeing the dark house should have alerted him to danger. Noticing Meg's car with the trunk open and some grocery bags inside, he realized his plan to pick up Juju and leave before they got home hadn't worked. Justin resigned himself to the fact that he would have to talk with them, convince them of the legitimacy of his concern. He grabbed two grocery bags and walked toward the door. It stood ajar.

Pushing it open with his elbow, Justin walked in, calling out, "Hello, Juju, Meg, M? I'm here and I guess we need to talk." He put the groceries on the counter. The house was eerily silent. Feeling the hairs on his arms rise, Justin walked into the kitchen, where he saw M sprawled on the floor, bleeding badly from a gash to her head. He grabbed a towel and knelt at her side, trying to staunch the blood while dialing 911. "Oh my God, M? Are you okay? Talk to me, M." Justin heard sirens, relieved by the rapid response. A paramedic with what looked like a large orange tackle box walked in. He crossed to M to assess her injuries and provide aid. A colleague fired questions at Justin, making notes on his laptop. Justin remained calm and answered the questions to the best of his ability. He stepped back to give the paramedics room and called Rob. It didn't take a genius to realize he couldn't go it alone anymore. Now wasn't the time for recriminations. He needed Rob's help.

****

Rob pulled in as the paramedics were loading M onto a stretcher to take her to the ER. He had thought to call in a suspected abduction and tell John, who pulled in right behind him. M had been slipping in and out of consciousness since the paramedics arrived. She needed a CT scan and a full workup for brain bleeds. John went with her, leaving Rob and Justin to talk.

While the crime scene team did their work in the house, the two men waited outside on the patio. The backyard stood in shadow, so Justin wasn't able to see the anger in Rob's eyes, but Rob knew he heard it in his voice and could see it in the set of his shoulders. Rob bounced on the balls of his feet like a boxer wanting desperately to beat the living crap out of Whitman. What the hell was he thinking?

"All right, Justin. I looked into the dates of your moves from city to city. You didn't show up until after the first murder had occurred. And the feds have been aware of the cop car being used. They haven't been able to discover how the killer is getting them. But you seem to have an idea. Now we are looking at a monster that just took the two most important women in our lives. I get it. You don't trust cops, but this is me and one day I might be your brother-in-law. You need to trust me, man. Using your baseball metaphor, it's time to call in the closer. Tell me what you know."

Justin had been standing with his hands in his pockets, staring at the ground, battling to control his emotions. The anger, frustration, and fear in his gut overflowed. Blowing out an exasperated breath, he explained everything.

"The feds are stupid and way behind the eight ball on this thing. They think the hooker in LA was the start of this crazed murder spree, but it actually started with my sister, Becky. His name is Eddie Paine. We were in shop class together in high school. Man, he's good, a genius with motors and body work. Back then, he used those skills to make money. He could take any junker and turn it into a beauty with a motor that purred like a kitten. We weren't exactly friends, but I had a grudging admiration for his work.

"After we graduated, I'd swing by his place every so often and check on his latest project. Sometimes my little sister Becky would come with me. She was a cheerleader and really cute, probably the most popular girl in school. But she was a tease and a pain in the neck. Eddie had it bad for her and she knew it. She'd wear provocative clothes and lean into him when he worked on a motor or stand over him so that when he rolled his creeper out from under the car, he'd get a clear shot up her skirt. I tried to tell her to knock it off, that Eddie was older and different from the high school boys she was used to. She just laughed.

"One day, she went over to his place without me. That was the last time we saw her. When I went to see Eddie, he denied seeing her that day, but I could tell he lied. When I told the cops, they talked with Eddie but found no evidence to tie Becky to him or his location. We never found Becky's body. They just assumed she ran away. I never gave up and watched Eddie for anything that would lead to Becky or help put him in jail for harming her."

As Justin's story unfolded, Rob tried to remember the information the FBI had about the early killings. It had started out with the beating and strangulation of a prostitute, then escalated to the cuts on the breasts and thighs. That was LA. Then the killer moved. He evolved.

Justin ran his hands over his face and sat on a patio chair. Hanging his hands between his knees, he continued. "I lost track of Eddie for a while after he left

LA. I figured his dad kicked him out and he couch surfed until he could save up enough money to get out of town. I scanned every paper and news outlet for missing women that fit Becky's description. Most of the hookers in LA had been young and blonde like Becky, so I figured that was his type. When I learned of one, I'd sell everything and move, hoping I could stay on his track long enough to catch him or at least stop him from taking someone else. But, God, Rob. He's good. He never leaves a trace.

"I hacked into the Henderson, Nevada police files on him. Yeah, I know, it's illegal. Shit, arrest me. I learned about the necklace and the branding. I remembered the ring. His old man promised to give it to him. His dad was a drunk and abusive. I remember Eddie coming to school with his lip cut from his dad, hitting him while wearing the damn ring. Then one day he showed up with a brand on the palm of his hand. God, how can a father do that to his son? Eddie finally had enough and beat the crap out of his dad. Eddie didn't wait for his old man to give him the ring. He took it and used it to brand his old man on the forehead. That was when his dad kicked him out, I guess. Eddie told everyone the story like he was proud of it. He showed it around to all the guys. It was an antique coin set in a big silver ring. It had a man hanging from a scaffold on it and the words End of Pain."

Rob looked at Justin, remembering the coin John had found at the drying beds. The one Meg had researched for her lecture. Puzzle pieces began to fall into place. It explained why he hadn't branded any of the other girls since they'd discovered Kathy's body. He'd somehow lost the coin when he dumped Kathy

Erickson's body. That was when John found it. Unfortunately, outside of Kathy, none of his other victims had the brand. All he had was Justin's word to tie the coin to Eddie and the murders. They needed more. Rob refocused his attention as Justin continued.

"I think Eddie thought it fit that he was providing the end of pain to these women. Or maybe he was exorcising his own pain by hurting them. I don't know. The necklace, though, that was so sick. Becky had one, and I guess maybe that was where he got the idea. I thought I could use that to track him and prove his guilt. I mean, he had to have them made, right? But I never discovered where he got them. Then I thought, shit, he is so damn talented at body work that making a necklace like that would be easy. He fabricated them all by himself. I tried to contact the FBI and share what I had, but just like LA, I didn't have any proof and they blew me off. I mean, who puts any store into what a twenty-year-old kid says? One that is more grease monkey than wealthy business man. So, as you already figured out, I followed his path of murder. I never knew when he'd move on and didn't know where he'd gone until I read about a killing that matched his MO or found a report of a missing girl with blonde hair. I landed here after I read about Linda Bjorek. That was the first killing in March, if I'm not mistaken."

Rob sat down, taking in everything Justin said. When Justin mentioned Linda as victim number one in Alton, he knew everything Justin told him was spot-on and that they needed to work together to rescue Meg and Juju. "What about the cop cars? How does he get them? Do you know?" Rob asked. It remained something the feds hadn't been able to figure out.

"He's that good, Rob. Like I said, everyone in shop class was in awe of his incredible talent. Even in high school, he could work miracles with old junkers. Best I can figure is, he either finds an old car that is a model year or two behind the current police force units or takes one that has been in an accident and refurbishes it. No one has ever found the vehicle he used after he moved on. I'm guessing he burns it or chops it up, disposing of the parts piecemeal in various junkyards." Justin's voice took on a more desperate tone. He was pulling at his hair. He grabbed Rob's arm and squeezed for all he was worth. "Rob, I've been following him for the last ten years. I know him. He doesn't start hurting them right away, but we don't have much time."

Rob put his hand on Justin's shoulder and gave it a squeeze. "I know. I figure we have less than five days. Let's go." The two got into Rob's car and drove to the PD station. Rob called the FBI profiler on the way, and they set up a zoom meeting to share the additional information Justin could provide. Six hours later, they thought they knew the type of building Eddie Paine might use as his lair to hold Meg and Juju. Now all they had to do was find that building. Not a simple task. As the profiler astutely observed, "It's like finding a needle in a haystack."

No one took a break from the search.

Chapter 32

Juju felt the motion of the car. Her head ached and when she tried to move, realized her hands were bound and he had used the seat belt to secure her in place. She remembered seeing him push M. She'd hit her head on the edge of the counter. M had gone down like a ton of bricks and Juju could still visualize the blood. She watched as he backhanded Meg, falling in a heap at his feet. Then he'd grabbed her. That must have been when he used the chloroform. She remembered the cloth over her nose and the sickly smell of something sweet, just like they write about in all those books about kidnapping. Then, nothing.

Now, she lay on the rear seat and closed her eyes. She could taste the bitterness of the drug on her lips. It all came back to her. Justin was right. She had been in danger. She was alone with a killer. No one knew where he was taking her. Saving herself depended on her own resources. She tried to figure out where he was taking her, but couldn't see any passing landmarks from her position. She could tell they were on a highway from the regular passing of streetlights overhead. Feeling a sway and tilt of the car, she thought he turned. It seemed like they were now traveling on a surface street. They must have left the city because she saw fewer street lights and couldn't hear a lot of other traffic.

With wide eyes staring, she saw him look over his shoulder, an exultant smile on his face. "It's okay, baby. That headache will go away in no time. And we'll be there soon." He turned back to the road and started singing in an off-key tenor, "She can kill with a smile…"

Fifteen minutes later, he turned onto a side street. She felt the car rock over uneven pavement pocked with potholes. She listened to the sound of tires driving on gravel. Next, she heard a power gate sliding open along its metal tracks and the squeal of the cable grinding through the pulley. The car bumped over tracks. Juju saw him reach up to the visor and push an automatic door opener. As she watched through the rear window, the frame of the big metal door passed overhead. She noticed a faded sign reading 'AAA Auto Body & Paint'. The vehicle drove through the door. The killer shut off the engine, closed the huge garage door and turned toward her in the back seat.

"Welcome home, honey." He flashed a smile at her. Extending his hand over the back of the seat, he stroked her hair. "Well now, let's get you situated, shall we?" He climbed out and opened the back door to the car. Unhooking the seat belt that had secured Juju in place, he pulled her from the back seat. Even though the lights were dim, she could make out the interior of a metal building with several cars in different states of repair.

She let her body go limp, but he slapped her. "Stand up and walk!" he ordered. Whimpering, she struggled to stand and walk. Still, he had to haul her across the cracked concrete floor. Juju dragged her feet, pretending to stumble so she could take in her surroundings. She noticed large oil stains on the concrete, suggesting they came from stored cars. It looked like a paint booth on one side of the room. A car parked in a three-sided room off to the side had its windows taped off. She could see the paint hose hanging from a rack overhead.

She tripped over an old rug sitting in front of a sagging couch and coffee table, creating a living area in the large open space. Seeing an upright piano off to the side horrified her. An unmade bed behind it frightened her even more. The sheets were a dull dirty blue, the pillow squished flat. He led her through to a small room at the back of the shop, drew a bolt on the door, and shoved her inside. The dark room smelled of old urine and something else, even worse. She cowered against the wall, frozen in place, hands still bound, fearing to move. Slamming the door behind him, he walked away. She stood riveted to her spot, her ears keenly perked at every sound. Juju heard the trunk of the car release.

Several minutes later, Juju heard the sound of something hitting the hard concrete followed by Meg's voice crying out in pain. *Oh, my God. He's got Meg too*. The sound of him pulling Meg from the trunk of the car registered in Juju's terrified brain. She listened as Meg fought back, wondering where she got the courage.

"Take your hands off me, you bastard!" Meg's voice sputtered with words of anger and hate.

A calm, cruel voice responded. "Shut up, bitch. I don't want to hurt you. Yet." The tear of tape and Meg's hiss followed by the sound of him dragging her across the room carried to Juju. A sharp slap sounded when he clearly grew tired of Meg's lack of cooperation. Juju heard an exclamation of pain from her sister.

Throwing open the door to the dingy dark room, he switched on an overhead light bulb enclosed in a wire cage. He pushed her through the door, where she stumbled and fell to her knees.

Meg turned outraged eyes to him. "What the hell do you think you're doing, you sick bastard? Let me go. What did you do with my family? You won't get away with this!"

"Let's see, Meg. What do I think I'm doing? I'm having fun. Aren't you? What have I done with your family? Well, don't know about the crazy old lady. She's probably dead. Hit her head pretty hard—lots of blood and all. But here is your lovely sister. Oh, and by the way…I will get away with this. I have countless times before." He snickered maniacally and slammed the door in their faces.

Meg gasped. She looked in the direction he'd indicated with a tilt of his chin. JuJu cowered against the wall, tears streaming down her face. He had them both. Using an old straight-back chair, she pulled herself up to stand. She had been stuck curled up in the trunk for so long her legs had gone to sleep. Seeing Juju's bound hands, Meg steadied her shaky legs and walked over to her. "Here, let me see if I can get that duct tape off." Meg calmly pulled on the tape, working to keep the fear and panic from her voice. It took some time, but Meg undid Juju's hands. Once free, she crushed Juju to her, hugging her, stroking her hair and shushing her with soft words of comfort.

"Are you hurt?" Meg asked, examining Juju from head to toe, looking for injuries.

Juju ran trembling hands up and down her arms, shaking her head. "I don't think so. Meg, your lip is bleeding. He hit you. I heard it. Are you hurt?"

Meg touched her mouth, then stared at her fingers when they came away with blood. Wiping it off on her pants, she ran her hand over her cheekbone, wincing at the pain. "I think I bit my lip when I fell. He clocked me. I'll probably have a black eye, but I'll survive."

Panic rising, Juju blurted out, "I hope so, Meg. I hope we both survive."

Meg took Juju by the shoulders, shaking her to get her attention. "Stop it right now. We can't afford to lose our heads." Meg led Juju to a chair, pushing her down to sit. Juju sniffled, blew out a deep breath, and pulled it together.

"Okay then, that's good. This is what Justin meant, isn't it, Juju? He was afraid this madman would take you, and now he has. Well, the bastard has bitten off more than he can chew, taking us both. The Lawrence sisters aren't so easily conquered. Now, let's see what we have here, okay?"

Meg looked around the small room. A mechanic's work light hung from a hook in the ceiling, illuminating the space. The electrical cord snaked across the ceiling and out of a small hold drilled in the plywood wall. A second unmatched chair sat next to a small square table, in addition to Juju's chair. The room had a double bed, iron headboard, nightstand, and a five-gallon bucket, like those from building supply stores. Meg walked over to the bucket. It didn't take a rocket scientist to figure out the source of the stench.

Using two fingers, she cautiously lifted the thin blanket covering the bed. Thankfully, the sheets looked clean, if somewhat worn. She lifted the mattress to check for vermin and noticed the handcuffs attached to the headboard. Biting back a cry of alarm, she pulled the covers back to hide them. Next, Meg went to the door and checked the handle. The lock seemed substantial and the door stronger than they'd be able to break down.

She limped around the perimeter of the room, painstakingly searching for anything that could be a weapon or a potential tool for escape. The chairs were her first thought. They were light enough to swing at someone, but he'd chained them to the wall. Meg walked over and put her ear to the door. She heard him whistling and shuffling about and the sound of a refrigerator opening. It sounded like he was walking toward the door so she leaped back, placing herself between it and Juju in a protective stance. When he banged on the door, both girls jumped and Juju clutched Meg's hand. He slid open a small window in the door and gazed in at them.

"You ladies go stand on the far side of the bed. I have some water and a couple of sandwiches. Don't want you wasting away to nothing…" Dark crazed laughter bubbled up from deep in his chest while Meg took Juju and they moved back.

"Very good. Allow me to introduce myself. I am Eddie and I am honored to have you as my guests. Now, as long as you behave yourselves and play nicely, I won't have to restrain you, understand? Let's make this as pleasant as possible for all of us. You won't be here that long." He placed the food and water on the table and as he was closing the door, called out, "*Bon appetite!*"

Meg put her arm around Juju and sarcastically commented, "Won't be here long? Oh, gee, what a shame. This place is almost better than the Waldorf Astoria."

"Or maybe the Savoy in London." Juju said, giving her sister a tremulous smile.

Juju was working hard to be brave, but Meg knew she'd have to be the strong one. Once sure he had left, she drew in a deep breath, squaring her shoulders. "Well, as much as we will hate to turn down his hospitality, what say we find a way out of here? Let's review what we know."

As they ate their day-old convenience store sandwiches, they reviewed the drive; the time it had taken to reach their destination, and what they could tell from the feel of the roads they'd traveled. Meg started out.

"Let's see. He entered the house about six-ten. It's now seven-thirty, so we couldn't have traveled very far. Juju, were you unconscious the entire time?"

Juju took a swallow of water to wash down the stale bread of the sandwich. "I came to during the ride. He strapped me down on the backseat and I couldn't see out the side windows, but I could see through the back window. There were streetlights passing overhead. They weren't the big stanchions, like on a freeway. It was more like lighting on a boulevard. I think he took a cloverleaf exit and then we sat at a stoplight for two to three minutes. I could see the reflection of the red light on the window. He turned left onto a surface road. He was driving fast. Not as fast as on a freeway, but faster than the speed limit on a neighborhood street. There were street lights again but nothing else. I think I heard a train. Maybe Davidson Street. It felt like the route I take to campus. From there, I think he turned left."

Juju described what she'd seen as he walked her to their cage, the cars and mechanic's equipment, the Auto Body & Paint sign. Both Juju and Meg had lived in Alton all their lives. They were familiar with the area. Meg closed her eyes in order to visualize the route, while Juju recounted what she'd seen. Everything pointed to him going somewhere on Greenway. The only cloverleaf she could think of was onto Davidson. Running through everything they'd both observed, Meg wondered if it could be the industrial park off Davidson by Park Springs. She had never driven through the industrial park, but she thought that most of the businesses there were light industrial; machine shops, auto body, towing companies, and vehicle storage. The signage fit and it backed up to a large undeveloped floodplain and a trailer park.

"This is better than I thought," Meg said with some hope in her voice. "We're probably still in town." Both girls looked hopeful and began calling for help. Exhausted after ten minutes, they sat on the edge of the bed, holding each other.

"We can't give up. If we can get out, help isn't that far away. Now we just have to figure out how to escape." Juju looked at Meg and together they looked around at the room. It looked like a shipping crate built of 2x4 studs; the exterior sheathed with plywood. He'd constructed the ceiling of 1x3 slats covered with more plywood. A wire cage protected the socket that held the lamp, but still might be useful for something. "Let me think a little. I might have some ideas," Meg said.

Meg considered the corded socket holding the light

bulb. If she could remove the light bulb, she could break it and use the jagged glass as a weapon, but he'd figure it out because it would be dark. Scratch that plan. How about the chairs? He'd chained them to the wall, but maybe they could remove a spindle or brace to use as a weapon. This idea held more promise, as the chairs were old and rickety. Hell, if push came to shove, they could throw the bucket of their waste at him. It would take him by surprise and might distract him enough to enable them to run out the door. All these things flashed through Meg's mind and she stored each one in place, waiting to see what he had planned next.

****

Eddie lay sprawled on the couch with his feet propped on the coffee table. He rested his head back on the cushion, eyes closed. He had a two-finger grip on the neck of a cold bottle of beer. Bringing it to his mouth, he sipped, envisioning the fun he planned to have the next few days.

Eddie checked his watch. It usually took about thirty minutes before they started to scream for help. He chose this particular location because of the empty buildings surrounding it. His building stood solitary, surrounded by a cyclone fence with wood slats woven through the mesh for privacy. Other vacant lots and metal buildings sat beyond them. A small industrial park, it housed wholesale carpet, discount tile, automobile storage, and paint and body shops. No one stuck around after six p.m. No one would hear them. True to form, the girls began beating on the door and calling for help. Ah, what sweeter music. Eddie smiled, taking another sip.

Chapter 33

Setting his phone down, Rob pinched the bridge of his nose, blowing out a frustrated breath. He crumpled his coffee cup and threw it at the waste can to join the other two dozen they'd gone through in the last few hours. Between Justin and the FBI profiler, they had come up with the most likely place for Paine to hide out, but without specific direction or distance, their guess was as good as anyone's. Using a large map, they mapped out each body dump site and the center of the college campus. Except for Amy, the killer favored Alton for dumping his victims. She was an anomaly. They would exclude her for now.

They then drew a radius of 25 miles from each. Where each circle overlapped, they zoomed in to see the type of neighborhood. If residential, it went to the bottom of the list. They considered this the least likely location for Paine's hideaway. If the neighborhood was retail, still probable, but not likely. Industrial was more promising and if light industrial with automotive related businesses? It jumped to the top of the potentials list. But they had no description of a vehicle or Paine outside of a 10-year-old picture from the high school yearbook the FBI had tracked down. They'd have to go door to door and canvas everyone about suspicious activities. No one had to remind them the clock was ticking.

Nine o'clock at night and no one expected to have any eyewitnesses to an abduction, but the Alton Police Department finished canvassing the Lawrence neighborhood to see if anyone had seen anything. They asked for any doorbell camera footage. The neighbors across the street from the Lawrence home were the best option, but tonight was the weekly family fun night. No one was home.

At midnight, Pete insisted Rob and Justin both take a break. The station provided a sleep room in the back of the squad room for just this type of situation. Pete pushed both men to grab some shuteye. They'd be useless without rest. Pete would oversee the canvas of 24/7 business in the targeted areas. Without more information, it would be the best they could do for now.

****

At five a.m., Rob sat in the conference room, coffee mug in his hand and his eyes glued to the map. Canvassing and patrols wasn't enough. What else did they have? What gave them an edge?

He poured a second up of coffee and walked back to the squad sleep room, thinking he'd rouse Justin, only to find the man staring at the ceiling. They grunted at each other as Rob handed the mug of coffee to him. Pulling himself up, Justin wiped a weary hand across his face.

Rob led the way back to the conference room where the two men sat contemplating their coffee and the situation, silent, forlorn.

When 6 a.m. rolled around, Rob gave John a quick call to check on M. He cradled the phone against his shoulder, under his chin. "How is she, John?" He looked over at Justin. Relief filled his eyes, and he nodded into the phone. "I'm glad you're there with her."

Having spent the night at the hospital with M, John passed along her status, his tired voice giving testimony to his long vigil. "She's hanging in there, Rob. M needed eight stitches for a two-inch gash to her skull. They had to shave off half her hair to patch her up. She was right pissed when she learned that. The dear girl has a concussion, but she is alive and should be able to go home in a couple of days. She is more worried about the girls than herself."

"Tell her to focus on getting better and that we're working on finding the girls."

"She knows that, but, well, it's hard not to worry. She asked me to run by the house to pick up her robe and a change of clothes. I'm heading out to do that now."

"Okay. Call me back if anything changes. Yeah, thanks. Goodbye." They hung up, promising to keep each other in the loop.

At 8 a.m. Rob and Justin joined the patrol cars driving through all the industrial parks in Alton. There turned out to be too damn many to number, some of them only a few blocks from the Alton PD headquarters. The problem continued to be they didn't know what they were looking for. The dead ends and passing time ate a hole in Rob's heart.

****

John drove over to M's house. It looked scary when he pulled into the drive. Crime scene tape stretched across the entry to the carport served as a dark reminder of the violence and kidnapping. John looked toward the front door. Going in that way, he'd avoid the side door with the fingerprint dust brushed on the handle and around the doorjamb. When the Lawrence ladies were there, they filled the house with love. Fear and dread filled it now. He pulled his jacket tighter around his shoulders and climbed out of the car just as young Barrett Sutton from across the street rode up on his skateboard.

"Hi, Mr. John. I saw all the police cars and ambulance last night. Is everyone all right?"

John reached over and ruffled Barrett's dark brown, curly hair. The ladies had a soft spot in their heart for the little nine-year-old scamp and his sister Leoni, who made a bundle off John this past year selling girl scout cookies. They were both sweet kids.

"Thank you for asking, Barrett. Ms. M is doing well. She'll be back baking cookies for you in no time. Well, I have to go now. Just came by to pick up some things for Ms. M." John turned to walk into the house, but Barrett still tagged along.

"What about Ms. Juju? I saw that man. He put her in his car. Was she hurt, too? Didn't he want to wait for an ambulance?" John stopped dead in his tracks. Kneeling down, he grabbed Barrett by his shoulders. "What did you say?"

"That man. He carried Ms. Juju to his car and then drove off. I think he put Ms. Meg in the trunk. I thought that was strange. Isn't that strange, Mr. John?" John crushed Barrett to his chest.

"Oh my God, Barrett, oh my God. Yes, that is very strange. He probably took Ms. Juju and Ms. Meg to a different hospital than the ambulance took Ms. M. Did you happen to notice what kind of car he was driving?" John held his breath.

"Oh, yeah, sure I did. It's the same kind of car my sister's boyfriend drives. A silver Hyundai Elantra. His has a big dent in the back bumper. This one didn't, so I thought he might have had it fixed. Dad says it's a POS. I know what that means. Do you, Mr. John?"

"I certainly do, Barrett. Thanks for telling me about Ms. Juju and Ms. Meg. Say, do you mind if I call my friends Mr. Rob and Mr. Justin? They might not know what POS stands for."

"Sure, you go ahead, Mr. John. See you later," Barrett said as he wheeled away on his skate board without a care in the world, not realizing he'd just provided a key piece of evidence.

John wasted no time dialing Rob's cell, while he drove like a bat out of hell to the station. M's clothes could wait, the girls couldn't. When Rob answered his phone, John filled him in on Barrett's observations. Rob hung up and looked at Justin with a hopeful expression. They'd just received another piece in that 1000-piece puzzle.

Chapter 34

Meg and Juju exhausted every option they could imagine. Working to maintain her calm, Meg attacked their captivity like a research project. To identify the meat of the subject, she had to break down each layer and peel back the facts. She wondered if Eddie had given them any clues of which he was unaware. Meg reviewed his comments and his voice. 'You're my guests.' 'Play nicely.' 'Won't be here long.' What did he mean by that?

Meg feared she knew. She'd been privy to the university leadership meetings. The meetings involved the additional security because a killer appeared to be targeting co-eds. Rob worked the case, so Meg knew Eddie killed the other women. Thinking about it clinically, Meg knew he would kill her and Juju, unless they could change that.

"Juju, we need to rest. We can't hope to escape if we are tired and weak from lack of food or water. We must be strong and ready to do whatever we can to escape." Meg knew she would do what she could to give Juju the opportunity to escape, even if it meant sacrificing her own life. "Juju, if the opportunity presents itself to either of us, we must be ready and willing to run. No hesitation, no looking back. Run like hell and get help. Do you understand what I am saying?"

Juju nodded. Meg had been protecting her since their folks had died and would continue to do it. Juju's expression changed from frightened to determined. "Meg, you have protected me since mom and dad died. I won't let you do it anymore. Whatever happens, we fight together. Whatever happens, happens to us both."

They cocked their ears, trying to hear anything from their captor, looking for clues about how he planned to proceed. The building had grown deadly silent. Meg led Juju to the bed. They wrapped themselves in the ratty blanket, seeking warmth and solace in each other's arms. While Juju dropped into a troubled doze, Meg lay staring at the ceiling, taking small comfort from the knowledge that they had something their captor didn't. They had each other. She also knew there were two very determined men who loved them. It just might be enough. Meg closed her eyes and prayed.

****

Eddie came to the door of their room a second time. He slid open the little window and peered in. "Still alive and kicking, I see. Oh, and how cute. Taking a little nappy-poo. Wipe the sleep from your eyes, girls, cause I'm getting a little lonely out here by myself. You, Meg! Step back against the wall. I'd like Juju to come out and play." The two girls exchanged terrified glances. Meg held Juju tighter, hatred burning in her eyes.

"No, Meg, not to worry. I only mean the piano. You see, I have heard Juju play, and she is really, really good. It is a beautiful thing. Just what we need to calm our nerves, don't you agree? Now, get out here, Juju, or I'll come in and hurt your sister." Juju rose from the bed. Meg stood defiantly with her. She reached out, taking Juju's arm to stop her.

Eddie kicked the door, causing both women to jump. Snarling, he yanked the door open and shouted, "I told you to stand against the wall, Meg. Don't push it!" A small knife glinted in his hand.

Shaking her head, Juju pried Meg's steel grip from her wrist. She gave an almost imperceptible nod. This might be their chance. Juju walked to the door, turning before she stepped out, and gave Meg a long look as Eddie closed the door and led her away. The silence drove Meg crazy with worry. She paced the one-hundred square foot room, wringing her hands until she heard the start of 'She's Always a Woman'. Meg drew in a shaky breath. As long as she could hear the piano, Juju was safe. But how long would that last?

Meg used the time Juju entertained Eddie to circle their small prison, feeling around studs, the plywood sheathing, corners, and door jamb. She didn't find any loose nails or gaps. She checked the chairs and table, nightstand and bed frame, finding nothing to enable them to escape. Ready to give up, Meg heard what sounded like a grinder being powered up. Running to the door, she pounded on it, shouting. Panicked, she stepped back and rubbed her fingers over her forehead and through her hair, thinking the worst. The grinder stopped and muffled voices carried through the wood walls. Meg heard Juju's tentative response to something Eddie said. Then she heard Juju play the piano again. Hugging herself, Meg reminded herself she needed to hold it together, stay in control. Until Rob found them, and Meg prayed he would, she and Juju needed to look for every opportunity to escape.

The grinder scared Meg, though. She wondered what the hell Eddie was doing. Eight songs and what felt like an eternity later, he opened the door and made a mocking bow to Juju, gesturing to her to enter the room. She held a gold chain in her hand and handed it to Meg. At the end of the chain was an expertly crafted 'Meg' in a swirly handwriting font. It matched in style to the one Juju had received with the flower delivery earlier in the month. Eddie stepped in just far enough to drop a bag of Corn chips and a liter bottle of diet soda on the table. He closed the door. The girls ate the chips and passed the bottle of soda back and forth between them. Eddie turned out the lights. Lying down, they eventually fell into a fitful sleep, holding tight to each other, afraid for their lives.

Eddie had gotten smart and taken their watches. He continued to supply them with stale sandwiches and diet soda. One time he included a box of hostess cupcakes. The sugar gave them extra energy, but the resulting stomach cramps resulted in the five-gallon bucket being used and emptied several times. Without windows, Meg had no way to tell the day or time. Hours of inactivity and terror took its toll. Juju's once lovely hands showed the ravages of cuticle picking and chewing.

Eddie asked Juju to play piano for him two more times. He usually requested Elton John or Billy Joel, but this time, she chose the special piece she'd written for Justin. A musical prayer for their salvation, perhaps. Eddie didn't like it and pulled Juju from the keys, slamming the lid down. When he escorted her back to their small prison, she sank into the chair and hugged herself, trembling.

Noticing their bucket, full again, creating a miasma of eye burning odor, Eddie sneered. "Jesus, you girls sure pee a lot. Well, hell." He went to get another bucket. Returning, he knocked and called through the door, "Put your full bucket by the door and step back." The girls did as instructed. Eddie opened the door and exchanged a fresh bucket for the almost full one. He saw their eyes dart to the door. Juju exchanged looks with Meg. Now would be when she should run. Meg's eyes told her to go.

"Please, please, do what you want with me, but let my sister go. You said you liked her piano playing," Meg begged, falling to her knees at Eddie's feet. She grabbed him around his legs, pressed her face to his crotch. Eddie was standing in the open doorway. She was hoping she could distract him so Juju could get away.

"Don't even think it," Eddie snarled. He looked down at Meg. He grabbed a handful of her hair and yanked her up to stand. "I might enjoy your face in my crotch later, but for now, bitch, hook yourself up." He shoved her hard against the headboard. "Get on the bed and put on the handcuffs."

When she hesitated, he jumped in and grabbed Juju by the hair. Pulling her head back, he held the small knife to her neck. "Now!" Spit flew from his curled lips, hitting Meg's face as she shivered and tried to do as he told her. Her hands were shaking. Lying down, she fumbled several times, finally succeeding to cuff herself to the headboard.

Keeping hold of Juju, Eddie walked over to check the cuffs. Eddie nodded, satisfied. Meg watched in horror as, with an iron grip on Juju's upper arm, he propelled her to the chair, pushing her down. Juju cowered; eyes squeezed tightly. Then he did the most bizarre thing. Eddie pulled a brush from his pocket and began to brush Juju's hair. Counting under his breath, he used long, sinuous strokes to comfort and relax her. Even though the touch came from a killer, Juju closed her eyes, her chin sinking down to her chest, mind blank, tension bleeding off. When he reached one hundred, he used his finger to separate strands of her hair, plaiting it into a single French braid. He pulled little wisps of hair loose around her face. It looked soft and feminine. Then he knelt at her feet. Using the tip of his finger, he raised her face and gazed into her eyes. Meg felt sick as she listened to him sigh.

"You are beautiful. You'll help me end the pain, won't you, Juju?"

"NOOOO!" Meg screamed. She pulled violently at the handcuffs, bruising her wrists. Juju pushed up and against a surprised Eddie who fell back against the bed. She made a run for the door, but Eddie was too fast. He leapt, knocking her to the floor. Juju clawed at the floor, dragging herself away. She gripped the door frame and, using her legs, kicked Eddie, solidly catching him on the chin. His grip loosened. Scrambling to her feet, Juju stumbled once, then ran out the door of the little room, toward the garage door, to freedom.

Eddie shook his head and grinned at Meg. "Oh, the fun is just beginning." He ran out of the room after Juju. Meg heard the commotion, the struggle, Juju's screams, the sound of a palm striking flesh and finally, Eddie laughing.

When Eddie returned, he had a bruised and

bleeding Juju in tow. Her blouse showed grease stains from when she'd fallen. She'd torn her pants and scraped both knees. A small trickle of blood ran from the corner of her mouth, where Eddie slapped her. He pulled Juju over to the chair. Using a second pair of handcuffs, he secured her to the chair back.

Panting a little from his efforts, he inquired, jeeringly, "There. Is everyone comfortable?" Waiting for an answer, he grew angry. He back-handed Juju. Her head snapped to the side from the blow. Her face hit the table, opening a small cut above her left eyebrow. "I asked if everyone was comfortable!"

Meg cried out for her sister and struggled again to free herself. Eddie watched the blood from Juju's cut run down her face. Running his tongue over his lips, he swallowed. Feeling the power the violence always brought him, he walked out.

Meg closed her eyes, choking back the sobs threatening to burst forth, listening to the whimpers coming from Juju. They had to have faith. "You're okay, Juju. We're okay. Justin and Rob are looking for us. They'll find us."

The sound of a car starting and the garage door rising meant Eddie was going out. They had a little more time to live.

****

Eddie enjoyed watching the girls grow more fearful every time he stepped into their little room. He hadn't even started having his fun. There were so many possibilities, he didn't know where to begin. Eddie needed air. Switching up cars, he took his ubiquitous silver Elantra for a drive. He enjoyed driving through the university campus, past Lucky Lucy Burgers, recalling all the fun times he'd had with Debbie. Feeling a little hungry, Eddie considered what to have for dinner. He thought his girls deserved a special treat. Heading to Braum's for burgers and a quart of ice cream, he was waiting in the drive-thru when he noticed several police cars heading toward Bowen, then turning south. He laughed out loud. "Wrong way, stupid heads. Wrong freakin' way!"

Returning to the body shop, he waved to the guys at the discount carpet place as they left for home, making sure they'd turned the corner before entering his building. Whistling softly, he opened the door. "Dinner, ladies. Shall we dine together?"

Eddie released one of Juju's hands so she could sit at the table to eat. Laying out her burger and fries. He placed her napkin in her lap with a flourish. When he went to do the same for Meg, allowing her to sit on the side of the bed, he noticed the necklace on the nightstand. His hands curled into fists and his breathing grew heavy with controlled anger.

"Meg, why aren't you wearing the necklace I made for you? It's yours and I want to see it hanging between your lovely breasts." Eddie pulled his knife, testing the edge with his thumb. "Maybe it's time to have a little fun. Juju, you can watch." He chortled and stepped to the bed.

"Let's see, first, I guess I need to help you get undressed. Hmmm, these buttons are so tedious. I'll use my knife, shall I?" Eddie used the point of the knife to cut the buttons slowly off Meg's blouse. He took the necklace off the nightstand and placed it around her neck. He laid the 'Meg' pendant lovingly between her breasts, brushing his fingers across her bra and making smacking sounds with his lips. Standing back to admire the sight, he smiled and said, "Oh, yeah. Nice. Very nice."

He released Meg's hand from one cuff so she could eat. When she reached to pull her blouse closed, covering her nakedness, Eddie simply said, "Unh, unh, unh."

The three ate in silence. Juju crying quietly with fear, Meg angry with embarrassment, and Eddie smiling with glee.

When everyone finished their meal, he cleaned up their trash, rehooked their cuffs, and walked out.

Eddie sat down on the beat-up couch and closed his hand over his crotch. God, he had one hell of a boner. Playing with those girls was going to be so much fun. What a rush to look into their eyes, read their fear. He'd give them a few more hours and then he'd begin his work. Meg first, then Juju. While he was daydreaming about the fun he expected to have with Meg and Juju, he'd been rubbing himself and felt a shudder as he came in his pants. *Ahhh, so good, so damn good.*

Chapter 35

Leaving Justin to work with the FBI regarding the police vehicle angle, Rob and Pete drove to the Sutton residence. Keith Sutton opened the door and ushered Rob and Pete into the living room. Passing Mrs. Sutton and the children coloring at the kitchen table, they smiled a greeting, excusing the interruption. Seeing the police officers, Barrett jumped up and ran to Rob. Holding his arm, he choked out his concerns.

"Detective. I saw that man take Ms. Juju and Meg away. Is he a bad man? Is he going to hurt them?" Mrs. Sutton put her arms around the boy, tugging him away. "Honey, let the police talk with your father."

Tears threatening, Barrett pulled away from his mom's grasp, turning back to Rob. "I saw him. I saw his car. I can help!" Mrs. Sutton reached out again, but Rob stopped her. He shook his head and then knelt down, taking Barrett by the shoulders.

"Yes, Barrett. He is a bad man. He wants to hurt Ms. Juju and Ms. Meg, but we won't let him do that. We are going to stop him. Mr. John told me you saw the bad man. You saw the car he drove. It's going to help us find him." Rob looked over his shoulder at Keith Sutton, seeking his permission to question Barrett further. Getting an affirmative nod, Rob stood and walked Barrett to the sofa.

Pete took the chair across from the two and pulled

out his notebook, ready to record new clues. Rob patted Barrett's knee to settle him and started with easy questions. Questions that helped put the boy at ease. "Mr. John says you're nine years old. You're pretty tall for your age. Play any ball?"

"Um, yes, sir. I play with my friends. Dad says I can join a real league this summer." Barrett visibly relaxed with this line of questioning. Rob let it run its course for a few minutes more, asking what position Barrett liked to play, talking about the Patriots. When he judged Barret comfortable enough to focus, he moved to the interview questions.

"Barrett, Mr. John said you saw the man that took Ms. Juju and Meg. Can you tell me where you were when you saw him?"

"I was in my fort. My dad built this really cool tree house. I sit up there a lot. Sometimes I sit up there and watch my sister and her stupid boyfriend, Mark, play kissy face. Yuck!" Mr. Sutton cleared his throat and raised eyebrows at his son.

Barrett shrugged and continued. "Well, it is yucky. Anyway, I can see everything from up there and no one knows I'm there. I saw Ms. M and Ms. Meg come home from grocery shopping. They said something about the ice cream melting and I thought I might go help carry the groceries in and maybe I could have some. Ice cream, that is. Before I could climb down, this car pulled into the driveway. It was a Hyundai Elantra, silver, just like Mark's. I thought it was weird that he parked across the street, but then this other guy got out of the car. He went into the house and after a while, he came out carrying Ms. Juju. She looked like she was asleep. He put her in the back seat."

Mrs. Sutton stood next to her husband, listening. She gasped, bringing her hand to her mouth. Rob gave a warning glance to the Suttons and brought a momentarily distracted Barrett back to the subject at hand. "That's very good, Barrett. What else did you see? What happened next?"

"Well, then he went back into the house and when he came back out, he was carrying Ms. Meg. She looked different."

Rob's face turned ashen, and his right hand curled into a fist. "Different, how?" He wanted to shake the child. Was she hurt? Was she bleeding? Drawing in a measured breath through his nose, Rob got his fear under control.

"Well, she wiggled, like she was waking up. She groaned, I think. Maybe said 'no'. She tried to push away from the man, but he held her tighter. Then he dumped her in the trunk and covered her with a blanket."

"Okay, Barrett. Now, I want you to think carefully. Did you see if Ms. Meg was bleeding?" Rob held his breath while Barrett screwed up his face and closed his eyes.

Grinning confidently, Barrett puffed his chest. "Nope. No blood. I'd remember that!"

Rob threw Pete a glance and stood. He needed to pace off this unbearable tension and blessed relief. No blood, no blood. Rubbing his hand over his face, he returned to the sofa and sat next to Barrett. They knew Eddie Paine was the killer. What they needed to learn is where he took his victims. Placing his hand on the boy's shoulder, he guided him through the rest of the interview. It yielded nothing more.

****

Eddie changed into the cop uniform he'd snatched from the dry cleaners. It turned out to be ridiculously easy to come by what he needed for his charade—if not a dry-cleaner, then the thrift store or an online supplier for police uniforms. He checked to see that everything was in order, then went over to the tarp and uncovered his pride and joy. A perfect match to the current APD squad cars. He'd rescued it from the crusher and refurbished it to use on his little escapades, finding his 'girlfriends'. Eddie flipped the switch to the paint booth exhaust fan. The sound of it would cover any screams for help from the girls. He drove the car out the garage door, closing it behind him. He'd be back soon from his little errand and the fun could begin. Zipping into the convenience store, he sauntered in, ignoring the pot head behind the counter. He picked up his usual order, walking out with a sack containing two generic cheap pepperoni pizzas and some bottled water.

****

Justin filled in the gaps with the FBI agent on past cases, hoping it would give them a clue on where Eddie holed up now. The only clues Eddie had ever left behind were the bodies of the dead girls, and nothing Justin added helped define a location for his current lair. Using the overlapping parts of the radius and the neighborhoods identified as the most likely to house a hidey-hole for Paine, Rob deployed unmarked cars and drones into the air, looking for a silver Hyundai Elantra. They'd been at it for hours. The clock kept ticking; they were coming up on the 53rd hour.

Rob and Justin sat at a light waiting to turn into a light industrial park behind the Townlake Trailer Park, as part of their spiral search pattern, when a blue and white pulled onto Davidson in front of them. Thinking the patrol car had covered this industrial park, Rob turned around and headed back. Stuck at another red light, they noticed the patrol car pull into the lot of a small convenience store four blocks down the road. An officer climbed out and walked inside. They watched him come out of the convenience store with a sack. Returning to his car, he drove off; crossing the intersection after the traffic light had turned red, narrowly avoiding a collision with a Honda mini-van. Rob watched in disgust. Patrol was getting sloppy, flaunting simple traffic laws. He and Justin turned the opposite direction and continued their spiral grid search.

When the sun peeked over the horizon, Rob and Justin headed back to the station for much needed coffee and to regroup with the next shift of officers that would be searching. Pete led that shift while Rob and Justin took a break from the physical search, focused on what other information they had that could provide a viable lead, and grabbed any shut-eye they could. Walking in the side door, Rob threw his jacket on the chair and shifted his shoulder holster to ease his back and shoulders as Gillespie walked into the duty room.

"Hey, Earl, I just watched patrol car twenty-seven run a red light and almost get T-Boned by a mini-van. Who is the knucklehead driving that one?"

"Twenty-seven you said? You must have seen it wrong. Twenty-seven was in that freeway pile-up last February. They totaled it; sent it to the patrol car graveyard."

Rob looked at Justin. Jesus H. Christ. Another

piece of the puzzle. They ran out to his car and made a beeline to the convenience store. Pulling into the lot, Rob and Justin jumped out of the vehicle. They looked at the dirty windows covered in cigarette decals, lotto advertisements, and an illuminated 'open' sign operated by a pull chain. Walking in to speak to the store clerk, Rob showed his badge, then pulled out the old picture of Eddie Paine and showed it to the store clerk.

"Do you recognize this man?" Rob asked.

A frowzy headed stoner looked at Rob through bloodshot eyes. He wasn't freakin' Stephen Hawking by any means, and probably higher than a kite. Rob wasn't holding out much hope for an ID off the photo.

Scratching his chest, the clerk yawned and took the photo, scrutinizing it intently, tilting his head from side to side. "Nah, man. Never seen that dude before."

While Rob asked additional questions of the genius clerk, Justin impatiently paced the aisles of the small store. They sold the usual; chips, soda, beer and some convenience foods—Mac n Cheese, Hamburger Helper, frozen breakfast burritos, and TV dinners. Suddenly, it clicked in place. He rushed up to the clerk.

"Hey, man, there was a cop in here earlier. Does he come in often?" Justin asked, holding his breath.

"Oh yeah, dude comes in a couple of times a week. Not a very good cop, if you ask me. Hell, one time there was this kid buying beer. He was standing in line right behind the guy, ya know? He didn't look legal to me, but his ID checked out. I mean, what was I to do? I can't just NOT sell the beer if they have ID. The cop just stood there and didn't say a thing. Real A-hole, ya know? You'd think he'd be a little more helpful. That's okay, man, cause he'll get what's coming to him.

Karma and all, ya know? I figure he'll end up with hemorrhoids or a heart attack. I mean, he doesn't eat very healthy. Usually buys junk food—Corn chips and frozen pizza. And not the good frozen pizza. No—he buys that cheap shit. Cardboard with tomato sauce, ya know?"

Rob and Justin looked at each other. "Yeah–not the good stuff at all." They thanked the clerk and ran to the car. Rob got on the radio and called the station. "Gillespie, call the team–tell them to head to the industrial park off Davidson and Park Springs. The one by the old Chicas Locas titty bar. Send the drones that way, too."

Chapter 36

The girls clung to their prayers as their only lifeline. With each passing moment, the hope that Rob and Justin were drawing closer remained firm. Every minute they remained alive increased their chances of being found.

The building had been silent since Eddie had cuffed them and left. They thought they might have heard engines and car doors slamming earlier, but no one entered the building. Both women called out for help, but their screams went unanswered because Eddie had cranked up his spray booth exhaust fan. Meg knew it would mask any noise made in the building, no matter how close the neighboring businesses were or how loud they yelled for help. None of the neighbors would find the sound of a huge exhaust fan running suspect. Everyone knew the building housed a body shop. He worked on cars. A sign on the building said so.

When Meg and Juju realized the exhaust fan kept anyone from hearing their cries for help, they grew quiet. Their dark thoughts turned inward. Juju nervously rocked back and forth. When the chair shifted, she heard a sharp crack. Gasping, Juju stopped moving and looked at Meg. Rocking a bit more, the light of hope grew in her eyes. Eddie thought he was clever, using the exhaust fan to mask their screams for help. What he forgot is that it masked noises from inside their little room, as well. Juju continued to rock; harder this time, toward the weakened spoke. When it snapped, the handcuff attached to the chair fell free, leaving the other one dangling from her wrist. She turned and, using her full body weight, smashed her foot down on the seat of the chair, breaking it in half. The chain that had been holding it to the wall fell, no longer connected. Juju raised the chair bottom, inspecting it with a malicious curl to her lip. It had split down the middle of the seat, leaving two of the legs attached. They formed a handle she could use to swing the chair bottom like a bat. It would make an excellent weapon against Eddie. The other two chair legs and back spindles sat in a heap, ragged and broken. She kicked it under the table. Placing her makeshift weapon against the wall by the door, she went to Meg and together they worked to release her from the headboard. After a frustrating ten minutes, they saw how fruitless their efforts were. "Meg, I can't get you free. It's a damn metal headboard. I can't break it."

"Juju, when Eddie comes back, you must do whatever you can to escape and go for help."

"I don't want to leave you with him," Juju cried in terror.

"You have to–at least long enough to run and get help, otherwise he'll hurt us both."

Juju gave Meg a hug. "I love you, Meg. We're going to get out of this." They heard the rumble of the garage door opening.

"Juju, open my blouse. Expose my breasts." Juju grasped what Meg was thinking and quickly did as she instructed. She returned to the second chair, sitting as if still handcuffed, hoping Eddie wouldn't notice she'd moved closer to the door. Then, holding fast to their fear, they waited, wondering if now would be when Eddie hurt them. When Eddie came back in, she would be in position to attack him, smash his head and, God willing, knock him out so they could make their escape.

Meg heard the grinder start up. She recognized the sound of metal scraping against stone and knew Eddie sharpened his knife. She pictured him checking its razor-like edge on the hair of his forearm. When the badly whistled strains of 'Uptown Girl' sounded, she exchanged meaningful looks with Juju. They listened to his steps carry him toward their little room.

"Ready or not, here I come, girls. Been looking forward to this all day."

Opening the door, Eddie cast a cursory glance toward Juju sitting in the chair, then turned his attention to Meg lying on the bed. Her eyes shone bright with fear, but Eddie only stared at her bared breasts. Mesmerized, he licked his lips and stepped toward the bed.

"Ooh. Somebody wants to play, huh?" Stooping, he snickered at her cry of pain as he sadistically squeezed a breast.

Meg saw Juju stealthily stand and move toward her weapon and Eddie. As she crept forward with a look of steely determination, Meg cried all the more and begged him to let them go. With her enormous eyes, she pleaded with Eddie, hoping to distract him from anything else in the room. She bargained with him, offering to do whatever he wanted. Eddie scoffed. He sat on the edge of the bed, laughing at Meg's poor pathetic pleas for mercy.

Juju raised the broken chair over her head, swinging it with all the strength she possessed. It caught Eddie on the side of his head. The force of her blow sent him pitching forward against the bucket of waste, tipping it over. He came to his hands and knees, trying to rise. Juju pounded his head again. He fell face down in their muck and didn't move.

"Oh my God, Juju. Run for help. Hurry before he comes to!"

"Wait, wait," Juju cried. "He put the keys in his pocket. I can unlock your handcuffs. We can escape together." As she rifled through his pockets, Eddie moaned and tried to push himself up.

"Juju! Now! Run! You are my best hope. Go!"

Juju did as told, sprinting for the door. Bursting out into the bright sunshine, she ran toward the building next door, only to be intercepted by Rob and Justin pulling up as she crossed the parking lot. Gravel spit and the car fishtailed as Rob slammed on the brakes. Justin was out of the car before Rob brought it to a complete stop. He seized Juju, crushing her to his chest.

Dropping the car into park, Rob hopped out. "Where is Meg? Where is she?" he cried out to Juju. She pointed toward the door to the metal building.

"In there. There's a room in the back. I knocked out Eddie. Help her, Rob, help her!"

Rob didn't need to be told twice. Running to the door, he rushed into the building, gun out and ready. It took precious seconds for his eyes to adjust to the dim light. He didn't notice a bleeding Eddie holding his knife to Meg's throat at first, but when he did; he stopped short. "Put the knife down, Paine," he said calmly, pointing his gun directly at Eddie.

Eddie burst out with a cruel laugh. "I don't think so, Rob. Oh, yes. I know who you are. I know who everyone is. Been watching you fall in love with Meg. Made the waiting even more titillating. As you can see, I have Meg and I have a knife at her throat. I think that means the odds are in my favor. No outs, bases loaded and I'm the designated hitter. You need to drop your weapon and step aside. Little Miss Meg and I are going to walk out that door and leave. I may or may not let her go when I get away but, you love her so you won't try to stop me. You won't take the chance that I'll just kill her right here and now. Put your gun on the table by the door and step over to the piano. You carry handcuffs, don't you, Rob? Sure you do. Go on! Cuff yourself to the piano leg, then toss the keys."

Rob read the fear in Meg's eyes, felt the fist of fear tighten around his heart. When he hesitated, Paine pressed the point of the knife a little firmer. The sharp point drew a soft hiss from Meg. Blood trickled down her neck. "Do it, Adams. Do it now!"

Rob did as Paine instructed, hooking himself to the piano with the cuffs, pitching the keys to Eddie. He opened a clear path for Paine and Meg to walk out.

Using his forearm, Eddie held Meg firmly against his body while pressing the point of the knife against the tender skin of her throat. They moved toward the table.

Eddie smirked. "One little nick, Rob. One little nick." Eddie took Rob's gun, tucking it into his waistband. Glancing at the door and back again at Rob, Eddie maneuvered Meg toward the door. He peered out to where Rob had pulled in. The car sat just outside the garage door. Rob had left the door open, the engine running. Juju was nowhere to be seen. Feigning disappointment, Eddie stuck out his lower lip.

"Juju has flown the nest. Oh, well. I have Meg. And a bird in the hand." He laughed manically. "And, Rob, your goose is cooked."

As Eddie stepped to the opening, he turned and kicked over a five-gallon container of paint thinner, knocking off the lid and spilling the highly flammable liquid across the floor. Pulling a wooden match from a tin container hanging on the door frame, he used his thumbnail to light it. As the flame of the match ignited, he pitched it toward the thin stream of paint thinner. A small blue flame picked up a drop or two of the solvent and then, with a whoosh, jumped to the larger spill and leapt across the floor, following its trail toward the piano and Rob. Eddie took a second to enjoy the scene. Rob would be toast. He backed out of the door, holding Meg by knife point. They walked to the car. Opening the back door, he used the hilt of the knife to strike Meg, stunning her, and shoved her into the back seat. He turned to climb into the driver's seat as Justin came barreling out of nowhere and tackled him, taking him down to the hard packed gravel. The knife flew from Eddie's hand. He and Justin grappled, rolling back and forth until Justin got the upper hand.

Pinning Eddie on the ground, Justin whaled on him, beating him about the face and head, yelling out a name with every blow he landed, starting with Becky. Back up arrived and Pete jumped out, running to where the two men fought. He dragged Justin off Paine before he could do more damage. Pete handed a bloody and beaten Paine off to the patrol officer, who cuffed him and put him in the back of a squad car. Pete looked around for Rob and Meg.

Juju ran up to Justin and together they opened the back door to check on Meg. Only dazed, she came around quickly. "Rob, where is Rob?" She saw the fire. "Oh, my God. He's inside!"

****

The flames swiftly engulfed the entry to the building, spreading rapidly. Rob looked around for another way out. A door in the back wall was his only option; but would he be able to drag a piano that weighed close to 400 pounds that far over uneven concrete? And then, would the damn thing fit through the door? No time to waste. He put all his muscle into it and pulled the instrument across the concrete floor, watching as the flames worked their way around the paint cans. The fire reached the tattered sofa, eating at its frayed and faded cover. Next came the bed. The smell of burned feathers filled the air as the flames consumed the pillows. Then the fire reached a plywood enclosure; the wood feeding the hungry flames. A pile of old tires stacked in the corner smoked, cutting visibility and adding to the acrid air. If the flames didn't get him, smoke inhalation would. Rob just kept pulling toward the back exit and the stack of grease and paint solvents. *Shit.* The hell with flames and smoke inhalation. Now he had to worry about being blown up. Things were definitely not going his way.

A fire truck pulled up and quickly deployed their equipment. Pete frantically coordinated the emergency vehicles, then tried to gain access through the front. Justin could see entry from that direction was impossible. He ran around the building, looking for a second entrance. Arriving at the back, he saw a gray metal security door without a handle on the outside. Justin didn't see any other way in. Rob was trapped.

Justin stood staring at the door in horror when he heard a pounding coming from inside the building. Suddenly, the door burst open. Rob threw himself out, knocking Justin to the ground. Instantly seeing the problem, he and Rob worked to pull the piano through the narrow opening. They heard the telltale whoosh of flames sweeping toward them, rushing to feed on the fresh supply of oxygen created where Rob burst through the door. When the flames hit the solvents, the building would explode.

With herculean efforts, the two men prized the piano through the small doorway. They pulled it far enough away to turn it and crouch behind when the building gave a groan and shudder and exploded. Pieces of sheet metal shot into the air and small bits of shrapnel strafed the sounding board of the old instrument. The pings, tings, and clangs made by each impact on the strings made sweet music as it stopped the fragments from striking either man. The fan blades of a commercial exhaust fan spun up and out of the roof, crashing to the ground ten feet away from them.

Pete came around the back of the building and, spying Rob cuffed to the piano, reached into his pocket and pulled out keys, releasing him. Rob grabbed Justin by the shoulders and croaked out, "Meg? Is she safe?"

"Yeah, and Paine is in custody. Come on, Rob, let's get you some medical attention."

The guys limped around to the front of the building where Juju and Meg broke through the fire lines beating the EMT's to the men.

Chapter 37

The FBI took over the case, placing Eddie Paine, aka 'The Traveler,' into custody. They invited Rob to watch the interrogation from the observation room. They preferred local law enforcement not to take part in the questioning. It didn't make Rob happy. FBI Special Agent Hardy had the details from Justin. Having the additional information would leave Paine little room to prevaricate. Rob requested permission for Justin to observe with him. Standing with his arm in a sling, he stared through the two-way mirror at the face of a deranged killer.

Paine played with the handcuffs securing him to the table. Steri-strips applied by the paramedics covered the facial lacerations he received when Justin subdued him. Paine cried assault by a civilian and police brutality. But every witness corroborated Pete's story that Paine sustained the injuries during the rescue of Juju and Meg. His attorney advised Paine to set that complaint aside. Snarling angrily, he clamped his hand around the paper coffee cup and lowered his head to slurp a sip.

"Mr. Paine, my name is Special Agent Hardy. We are recording this session for the records. You have been read your rights and chosen to be represented by Warren Dooley, a public defender. Is that correct, Mr. Paine?"

Paine stared at Agent Hardy with a smirk on his face. Eddie leaned back in his chair, a sneer distorting his mouth. "Yeah, I heard my rights and I understand them. So what the hell?" Eddie spat indignantly. Afraid he'd let his mouth overload his ass, Eddie's attorney placed his hand on Eddie's arm to silence him.

"For the record, I'm Attorney Warren Dooley. My client understands his rights, Agent Hardy, and has retained me to represent him. May I inquire what charges you are bringing against Mr. Paine?"

Agent Hardy leaned back in his chair and looked at the two-way mirror. "Well," Hardy explained expansively, "aggravated assault, kidnapping, attempted murder of a police officer, to start. Mr. Paine, you could make it a lot easier for yourself if you'd explain your actions."

"I didn't do anything wrong. Those women wanted to come with me. When that police officer burst into my building, I feared for my life. I had to defend myself. You always hear about police showing up at the wrong address, shooting the wrong people. You got nothing." Attorney Dooley tried to stop Eddie from speaking. The more he said, the more avenues the FBI would have to explore.

"My client is confused, Agent Hardy." Dooley smoothed a hand over his oiled, closely cropped hair. The man was slick and almost as perverted as his client. "He is a good-looking young man and many women would enjoy spending time with him. It's not a crime to have sex with consenting adults."

"No, Mr. Dooley, you are correct. It isn't a crime to have sex with a consenting adult, but we have evidence that suggests consent was not given. But let's not get ahead of ourselves. Let's discuss the aggravated assault."

The questions went on for two hours when Paine's attorney called for a break and some food. Things were not going as he expected. He wanted some private consultation time with Eddie. When they resumed, Eddie agreed to the charges of assault but denied all other charges. They had enough to hold Eddie Paine. The interrogation would continue the next morning.

Relentlessly, over the next two days, Agent Hardy wore Paine down until his attorney recommended he plead guilty to the charges of assault and negotiate a plea deal.

That was when Hardy brought in the big guns and pulled out the murder charges. Dooley smirked. "That might be a little difficult without any evidence. I've reviewed the files and there is no DNA, no fibers, no witnesses."

Eddie, feeling emboldened, leaned back in his chair. "Yea, you can't prove a thing and I'm homeless due to the poorly executed arrest and fire. I'm considering a civil action against the Alton Police Department."

Dooley nudged his client's knee under the table and tried to regain control of the conversation. "My client is distraught. But be advised, our legal team is considering pursuing appropriate legal recourse."

Hardy's color rose from pink to red to puce. Eddie smirked at him and at the mirror. He figured Rob was watching.

Hardy knew he'd gotten as much as he could from this interview. Gathering up his papers, he turned a scornful look to Dooley and Paine. "You may think so, but rest assured, we are pursuing evidence and will find it. Meanwhile, Mr. Dooley, your client is remanded into custody for the aggravated assault and kidnapping of Meg Lawrence, Juju Lawrence, and the attempted murder of Detective Rob Adams."

Chapter 38

While the FBI worked to tie Paine to the murders in California, Arizona, and San Antonio, Rob concentrated on finding the evidence to pin him down on the murders in Alton. He was damned if the bastard would walk on Kathy, Debbie, and Amy. Knowing Mia Hansen was the strongest tie to the kidnappings, he prepared a photo line-up with eight pictures. He included Paine, similar looking men and Justin Whitman. Since Mia was still recovering from her injuries, he called to schedule a visit to her home.

Douglas Hansen answered the door to Rob and Pete with a grim expression on his face. His little girl still suffered nightmares from the ordeal. The dark shadows under his eyes gave witness to his worry. Pete understood. He gripped the hand of a fellow father, extending support and comfort.

"Thank you for giving us time with Mia." Pete laid a reassuring hand on Hansen's shoulder. "We understand your reluctance. The sooner we can close the case, the sooner Mia can focus on healing. Having the killer behind bars is a good first step, and we hope Mia can help us do this."

Douglas Hansen nodded, then turned worried eyes toward the family room that had been converted to Mia's bedroom while she healed. Mrs. Hansen waited with Mia. "Then let's do this."

Rob let Pete handle the interview and the showing of the photo line-up. Mia faltered when Pete first handed her the photo card. An audible gasp escaped her lips. Her hand darted toward Eddie's photo but pulled back. Pressing her lips together, Mia studied each photo. They could see her struggle to overcome the fear elicited by looking at the face of her assailant, read the determination on her young face. Rob watched her closely. She held up well and would do so on the stand when the time came.

Mia's slender fingers ran over each photo. You could see when they flicked over the ones she knew were not Paine. When she came to Justin's picture, she hesitated, running her index finger over the cut of his jaw, the curve of an ear. Then her hand moved on to Paine, fingertip following the same pattern. Turning the card to Pete, she tapped the two photos. "These two could almost be the same person, but I can see the difference. I know the difference." Mia handed the card back to Pete, her finger pointing at Paine. "This is the man. The one that took me. That hurt me."

Pete took the card. "You are certain, Mia?" he asked, already knowing her answer.

"Yes, Detective Bonnert. This is the man. It's in the eyes. But there is something else. Most people wouldn't even notice it, but my being so short? When we were walking to the car, sharing the umbrella? I noticed the small scar just under his ear. I remember thinking it might be a scratch from a cat or dog. That's probably why I fell for his new puppy story." She had just enough derision in her voice to cause a concerned look from her mother. Mrs. Hansen tut tutted, patting Mia's hand. "It's okay, Mom. I was stupid and naïve.

My world has changed. I have seen evil. I also see good. Being a little wiser now, I can distinguish between the two."

Rob took the wheel as he and Pete drove back to the station, thinking Mia had learned a hard lesson but she was alive and would be stronger because of it.

****

Rob called the Tarrant County District Attorney. Getting Howard Wooton on the line, they reviewed the outcome of the interview with Mia Hansen. "That's good, Rob, but I could use some physical evidence. Are we sure we don't have anything?"

Rob hung up feeling discouraged. He ran over every possible item in his mind once again. The fire had destroyed everything, eliminating any hope of physical evidence. Then he considered what had survived. What if they could lift evidence off that? Rob didn't know what might have survived the explosion and fire. Rubbing his fingers over his forehead, Rob expelled a frustrated sigh. He reviewed everything that had occurred, relived the fear he'd felt when Eddie held Meg at knife point. Suddenly, the light bulb lit up.

"Pete, what happened to the knife Eddie had when Justin tackled him?"

Pete scratched his head. "Justin hit him pretty hard. The knife flew. I'm sure the crime scene guys picked it up. Must have. Let me look at the list of items logged in as evidence." Pete pulled the form up on the computer. "Good Lord, it's right here. Logged as found outside the perimeter so they bagged it but didn't put it on the priority list for processing. No one connected the dots."

Rob slapped a triumphant fist into his palm. "Let's take a run to evidence and the medical examiner's office."

Rob listened to complaints about the rush job and then the white-coated geek at the ME's office drone on about the entire process of checking for blood and prints. TMI, he thought, giving the tech a piercing gaze. "Moots, can you just tell me the time without going into the details of how the watch is made? Please?"

The coroner's lab nerd looked momentarily wounded, then preened. "They always try but rarely succeed. The knife has traces of blood from your victims. And, prints from your suspect!"

Rob almost hugged the man. "Moots, I owe you!"

"Schedule an interview with Paine. We're going to cook him." Rob knew they'd hit for the cycle with the blood and prints on the knife. The DA's office would run with it, but Rob wanted to tie it up with a bow. He wanted Eddie to sweat; to confess his crimes.

****

At two-thirty p.m., Eddie Paine, wearing an ill-fitting orange jumpsuit, sat waiting with his attorney. Warren Dooley stroked his oiled hair, thinking this would be when the Alton Police confirmed they had nothing and the DA released his client on bond, pending a trial he felt confident he'd win.

At two-thirty-five, Rob and Pete entered the room. Rob looked angry, while Pete, the elder, more seasoned detective, scolded him with his eyes.

Setting down the file, Rob took his seat and sighed. "Mr. Paine, I have a couple of things I'd like to review with you concerning the abduction of Meg Lawrence." Rob pulled the necklace Eddie had made for Meg from the file, laying the evidence bag on the table for all to see. "This is the necklace you gave to Ms. Lawrence, correct?"

Eddie gave the necklace a cursory glance and smirked. "Yeah. A little token of my affection since she willingly came with me for our little fun."

"Yes, so you say." Rob felt the start of an angry tic and dialed back his emotions. "This is a unique piece of jewelry. Mr. Paine, did you fashion this necklace yourself? The craftsmanship is exceptional."

Dooley watched the exchange between Rob and Paine. Something was up. He just couldn't put his finger on it. Eddie warmed to the subject.

"It is pretty good, isn't it? You can buy these necklaces online but mine are better. Girls like pretty things." Eddie had been studying his fingernails, surprising Rob that he didn't blow on them and buff them against his chest in a self-congratulatory way.

Rob returned Meg's necklace to the file and pulled out one with Debbie's name on it. He'd had a crude replica made of the one found on her body. "And this one? You made it too?" He pushed it toward Paine.

Eddie picked up the necklace to examine it, then tossed it back on the table. "Oh, hell no, this isn't my work. The one I made for Debbie was much..." Eddie stopped, realizing he'd just put his foot in it.

Rob smiled. "Much what, Eddie?"

Dooley jumped in, putting his hand over Eddie's, preventing his client from digging himself deeper, but Eddie pushed his hand away. "It's better. Everything I do is better. You think you know so much? You're nothing, and that asshole Whitman is nothing. He used to suck up to me when we were in shop class together, thinking I'd teach him how to do what I did. His little sister used to come along. She'd prance and look at me through her lashes, lips all pouty."

Rob sat back in his chair. He had one last piece of evidence that would put the final nail in Paine's coffin and he couldn't wait to show it to Eddie. "And this? Do you recognize it?" Rob pulled the coin from the file and laid it on the table. Eddie lunged, wrapping his hand around it. "Where did you get this? This is mine. My dad gave it to me."

"Are you sure? Someone found it when out walking." Rob shook his head.

"No, it's mine. I must have dropped it." Eddie's eyes had taken on a crazy, obsessive sheen.

"Well, it's an expensive historical piece. I can't just return it to you without knowing for certain it's yours. When did you notice it missing? Where did you lose it?"

Eddie rubbed the coin between greedy fingers. Rob watched the gears turning in his head. His eyes twitching back and forth. Eddie wanted the coin. "I think I lost it around Labor Day weekend. I don't know where, but look. It has markings on the edges, see? I had it in a ring. It must have fallen out when I was walking."

"Walking? You don't impress me as the type for fresh air and exercise," Rob said derisively, taking the coin back from Eddie's grasp. Eddie's eyes followed it avariciously as Rob returned the coin to the file. "I'm afraid that isn't enough to convince the lost and found department it belongs to you."

Eddie licked his lips, his eyes glued to the file where the coin had disappeared. "No, wait. I remember. I was at that place where those people go that like to look at birds. Someone had said they saw some hawks.

I wanted to see some hawks, so I went there."

"So, let me get this straight. You were walking at the Fort Worth Water Treatment drying beds, looking for hawks. You had this coin in your pocket and it fell out. Is that correct?" Rob wove the story in a convoluted way, hoping Eddie would follow it down the rabbit hole.

"Yes. No." Eddie grew agitated. His eyes never left the file holding the coin. "I was at that place, but the coin didn't fall out of my pocket. It was in a ring and it must have fallen out of my ring. The ring my dad gave me. It's mine. Those marks, it's from being set in the ring. Don't you know anything?"

"Oh, I know a lot and even more now, Eddie." Rob stood, gathered up the file. "You used your ring to brand your victims before you came to Alton. Just like your dad used it to brand you." Rob grabbed Eddie's left hand, turning it palm up. There, imprinted in the mound under his thumb, was a clear, clean circle and the image of a hanging man.

Eddie pulled his hand back, cradling it against his chest, rubbing furiously across the scar from the brand his dad had given him. His eyes shone with a crazy light, his lips curved by a crooked smile.

"You used it to brand Linda Bajorek, Patty Cruise, and Kathy Erickson but lost it when you dumped Kathy's body at the drying beds. That's why Debbie and Amy didn't have the brand and why you tried to buy it back from the person who found it. Eddie Paine, you are under arrest for the murders of Linda Bajorek, Patty Cruise, Kathy Erickson, Debbie Crawford, and Amy Winehurst."

Eddie stood, lunged at Rob, then fell back into his

chair, crying, "I need that ring. My dad gave me that ring. It meant something. They asked for it; Becky, Kathy, Debbie. All of them. They wanted it. They asked for it. So I gave it to them. I ended their pain."

Rob pulled Eddie Paine's fisted hands from the evidence file and walked from the room.

Agent Hardy stepped out of observation. Rob had gone rogue with the interview, but in light of its success, he opted to overlook it. Rob turned the file and evidence over to the FBI. Hardy added it to their long list of victims. Over the next two days, Paine confessed to a string of murders from California to Texas; often bragging about how he duped the victims.

California claimed first dibs because he murdered his first victim there. But the Tarrant County Prosecutor hoped his argument that Paine, being apprehended in Texas, should be primary. Everyone involved in the case wanted Texas to get him first. Texas had the death penalty. California could extradite Paine when he was dead.

Justin felt a flood of emotions when Paine told them where to find Becky's body. He called his mom, letting her know he'd be coming home to bury Becky. Juju accompanied him. She wanted to invite Justin's mom to return with them to live in Texas.

Epilogue

Rob stood with Justin at the small reception following the President's Day Program. Under the direction of the new music teacher, Juju Lawrence, the children performed patriotic renditions of Yankee Doodle and America.

Paine stood trial in California. They sentenced him to nineteen consecutive life terms for the murders he committed in the southwest. He'd live a comfortable life spinning out the details of his killing spree and doling out the location of bodies to the families, allowing them closure.

Justin sat through every day of the trial, his mother at his side. It provided him with the closure he yearned for and needed. No more questions. His mom was whole, his dad could rest in peace, and Becky was finally home. When he returned to Texas, his mother accompanied him. He helped her find a townhome near the Lawrence home while he and Juju house hunted for a place of their own. They set the wedding for April, just before spring break, so the honeymoon wouldn't interfere with Juju's teaching. John and M snuck away to Vegas for a wedding chapel ceremony and returned *fait accompli* in mid-January.

Rob let his gaze circle the room. His eyes fell on Meg, serving punch and laughing at something a blushing Ben was saying. He sighed into his glass, feeling a contentment he'd always longed for. When he looked back at Meg, he found her gazing at him, a Mona Lisa smile on her lips. Oh, yes, he thought. Contentment. He heard the strains of 'yours, yours, yours' from '*1776*' play in his head.

A word about the author…

Musician, actor and retired sales & marketing rep, CA Humer, Cheryl to her friends, grew up in small town Wisconsin. Music, dance and performing were passions growing up, but she always felt a tug toward writing. Tamping down her creative side, Cheryl chose business and sales–relegating her artistic inclinations to a side-line. When her creative hunger bubbled to the surface, she satisfied the urge to write by creating marketing campaigns, scripts and newsletter articles. Now retired, the book that percolated in her imagination for decades has found its release, along with several others waiting to break free. Before, music and acting were her all-consuming passions. Now, Cheryl can't stop imagining or writing.

Cheryl and her husband live in the Fort Worth metroplex with their cat. She enjoys travel, reading and a good glass of wine.

She enjoys hearing from readers. Please reach out to CAHumer0922@gmail.com and share your thoughts. She is also available for readings and signings, both local and via Zoom.